HEART QUEST®

HeartQuest brings you romantic fiction with a foundation of biblical truth. Adventure, mystery, intrigue, and suspense mingle in these heartwarming stories of men and women of faith striving to build a love that will last a lifetime.

May HeartQuest books sweep you into the arms of God, who longs for you and pursues you always.

Catherine Palmer

PRAIRIE ROSE

A TOWN CALLED HOPE

HEART QUEST

Tyndale House Publishers, Inc.
WHEATON, ILLINOIS

Visit Tyndale's exciting Web site at www.tyndale.com

Check out the latest about HeartQuest Books at www.heartquest.com

ISBN 0-8423-7420-5 (sc)

Printed in the United States of America

05 04 03 02
5 4 3 2 1

For my husband

Timothy Charles Palmer

Twenty years of promises kept.

I love you.

His name is the Lord—rejoice in his presence! Father to the fatherless . . . God places the lonely in families. Psalm 68:4-6, NLT

So you should not be like cowering, fearful slaves. You should behave instead like God's very own children, adopted into his family—calling him "Father, dear Father." For his Holy Spirit speaks to us deep in our hearts and tells us that we are God's children. Romans 8:15-16, NLT

CHAPTER 1

Kansas City, Missouri
May, 1865

TALKING to God from the outstretched limb of a towering white oak tree had its advantages. For one thing, it meant that Rosie Mills could see beyond the confining walls of the Christian Home for Orphans and Foundlings, where she had lived all nineteen years of her life. For another, she had always felt as if she were closer to God up in the old tree. That was kind of silly, Rosie knew. God had lived in her heart ever since she gave it to him one night at a tent preaching service, just before the War Between the States. But the best thing about praying in the oak tree was the constantly changing scene that unfolded below.

Take these two men coming her way. The first—a dark-haired fellow in a chambray shirt and black suspenders—minded his own business as he drove his wagon down the dusty street. He had a little boy beside him on the seat and a load of seed in the wagon bed. The other man followed on a black horse. All the time Rosie had been praying, she had been watching the second fellow edge closer and closer, until finally he was right behind the wagon.

"Seth Hunter!" the horseman shouted, pulling a double-barreled shotgun from the scabbard on his saddle. "Stop your mules and put your hands in the air."

The command was so loud and the gun so unexpected that Rosie nearly lost her precarious perch on the old limb. The milkman across the street straightened up and stared. Down the way, the vegetable seller and his son halted in their tracks.

"I said stop your team!" the horseman bellowed.

The man on the wagon swung around and eyed his challenger. "Jack Cornwall," he spat. "I might have known."

He gave the reins a sharp snap to set his mules racing lickety-split down the road. Jack Cornwall cocked his shotgun, lifted it to his shoulder, aimed it at the fleeing wagon, and fired. At the blast, Rosie gave a strangled scream. A puff of pungent gray smoke blossomed in the air. A hundred tiny lead pellets smashed into the seed barrels on the back of the wagon. Wood splintered. Seeds spilled across the road. The mules brayed and faltered, jerking the wagon from side to side.

"Whoa, whoa!" the driver of the wagon shouted. "Cornwall, what in thunder do you think you're doing?"

"Give me the boy, or I'll shoot again!" Cornwall hollered back.

"He's my son."

"You stole him!"

"He's mine by rights." The wagon rolled to a halt directly beneath the oak tree where Rosie perched. "I aim to take him to my homestead, and neither you nor anybody else is going to stop me, hear?"

"What do you want him for—slave labor?"

"You forgetting I'm a Union man, Cornwall? We don't trade in human flesh like you Rebs."

"And we don't go stealing children out from under the noses of the grandparents who took care of them since the day they were born."

"My *wife* took care of Chipper—"

"Wife?" the man exploded. He edged his horse forward, once again leveling his shotgun at Hunter. "You claiming my sister would marry some good-for-nothing farmhand?"

Rosie gripped the oak branch. The two men were barely three

feet beneath her, and she could almost feel the heat of their hatred. This was terrible. The little boy the men were arguing about was hunkered down in the wagon, terrified. He couldn't have been more than five or six years old, and as he peered over the wooden seat his big blue eyes filled with tears.

Rosie didn't know which of the men was in the right, but she wasn't about to let this Jack Cornwall fellow shoot someone. She spotted a stout stick caught in a fork of the tree. Maybe she could use it to distract the men, she thought as she shinnied toward the slender end of her branch.

"Your sister married me, whether you believe it or not," Seth Hunter snarled. "I'm this boy's father, and I mean to take him with me."

"I didn't track your worthless hide all the way to Kansas City to let you just ride off to the prairie with my nephew. No sir, Chipper's going south with me. My pappy's not about to let you work his grandson to the bone on your sorry excuse for a farm."

"I told you I don't plan on working him. In fact, I'm headed for this orphanage right now to hire me a hand."

"Hire you a hand," Jack scoffed. He spat a long stream of brown tobacco juice onto the dirt road. "What're you aiming to pay him with—grasshoppers? That's all you're going to be growing on your homestead, Hunter. Grasshoppers, potato bugs, and boll weevils."

"I've got a house and a barn, Jack. That's more than a lot of folks can say, including you. And any young'un would gladly trade that orphanage for a home."

I would, Rosie thought. She was beginning to side with Seth Hunter, even if he had stolen the little boy. The other man was big, rawboned, and mean-tempered. For all she knew he planned to shoot Seth dead with his shotgun. And right in front of the child!

The branch she was straddling bobbed a little from her weight as she inched along it toward the stick. Truth to tell, it was the boy who stirred her heart the most. Neither man had even bothered to ask the child what he wanted to do. And where on earth was the poor little fellow's mother?

"A house and a barn," Jack said, his voice dripping with disdain. "What you've got is dust, wind, and prairie fires. That's no place to bring up a boy. Now let me have him peaceful-like, and I won't be obliged to blow your Yankee head off."

"You're not taking my son." Seth stood up on the wagon. His shoulders were square and solid inside his homespun chambray shirt, and his arms were roped with hard muscle and thick veins. Badly in want of cutting, his hair hung heavy and black. His thick neck was as brown as a nut. With such a formidable stature, Rosie thought, he should have the face of the bare-knuckle fighters she had seen on posters.

He didn't. His blue eyes set off a straight nose, a pair of flat, masculine lips, and a notched chin. It was a striking face. A handsome face. Unarmed, Hunter faced Jack. "I already lost Mary, and I'm not—"

"You never had Mary!"

"She was my wife."

"Mary denied you till the day she died."

"Liar!" Seth stepped over the wagon seat and started across the bed. "If your pappy hadn't tried to kill me—"

"You ran off to join the army! We never saw hide nor hair of you for more than five years till you came sneaking back and stole Chipper."

"I wrote Mary—"

"She burned every letter."

"Mary loved me, and none of your lies will make me doubt it. We'd have been happy together if your pappy would have left us alone. He ran me off with a shotgun. I was too young and scared back then to stand up to him, but I'll be switched if I let him do it again. Or you, either."

"I'll do more than that, Hunter." Jack steadied the gun. "Now give me the boy."

"Over my dead body."

"You asked for it."

He pulled back on the hammer to set the gun at half cock. Rosie held her breath. No. He wouldn't really do it. Would he? She reached out and grabbed onto the stick.

"Give me the boy," Jack repeated.

"If you shoot me, they'll hang you for murder."

"Hang me? Ha! You ever hear of Charlie Quantrell, Jesse James, Bob Ford? They're heroes to me. I've joined up with a bunch down south to avenge wrongs done in the name of Yankee justice. Nobody messes with us, Hunter. And nobody hangs us for murder. Besides, I'm just protecting my kin." He pulled the hammer all the way back.

Seth stood his ground. "People are watching every move you make, Jack," he said. "They know who you are. Don't do this."

"Chipper, come here, boy."

"Stay down, Chipper."

"Hunter, you Yankee dog. I'll get you if it's the last thing I do."

Jack lifted the shotgun's stock to his shoulder. As his finger tensed on the trigger, Rosie gritted her teeth and swung her club like a pendulum. It smashed into the side of Jack Cornwall's head and knocked him sideways. The shotgun went off with a deafening roar. Like a hundred angry hornets, pellets sprayed into the street.

At the end of the limb, Rosie swayed down, lurched up, and swung down again. Acrid, sulfurous-smelling smoke seared her nostrils. As screams filled the air, she heard the branch she was clinging to crack. She lost her balance, tumbled through the smoke, and landed smack-dab on Seth Hunter. The impact knocked them both to the wagon bed, and her head cracked against the wooden bench seat. A pair of startled blue eyes was the last thing she saw.

"Glory be to God, she's awake at last! Jimmy, come here quick and have a look at her."

"Aye, she's awake, that she is."

The two pairs of eyes that stared down at Rosie could not have been more alike—nor the faces that went with them more different. The woman had bright green eyes, brilliant orange-red hair, and the ruddiest cheeks Rosie had ever seen. The man's green eyes glowed like twin emeralds from a gaunt face with suntanned skin stretched over sharp, pointy bones. He sucked on a corncob pipe and nodded solemnly.

"Seth Hunter, the lass has come round," he said. "Better see to her. She's a *frainey*, all right. She's so puny she'll keel over if she tries to stand up."

Her head pounding in pain, Rosie was attempting to decipher the lilting words her two observers had spoken when Seth Hunter's blue eyes—now solemn—appeared above her for a second time that day. He stroked a hand across her forehead. His hand was big and warm, his fingers gently probing.

"I don't feel right about us leaving her here, Jimmy," he said. "She's still bleeding pretty bad from that gash on the back of her head. But if we don't take off soon, I reckon Jack Cornwall will be back on my tail. I've got to get Chipper out of town. I want him home and settled as quick as possible."

"Sure, the wagon's loaded down with our tools and seed we came for," Jimmy said. "The *brablins* have their peppermints, and they'll be eager to start licking on them. If we set out now, we'll be home not a day later than planned."

"I know, but I just . . ." Seth touched Rosie's forehead again with his fingertips. "Ma'am, can you hear me? I want to thank you for what you did. I never expected such a thing. I owe you, that's for sure. If I had any money, I'd give you a reward, but—"

"Home," Rosie said. She didn't know where the word had

come from. She'd never had a home, not from the very moment she was born.

"We'll see you get home, ma'am," Seth said. "The delivery boy for the mercantile here said he recognized you. He's gone to fetch your mother."

Mother? Rosie studied the rows of canned goods, bolts of fabric, and sacks of produce that lined the floor-to-ceiling shelves in the mercantile. She knew the place well. She had been here many times, shopping for the orphanage's kitchen. She gradually recalled how she must have come to be lying on the sawdust-covered floor with her head throbbing like a marching band. She even knew the name of the man bending over her. But how could the delivery boy be fetching her mother?

"I don't have a mother," she said.

"No mother!" The ruddy-cheeked woman leaned into view and clucked in sympathy. She placed a clean folded cloth over Rosie's gash. "Can such a thing be true? Aye, lass, you're cruel wounded in the head, so you are. Perhaps you've lost your wits a bit. Sure, we wouldn't want you turnin' into a *googeen* now. Can you recall your name at all?"

"Rosenbloom Cotton Mills."

"She's disremembered the sound of her own name, so she has!"

"No really, that's who I am. Rosie Mills." She struggled to sit up, and the woman slipped a supporting arm around her shoulders. "My mother . . . you see . . . she put my name on a piece of paper."

"But you just told us you didn't have a mother."

"I don't. Not one I ever met, anyway. The piece of paper with my name on it was inside the stocking with me when I was discovered."

"You were discovered in a stocking?"

"I was a baby at the time. Newborn."

"A baby! *Ullilu*, Jimmy, did you hear the wee thing? She was left in a stocking."

"A foundling."

Jimmy pronounced the word Rosie had despised from the moment she learned its connotations. For nineteen years she had worn that label, and it had barred her from adoption, from marriage, from all hope of a family and a home. Taking no notice of the expressions on their faces, she pulled her pouch from the bodice of her dress.

"I keep the paper in here in this little bag I made from the toe of my stocking," she said. "As you can see, my name is written out very clearly: Rosenbloom Cotton Mills."

She unfolded the tiny scrap that was her only treasure. Everyone gathered around. As it turned out, there were many red-haired, green-eyed visitors at the mercantile that day, and most of them weren't more than three feet tall. Clutching red-and-white-striped peppermint sticks, they elbowed each other for a better look.

"Appears to be a stocking tag from that mill over on the river in Illinois," Jimmy said. "You remember, Sheena? We passed it on our way west, so we did."

"*Whisht*, Jimmy. If the lass says it's her name, who are you to start a clamper over it?" Sheena gave Rosie a broad smile that showed pretty white teeth. "Now then, we're to set out on our way home to Kansas in the wagon—Jimmy O'Toole and me, our five children, and our good neighbor, Seth Hunter. We're most grateful to you for the whack you gave that *sherral* Jack Cornwall. We never met a man as fine as our Seth, God save him, and we won't see him come to harm. So, if you think you'll be all right now, we'll—"

"Rosie? Rosie Mills?" A woman who had just entered the mercantile spotted the injured girl and clapped her hands to her cheeks. She glanced at Sheena O'Toole. "I'm Iva Jameson, the director of the Christian Home for Orphans and Foundlings. What on earth has happened to Rosie?"

"I . . . I was up in the oak tree," Rosie said meekly, dabbing at her wound with the cloth, "and then along came Mr. Hunter's wagon . . . and I—"

"You should have outgrown tree climbing long ago."

"But it's where I pray, ma'am."

"Rosie, shame on you for such tomfoolery—and at your age!"

"Maybe I should explain, ma'am." Seth stepped forward. "What happened was mainly my fault. I'm Seth Hunter, and I was on my way to your orphanage with my son this morning when things took a wrong turn."

"I see, Mr. Hunter." Mrs. Jameson eyed the little boy standing forlornly beside him. "Would this young man be your son?"

"Yes. This is Christopher. They call him Chipper."

"Chipper. Now, that's a fine name for such a strong, handsome lad." The director knelt to the floor. "And how old are you, young Chipper?"

"He's five," Seth said. "Listen, ma'am, we don't have much time here. The O'Toole family and I—we've got homesteads waiting for us over in Kansas, and we need to get on the trail."

"Are you a widower, sir?"

There was a moment of silence. "Well, yes," Seth said finally. "I reckon I am a widower."

"You're uncertain?"

"I just hadn't thought of it that way. My wife . . . Chipper's mother . . . I went to fetch her and I learned she had died."

"I'm very sorry about your loss, sir," Mrs. Jameson said. "These are difficult times indeed. I'm assuming you were planning to ask the Christian Home for Orphans and Foundlings to look after your son while you find another wife."

"A wife?" Seth's voice deepened. "No. Absolutely not. No, I'm taking the child with me."

"Oh, I see."

"I was on my way to the orphanage because I'm in need of a strong boy," Seth told Mrs. Jameson. "Maybe you can still help me.

See, I want somebody who can work with me on the homestead. There's plowing and planting and such, but I wouldn't push him too hard. In fact, if you've got a boy who's good with young'uns, I mostly want him to keep an eye on Chipper. I can't offer pay, but I'll give him room and board. I'll give him a home."

Rosie stiffened and took Sheena O'Toole's hand. Holding the cloth to her hammering head, she pulled herself to her feet. What had Seth just offered? *A home. I'll give him a home.*

"I'm sorry, Mr. Hunter," Mrs. Jameson said, "but we're not an employment agency. Why don't you place an advertisement in the newspaper?"

"I don't have time for that. I've been away from my claim more than two weeks already, and my fields need plowing. Don't you have somebody who could help me out?"

"I understand your predicament, truly I do," Mrs. Jameson said. "But all our oldest boys went off to the war. We don't have anyone at the Home much over twelve, and I don't believe—"

"Twelve would do. If he's strong, it won't matter how old he is. Look here, ma'am," Seth said, "I'm an honest man, I'm a hard worker, and I won't do wrong by anybody. I'm offering the boy a chance to get a good start on life. A home of his own."

Rosie sucked in a breath. *A home.* A chance to make her unspoken dream come true! She was strong enough to do most any job. She could learn to plow. She could plant and dig and hoe. And she knew she could look after that boy.

"I'm so sorry, Mr. Hunter," Mrs. Jameson said, "but I simply couldn't send a twelve-year-old off with a stranger. We find our children jobs in the city. With the shortage of men these days, even our younger ones are working at the liveries and helping with refuse collection—"

"Shoveling stables and picking up garbage? I can offer a boy a better life than that."

"But I can't just give you a child. It would be worse than slavery."

"Slavery? I'm holding out a chance at a new life. I'm offering this boy a future. I'll turn him into a strong, useful man."

"I'll be your man!" Rosie called out. She took a step and began to sway. Sheena leapt to her side, placing an arm around her waist to keep her from falling. "I'll go with you, Mr. Hunter. I'll help you with the plowing, and I'll take care of your son. I know I can do it."

Seth Hunter stared at her. The little boy beside him gaped at the unexpected declaration. Even Sheena O'Toole eyed her in wonderment. Rosie didn't care that she had astonished them all. This was her chance—and she intended to take it.

Mrs. Jameson turned on her. "Don't be ridiculous," she snapped. "The cook will be searching the whole house for you. At this hour of the morning, you're to be in the kitchen ladling out porridge."

"Yes, ma'am . . . but . . . but I believe I'll go to Kansas with Mr. Hunter instead. I'll be his worker. I'm good with children, and I can learn anything." She swallowed and forced herself to meet those bright blue eyes. "Sir, won't you take me with you? I'm nineteen—almost twenty—and I can do a good day's work. I promise you won't regret it."

So far Seth Hunter had said nothing. Rosie knew she was losing ground. Mrs. Jameson would never hear of her going away with a stranger. And what man would want a skinny foundling to help him on his homestead? But he had offered a future. A home.

"I'm a very good cook," she continued. "Just ask anyone. I bake the best apple pies. I can clean and scrub, and I know how to take a stove apart and black it top to bottom good as new. I'm wonderful at hoeing, and nobody makes pickles better than mine. It sounds like I'm boasting, but it's true, Mr. Hunter. You'll see how thankful you are to have me."

Seth looked her up and down, his blue eyes bringing out a flush in her cheeks and making the back of her neck prickle. She glanced at his son. Chipper was grinning. A broad space where he'd lost his two front teeth gave his face the look of a small, round jack-o'-lantern.

Mrs. Jameson harrumphed. "Rosenbloom Cotton Mills, I shall not tolerate such nonsense. And as for praying in a tree—"

"Mrs. Jameson's right," Seth said to Rosie. "I was mainly needing a farmhand. I don't reckon you'd be strong enough."

"I'm strong enough, Mr. Hunter," she countered, squaring her shoulders and setting the bloodied rag on a countertop. "Besides, you *owe* me. You said so yourself."

"Indeed you did, Seth." Sheena wasn't quite as tall as the younger woman, but her stocky stature gave her the look of a determined bulldog. When she spoke again, her voice held a tone of foreboding. "Speak the truth and shame the devil."

"I admit I'm obliged to the girl," Seth said. "She saved my life, and I intend to pay my debt by sending her a reward from Kansas. A dollar here, another there, as my crops come in."

"She wants to go with you to Kansas. That's the reward she claims," Sheena said.

Rosie's heart warmed to the woman at her side. Somehow, Sheena understood the depths of Rosie's need. Somehow, she *knew*.

"She's a *donny* thing, Sheena," Jimmy put in, "but she'll not last two weeks on the prairie before—"

"You're no great help to her, are you now, Jimmy O'Toole?" Sheena interjected. "She's a poor slip of a thing with no mother and never a home to call her own. She knew not a *stim* about our Seth, yet she saved his life, so she did." She fastened a glare on Seth. "Now then, Mr. Hunter, what do you have to say for yourself?"

Seth took off his hat and scratched the back of his head. He assessed Rosie and appeared clearly unhappy with what he saw. He crossed his arms over his chest and stared out the mercantile window for a full minute, his eyes narrowed and his jaw clenched. Finally, he gave a grunt of surrender.

"I reckon I'm going to take the girl." He turned to Mrs. Jameson. "I'll only need her for the growing season—six months at the most."

"Sir, Miss Mills is an unmarried woman." Her words were clipped. "You can't just take her into your home like that. It wouldn't be Christian."

"She can live in the barn."

"But Rosie isn't married!"

"A family down the river brought in a girl from Sweden, so they did," Sheena put in. "She takes care of their children and cooks their meals. Two or three families in Lawrence hired young women who used to be slaves to work for them. I even heard of a family—"

"But Mr. Hunter is not a family. He's a widower. He's a single man!" objected Mrs. Jameson.

"And that's how I'm going to stay, too," Seth said, turning on Rosie. "So if you have any crazy ideas about—"

"No," she said quickly. She had to reassure him—had to make this work. "All I want is somewhere to live."

"Don't be foolish, Rosie," Mrs. Jameson cut in. "You know nothing about this man. You have a place with us."

"A place, yes. But not a home." In spite of Mrs. Jameson's scowl, Rosie lifted her chin. "I'm going to Kansas, ma'am, with Mr. Hunter."

Seth hooked a thumb into the pocket of his denim trousers and cocked his head in the direction of the orphanage. "Go fetch your things. I'd just as soon be gone when Jack Cornwall talks the sheriff into letting him go."

"I don't have anything of my own to fetch, sir. I'm ready to leave this very minute."

"You don't have anything?" He frowned and glanced at Mrs. Jameson.

"We're an orphanage, Mr. Hunter," the director explained. "We do well to put food in the children's stomachs. Rosie's fortunate to have a pair of shoes."

Seth studied Rosie up and down for a moment, his blue eyes absorbing her faded dress, worn shawl, and patched boots. Finally he shook his head. "All right," he said. "Let's go."

Rosie pressed her cheek against that of the woman who had taken her in so many years before. "Pray for me, Mrs. Jameson. And give my love to the children."

She turned quickly so she wouldn't change her mind and hurried out of the mercantile. Seth Hunter lifted Chipper onto the spring seat, helped Rosie into the back of the wagon, and climbed aboard himself. Jimmy O'Toole settled his wife and their five red-haired children among the sacks, barrels, and tools. Then he joined Seth on the seat.

Rosie tucked her skirts around her ankles before allowing herself one last look at the Christian Home for Orphans and Foundlings just down the road. What had she done? Oh, Lord!

After releasing the brake, Seth flicked the reins to set his team plodding down the street.

"Don't give her bed away, Mrs. Jameson," he called as the wagon passed the Home's director, who was already marching purposefully back toward the orphanage. "I'll have her back in six months."

"It's a long way from Kansas City to my homestead," Seth said as the wagon rolled out of town. "Ever been to the prairie, Miss Mills?"

She was sitting bolt upright, her head held high as though she intended to drink in the sights and smells and sounds of everything along the way. A ragged bonnet covered the lump on her head, and only a few wisps of brown hair drifted around her chin. Skinny as a rail, she had a straight nose, high cheekbones, and a long neck.

If it weren't for her eyes, she'd be about as pretty as a fledgling prairie hen. But her eyes glowed, huge and brown, like big warm chocolates, and when she blinked, her thick lashes fluttered down to her cheeks in a way that made Seth feel fidgety.

"I've never been anywhere," she said, turning those big eyes on him. "Except to the mercantile and church."

"My place is a long way from any market or church."

"I don't mind, Mr. Hunter. The Lord promises, 'My presence shall go with thee, and I will give thee rest.' I'm not afraid."

"You're a brave lass, so you are," Sheena O'Toole put in. The children were nestled around her, busily sucking on their peppermint sticks. "In truth, at times the prairie can be a lonely place."

"Oh, I've been lonely all my life."

Rosie said it so matter-of-factly that Seth almost didn't catch the significance of her words. When he did, he knew he had to set things straight right away. He didn't want her getting any ideas.

"Look, Miss Mills," he said. "I agreed to let you come along because I owe you. I'm giving you room and board in exchange for hard, honest work. I don't promise any luxuries, and I won't require your company evenings or Sundays. I've been alone a lot of years, and I like it that way."

He knew she didn't fully understand his situation, but he had no intention of going into the details. He had shelved the memories of a brief young love, a secret wedding, and the tumult that had followed. He had lived as a husband for less than a month before his wife's parents banished him from their property. When he had learned he had a son, he was in the Union army and camped on a battleground three hundred miles away. He had not seen his wife again.

"The boy stayed with his mother," Sheena O'Toole whispered in explanation. "Seth was fighting in the war."

"My mama lives in heaven now," Chipper whispered, turning

his big sapphire eyes on Rosie. "She's not coming back to take care of me anymore."

Seth hadn't heard the boy speak more than a word or two in the days he'd had him. Chipper had a high, sweet voice, a baby's voice with a slight lisp from his missing teeth. But not much about him reminded Seth of Mary. Sturdy, black-haired, and blue-eyed, the child was a spitting image of himself.

"I bet you miss your mama," Rosie Mills said from the wagon bed.

The dark head nodded. "I do miss her. And I don't like *him*." He jabbed a tiny thumb in the direction of his father. "He's a Yankee."

"Oh, but he's much more than that. He's your papa, too. That means he loves you, and he's going to watch out for you."

"I don't care. I want to live with Gram and Gramps. I like them better than any Yankee."

Seth glared at the little gap-toothed face. He didn't know how to talk to a five-year-old. Mary's parents despised their son-in-law, and they had poisoned his own child against him. When he returned for a wife he hadn't known was dead, he had learned they'd lost their farm and were moving to southern Missouri. It was then he had decided to claim the son he had fathered. Now he was beginning to wonder if he'd made a mistake.

"Did you know your mama's love lives in your heart, Chipper?" Rosie asked, leaning forward and taking the child's chubby hand. "Why, sure it does. Whenever you're lonely, you can think about her."

"Where does *your* mama live?"

"She doesn't know, Chipper," Sheena said. "Poor Miss Mills never met her mama."

"But I know my father very well," Rosie said. "God is my father. He's always looking out for me, always wanting the best for me, always with me. If I need help, I can talk to him any time."

"Sounds like a better father than *him*." The thumb jabbed Seth's way again.

"I imagine he could be a pretty good papa in time. You'll just have to teach him, Chipper. Now, what do you think a good papa would do with his son while they were traveling to the prairie in a wagon?"

Seth frowned at the road. He didn't like this turn of conversation. Not at all. He wanted to concentrate on his land, to plot out every one of his one hundred sixty acres, to imagine how his crops would grow. He wanted to talk over new ideas with Jimmy O'Toole. He didn't know what to do about the little boy beside him. Or the woman with the big brown eyes.

"He'd sing," Chipper said. "A good papa would sing."

"Oh, that's easy." Rosie laughed at the boy's suggestion. "Come on, then, Mr. Hunter. What shall we sing on our way to the prairie?"

"I don't sing."

"I told you," Chipper said. "He don't even sing."

"Everyone sings," Rosie said. "It's the easiest thing in the world."

"That it is," Sheena agreed. "As easy as dreaming dreams."

"Here's a song about heaven, where your mama lives, Chipper. Let's all sing it together:

"Precious memories, unseen angels,
Sent from somewhere to my soul;
How they linger, ever near me,
And the sacred past unfold."

Rosie's voice was high and lovely. It wrapped around Seth's heart like a pair of gentle arms, warming and comforting him. He did his best to ignore her, but the pleading in the woman's sweet voice softened him.

"Precious memories, how they linger," he joined in roughly, keeping his attention trained on the road ahead.

"How they ever flood my soul;
In the stillness of the midnight,
Precious, sacred scenes unfold."

CHAPTER 2

THE TRAIL that followed the Kansas River toward the open prairie bustled with traffic as Seth Hunter's wagon rolled west. That first day of the journey, Rosie counted three stagecoaches filled with excited travelers heading for the frontier. Two more coaches returning east passed the wagon, their passengers worn and weary from the long journey. A pair of bearded prospectors led a plodding mule bearing their pickaxes and shovels, and dreamed of quick, easy riches. A group of dusty cowboys drove a large herd of cattle east toward the Kansas City stockyards. They had traveled all the way from Texas, the men called out as they passed. The ever-changing pageantry was enough to keep the five O'Toole children chattering, arguing, and speculating for hours.

Just before they stopped in Osawkie for the night, a swaying black buggy raced toward the travelers. "Mrs. Dudenhoffer near Muddy Creek is indisposed," the driver, a physician, called out as his horse rounded Seth's wagon. "We're afraid it may be twins this time."

"God save you, kindly doctor!" Sheena O'Toole shouted back. Then she shook her head at Rosie. "Twins. May the good Lord have mercy on the poor woman's soul."

Rosie knew the birth of twins could kill, and there was little anyone could do about it. A widower with small children would have a hard lot on the prairie. Any man in such a dire situation would be desperate to find himself a hardy new wife. And he couldn't be choosy.

Rosie mulled this thought as they crossed Rock Creek the following morning. At Muddy Creek a circuit preacher approached on his horse. He gave the travelers a friendly wave. "On your way home?" he called. "God bless!"

"Good morrow to you," Sheena replied. "Shall we have the privilege of a visit, sir? We homestead on Bluestem Creek. There are two families of us, and we've been without preaching all winter."

"Bluestem Creek? I'm afraid I always circle around you folks. Your creek runs too high to cross most of the year."

"Humph," Jimmy O'Toole grunted. "I understood you crawthumpers could walk on water."

Seth chuckled as Sheena gave her husband's shoulder a swat. "As you can see, Reverend, we're in grave need of prayer and preaching. Do keep us in mind."

"I will," the preacher said. "And I'll see if I can manage a visit."

Lifting his hat, he gave the group a broad smile and spurred his horse past the wagon. Rosie took note that with his bright yellow hair and well-cut suit, the preacher could almost be called handsome. Not in the same way Seth Hunter was handsome, of course, but the preacher was tolerable looking all the same.

As the wagon neared Indianola, Rosie pondered the unfolding panorama of the prairie and the hope it inspired. Toward evening, she came to a momentous conclusion regarding the six months she would spend on the Hunter homestead. She might actually find someone who would be amenable to the notion of marriage with a woman lacking pedigree, money, or a fancy education! In fact, she already had taken note of several prospects. A lonely widower. A traveling preacher. Even a Texas cowboy. The land was filling quickly with men in need of good, strong wives. The possibilities were endless.

Rosie glanced at Seth Hunter on the wagon seat beside Jimmy. Her new employer was in want of a wife, though he wouldn't admit it. He had made it clear that he would never allow another woman into his life. She suspected his first marriage had been one of true love—at least on Seth's part. He had devoted himself to a young woman whose family despised his northern heritage and abolitionist sympathies. In defiance of her parents and brother, he had married Mary Cornwall, written countless letters to her while he was away in the war, and laid claim to their young son so he could keep a part of her with him always.

Though she was dead to the world, it appeared that his wife was very much alive in Seth Hunter's mind. Rosie sensed it would take a special woman to win his heart—a woman who had much more to offer than the ability to bake apple pies and black a stove from top to bottom.

Though the travelers were just across the river from Topeka, Rosie spent her second night of independence sleeping under the open sky, an ebony umbrella sprinkled with stars. Seth had expressed concern that Jack Cornwall—assuming he had been released from custody and was recovered from the knock on his head—might be able to track the party down if they stopped in Topeka. Besides, Sheena wouldn't hear of allowing her *brablins* to spend a night in such a wild city.

The next day they began the long journey toward Manhattan. As the wagon rolled west, the land began to flatten, the trees gave way to tall golden grass, the streams slowed down and straightened into long silver ribbons. The sun beat on the travelers like a merciless golden hammer.

Throughout the day, the mules plodded wearily down the baked, dusty trail. Every twelve miles, they passed a station on the Butterfield stagecoach route—a refreshing, timely stopping place to trade and water the mule teams. Seth, in a hurry to elude his possible pursuer, paused as briefly as possible.

The sunburned O'Toole children grew restless during the long journey, the young ones whimpering and the older ones fussing at each other. Not even passing through the Potawatomi Indian reservation could perk them up. Seated between his father and Jimmy O'Toole, Chipper slumped over on the front bench, shoulders hunched. Sheena fanned herself as she mourned the lack of a canvas wagon cover, and Jimmy mopped his forehead.

"Why then, Seth, do you think that *sherral* Jack Cornwall is coming after us even now?" Sheena asked as the sun rose to its apex. Like a mother hen, she had settled her five children around her. The two youngest drowsed on her lap. "Sure, I won't have harm done to any of my wee ones."

"I doubt he'll be able to track me down right away," Seth said over his shoulder. "The sheriff had him in custody, and a couple of townspeople gave the story of what happened between us in the street. I hope Cornwall will stay locked up for a while, anyway."

"Aye, but then what? Does he know where you homestead?"

"All he'd have to do is ask around."

"Will he come for you?"

"It's the boy he wants."

"Chipper, you're a good lad, aren't you?" Sheena asked softly. "You don't want your papa to come to harm. Why then, let's have the preacher in Manhattan write a letter to your grandparents and tell them how happy you are."

The little boy turned and scowled at her. "I don't wanna live with no Yankee papa," he said, speaking aloud for the first time that day. "I want to go home to Gram an' Gramps. I want my mama."

"Enough about her," Seth snapped. "You have a papa, and I don't want to hear any more talk about your mama."

Rosie bristled at the man's harsh tone. Surely he could understand the boy missing his mother. Seth Hunter wanted a son, but he clearly had no idea how to be a father. If he intended to weld the two of them into a family, he would have to do better than chastise the little boy and forbid him to mention the mother he was so obviously mourning.

Rosie couldn't deny she knew little about the business of being a family. But after nineteen years at the Christian Home for Orphans and Foundlings, she did know a great deal about children. Above their basic needs of food, clothes, and shelter, they wanted kindness. Discipline. A good Christian example to follow. And fun. All children deserved fun.

"Let's play Cupid's Coming," she said, elbowing Erinn, the oldest of the O'Toole children. At eight, Erinn was well versed in the responsibilities of child care. "You and I will start, and we'll go around the wagon, ending with your mother. How's that?"

"Cupid's Coming?" Erinn asked, her green eyes bright. "But we don't know that game."

"It's easy. I'll start. We'll use the letter *T* for the first round." Rosie frowned for a moment, pretending to study the situation. "Cupid's coming," she told Erinn. "Now you ask, how?"

"How?"

"Tiptoeing."

"Cupid's coming," Erinn told her brother, six-year-old Will.

"How?"

"Talking," Erinn said.

Will turned to Colleen. "Cupid's coming."

"How?" she asked.

"Terrifying!" Will shouted, forming his hands into claws. Everyone laughed. Even Chipper managed a half grin.

Colleen nudged her father on the wagon seat. "Cupid's coming."

"How?" he asked.

"Ticktocking."

"Cupid's coming," Jimmy told Chipper.

"How?"

"Tapping."

Chipper looked at his father. Then he glanced back at Rosie. She gave him an encouraging wink.

"Cupid's coming," the boy said.

Seth gave the reins a bored flick. "How?"

"Tripping."

"Cupid's tripping?" Seth exclaimed. "Well, I guess that's the end of the game then."

"No!" the children shouted. "Come on, Seth! Play with us."

"Excuse me," Rosie cut in. "I'm afraid Mr. Hunter didn't take his turn quickly enough. He'll have to pay a forfeit."

Seth turned slowly, his blue eyes locking on Rosie's face. "A forfeit?"

She lifted her chin and stuck out her hand. "That's right. Pay up, sir."

Seth frowned and patted his empty shirt pocket. "I'm afraid I'm fresh out of—" He stopped, leaned out of the wagon, reached into the tall grass growing by the trail, and snapped the prickly head off a dry stem. He tossed Rosie the small black ball. "Purple coneflower."

She held the gift in the palm of her hands. "This is a flower?"

"Seeds. You'll have to plant them if you want flowers." Seth turned to Sheena. "I choose the letter A. Cupid's coming."

"A? Why, Seth, that's impossible!" Sheena squawked.

"Cupid's coming," he repeated.

"How?"

"Annoying," Seth said, giving Rosie a look.

The game faltered after that. The letter A only managed to make its way to Will, who came up with "apples" and was disqualified. He paid his forfeit with a peppermint-sticky kiss on Rosie's cheek.

She was tucking her purple coneflower seedpod into the pouch she wore around her neck when Seth pulled the wagon up to a small frame building, unpainted and sagging. "Holloway's Stagecoach Station," he called. "I've had enough of Miss Mills's songs and games for one morning. We'll stop here for lunch."

"Hurrah! Come on, Chipper!" Will grabbed the younger boy by the hand. "This station has a creek out back—with tadpoles!"

"Don't get muddy!" Sheena called. She woke the littlest ones and began handing them down to Seth and Jimmy one by one. "I pray Mrs. Holloway has some of those delicious pickles. I want to buy a few. I'd love the recipe, but Mrs. Holloway won't give it out. Selfish, if you ask me."

"Come on then, my treasure," Jimmy said. "You know you'll copy the taste of Mrs. Holloway's pickles in your own kitchen, as fine a cook as you are."

"Blather, blather, blather," Sheena said with a chuckle.

She and Jimmy walked toward the station as Seth lifted a hand to help Rosie down. She slipped her fingers onto his palm, aware of the hard calluses that bore testament to his labors. Lifting the hem of her skirt, she stepped onto the wagon wheel. Before she could jump down, Seth wrapped both hands around her waist and swung her to the ground.

"Cupid's coming," he said in a low voice. "Afflicting."

"Appalling," she shot back, meeting his steady blue gaze.

"Agitating."

"Alarming."

She pulled away from him and hurried toward the station door, aware that her cheeks must be as hot and red as a pair of sun-ripened tomatoes. Why was he tormenting her this way? Did he despise her?

"Agonizing," he said, following her with long strides.

She sucked in a breath and stopped. "Abusing."

He smiled. "Amusing."

"A . . . a . . . admitting."

"Admiring."

She stepped through the door into the cool shadows. "I can't . . . can't think . . . oh, alligator."

"Ha! Too slow. You lose." He stood over her, seeming twice as tall as he had in the Kansas City mercantile. "I'm afraid Miss Mills wasn't able to give an answer quickly enough. She'll have to pay a forfeit."

Rosie swallowed. "What do you want? You know I don't have anything."

"Agreeing."

"To what?"

"No more games. No more songs. No more silliness. Leave my son to me. Take care of him—feed him, see that his clothes are patched, make him go to bed at night—but that's all. Come fall, Miss Mills, I'm taking you back to Kansas City. I don't want Chipper sad to see you leave. He's *my* son. Got that?" He turned into the station.

"Cupid's coming," Rosie said softly behind him.

Seth swung around, a frown drawing down the corners of his mouth.

"Accepting," she finished. Spotting Sheena admiring a bolt of calico, she set off toward the counter.

As Seth chewed on a slab of salt pork as tough as old leather, he studied Rosie Mills from under the brim of his hat. He didn't like her. Didn't trust her. She was too cheerful, too perky. Worse, she was defiant. In opposition to his direct orders, she had continued her charming, winsome ways with the children. With her songs and games, she had easily won them over. Look at them.

Under the shade of a big black willow tree, Rosie had arranged everybody in a circle and was marching around tapping them one by one as she chanted:

"Heater, beater, Peter mine,
Hey Betty Martin, tiptoe fine.
Higgledy-piggledy, up the spout,
Tip him, turn him 'round about.
One, two, three,
Out goes he!"

In a moment, the whole pack of children was racing around like a bunch of prairie dogs with rabies. Rosie ran among them, her bonnet ribbons flying and her skirts dancing at her ankles. How could anyone who had nothing—no home, no family, not even a blanket or a spare petticoat—be as happy as that?

No, Seth thought, it just didn't make sense. In fact, it was downright suspicious. What was she after, this Rosie Mills? What was she planning to get out of this little adventure of hers? What scheme did she have up her sleeve?

Even worse than her unsettling cheeriness was the way Chipper responded to Rosie. Ever since Seth had reclaimed the boy, Chipper had spoken barely six words to him—and not one of them was charitable. Seth could hardly blame him. After all, until three days ago, they were complete strangers, and with little explanation he had scooped up the boy, toted him to his wagon, and driven off with him.

Sure, Chipper understood that Seth was his father. Thanks to his grandparents, the boy had been well versed in the story of the Yankee "scalawag" who had sired him. Chipper didn't like his father, didn't trust him, wanted nothing to do with him. But the child clearly adored Rosie Mills.

"Oh, Chipper!" she exclaimed as he tackled her, and she tumbled to the ground in a heap. "You caught me, you little rascal!"

"You're it, you're it!" Barefooted, he danced around her. "Rosie's it!"

"I can't!" She threw back her head, stretched out her long legs, and gave a breathless laugh. "You've worn me out, all of you."

"Let's go down to the stream again before Papa calls us to the wagon," Will suggested. "We'll catch a frog and take it to Bluestem Creek. Come on, Rosie! Come with us!"

"You go ahead. I need to catch my breath."

"Please come," Chipper begged, pulling on her hand in an attempt to make her stand.

"Really, sweetheart, I can't. Go with Will. He'll show you how to catch a frog."

Seth watched as the children traipsed over the hill and down the slope toward the creek. The moment they were gone, Rosie pulled off her bonnet and crumpled it in her lap. A pained expression darkening her eyes, she gingerly touched the back of her head. Then she began to take out her hairpins one by one. She loosed the thick ropes of her brown tresses. Her hair slid to her shoulders, then tumbled down her back to the ground in a puddle of shiny silk.

Seth stared. He'd never seen such hair. Long hair—masses of it—draped around the woman like a brown cape. Even more amazing was the great pile of it that sat in the grass around her hips. Rosie Mills had enough hair for three women. Maybe four. Unaware of Seth's staring, she bent over her knees and probed her head.

"Sheena," she called softly. "Sheena?"

Seth frowned. Sheena was inside the station buying pickles. Jimmy was with her, trading one of his famous knives for a cast-iron skillet. Rosie touched her head again and looked at her fingers.

"Sheena!"

"She's inside," Seth called. He set his plate of salt pork in the wagon bed and started toward her. "Something wrong?"

"My head. It hurts where I hit it the other day. I'm afraid . . . am I bleeding again?"

Seth didn't like the notion of getting too near the woman. His new employee had an unsettling way of looking into his eyes as though she could read his thoughts. And she smelled good. He had noticed that when he helped her down from the wagon. She smelled clean and fresh—like starch mingled with lavender. Most of all, he didn't want to touch that silky sheet of her hair.

"I shouldn't have been running," she was saying, "but I thought if the children played hard, they might sleep in the wagon this afternoon. It would shorten the trip for them. Would you mind taking a look at my bump, Mr. Hunter? If I'm bleeding, I think I should put some ice on it. Maybe the stationmaster would spare . . . Mr. Hunter? Would you mind?"

She turned those big chocolate eyes on him, and Seth walked over to her like a puppet on a string. Before he could stop himself, he was kneeling beside her and drinking in that sweet lavender scent. She sifted through her hair with long fingers.

"It's just there," she whispered. "Can you see anything?"

He touched the warm brown strands. "You've got a swollen lump—"

"Ouch!"

"Sorry. I don't think it's bleeding again. I could buy you a chunk of ice."

"No, I'll be all right." She threaded her fingers through her hair. "I would hate to spend good money on something that's going to melt. I just don't want to stain my bonnet, you understand. This is the only one I have, and it's very precious to me. Priscilla gave it to me two years ago, before she left the Home."

"Priscilla?"

"My best friend. When she married the vegetable seller's oldest son, he bought her three new bonnets—not to mention a green twill skirt, a pair of new stockings, and a wool shawl. Wool. Pure, white wool. So, seeing as she didn't need it, she gave this bonnet to me for Christmas."

Seth blinked. He'd never heard anyone rattle on the way Rosie Mills could. Despite the bump on her head, she jumped from one subject to the next like a rabbit in a spring garden. As much as he wanted to ignore her, Seth couldn't quite suppress his intrigue.

"Cilla lived at the Home three years," Rosie went on, oblivious to her employer's bemusement. "She came to stay with us after her parents died in a terrible fire. All her relatives lived in England, and they couldn't afford boat passage for her even though she ached to go to them."

"I'm sure she did," Seth managed, searching for an adequate response to the woeful tale. "Poor Cilla."

"It was very sad. But I wouldn't feel too sorry for her, if I were you. Cilla wasn't a foundling, you know. She came from a respected family, and she was very pretty. Blonde. Curls everywhere. Anyway, the vegetable seller's son decided she would make a good wife. So they married, and now she has a baby girl and another on the way."

"Not to mention three new bonnets, a skirt, and a pair of stockings."

The corners of Rosie's mouth turned up. "Don't forget the wool shawl."

"Lucky girl to win the heart of the vegetable seller's oldest son. Must have been true love."

"I don't know about that." She shrugged and began to twine her hair into a long rope. "What matters is Cilla's settled, and I miss her. I won't have this bonnet ruined."

Seth studied the wad of thin calico. The bonnet was a pathetic scrap, patched and frayed. Cheap cotton, it might once have been navy, but it had faded in the sun to a pale shade of cornflower blue sprinkled with small white rosebuds.

"Is that what *you're* after, Miss Mills?" Seth asked. "Bonnets and stockings and wool shawls?"

"Good heavens, no! Those are earthly treasures. The Bible tells us not to store them up. They won't last. I'm after something much more important."

"I figured as much."

She lifted her focus to the tips of the arching willow branches. "Faith," she murmured. "I want to grow in faith. Hope. The hope of heaven. And love. To share the love of my Father with people who've never known it."

"Lofty dreams." He gave a grunt of impatience. "Look, Miss Mills, you left everything familiar to risk traveling to the prairie with a stranger. You must be thinking you'll get something practical out of it."

Her brown eyes searched his face. "Yes," she said softly. She leaned toward him. "This is a secret, so please don't tell anyone. I've made up my mind. I want to get married, Mr. Hunter."

"What?" His heart jumped into his throat and froze solid. "Married?"

"Not to you! Don't draw back like a snake just bit you." She laughed for a moment as though the idea of anyone wanting to marry him was a great joke. "Of course not you. Someone else. Almost anyone will do. While I'm living on your homestead the next few months, I'm going to search for a husband. If I can find someone fair-minded and strong, a kind man and a hard worker, I'll ask him to marry me."

"You'll ask *him?"*

"Why not? I don't have a thing to offer but a pair of good hands and a strong back. Who would ask me?" She leaned back and giggled again as though this were the funniest notion she'd heard in weeks. "Oh, laughing makes my bump hurt."

Seth watched as she twirled the rope of her hair onto her head in a big glossy mound of loops and swirls. Still chuckling, she deftly slipped hairpins here and there. She gave her creation a quick pat to assure herself it was secure, then she swept her bonnet over it and tied the ribbons into a loose bow under her chin.

"Keep your eyes peeled for me, Mr. Hunter," she confided. "I don't much care what the man looks like or how old he is. It makes no difference how many children he's got. As long as he's good and kind."

"And hardworking."

"Yes." She studied him. "Why are you smirking at me, Mr. Hunter?"

"It just seems a little strange that you've made up your mind to go out husband hunting like a trapper after a prized beaver."

"And why not? The Bible tells us it's good for a man and woman to marry. I don't know why I should be obliged to spend the rest of my life working at the Christian Home for Orphans and Foundlings when there might be a lonely man somewhere who could use a good wife."

"I guess you never considered that it might be nice if the fellow loved you. And you him."

"Love? Please, Mr. Hunter. Have you been reading novels?"

Seth studied the woman's brown eyes. He didn't know what had made him kneel under the willow tree and talk to this creature in the first place. She jabbered like a blue jay. She giggled like a schoolgirl. He didn't trust her around his son. No telling what ideas she might put into the boy's head. Any woman who would walk away from a secure position to go to work for a stranger . . . any woman who would set out on her own in search of a husband . . . any woman who would ask a man to marry her . . . any woman like that was too downright bold. Too forward. Too impetuous. It just wasn't proper.

Rosie Mills didn't seem to have the least idea what love was all about. She would marry a man the way a store owner would take on a hired hand. No feeling. No emotion. No passion behind it.

That wasn't how he and Mary Cornwall had felt about each other. He had been half crazy over that girl. The way she swayed when she walked had set his heart beating like a brass band. The way she batted her eyelashes at him turned his stomach into a hundred butterflies. And when she had stood on tiptoe to kiss him on the cheek that afternoon in the barn . . . well . . .

Seth hadn't known Mary very long when he asked her to marry him. But the way she made him feel was love. True love. No doubt about it.

"I don't know a thing about love except what the Bible says," Rosie announced, cutting into his pleasant memories. "Love is patient, kind, forgiving. Never jealous or proud. Love is never demanding or critical. I imagine I could love just about anybody, Mr. Hunter. Couldn't you?"

"Nope." He stood and swatted the dust from his knees with his hat. "I hate Jack Cornwall's guts, and if he tries to take my son again, I'll kill him."

"Kill him?"

"Besides that, I'd never marry some bold, insolent woman who thought she could do the asking. If I ever marry again, I'll have more in it than patience, kindness, and forgiveness. You don't know the half of what it takes to make a marriage."

Rosie got to her feet. "Maybe I do know the half. I may never have had a family to grow up with or a man turning somersaults over me, but I watched the family who lived across the street from the Christian Home. I climbed up in the white oak tree every morning to say my prayers, and I studied that family. I saw how they lived, working together day and night. I watched the children grow. I saw funerals and weddings and birthday parties."

"Working together day and night is not all there is to marriage," Seth said, growing hot around the collar.

"Maybe it's not all, but it's half!" Rosie Mills tilted her chin at him, her brown eyes sparking like coals. "Half is what *you* know—the kind of love that forces a man to marry a girl against her parents' wishes, love that makes him write her from the battlefield and steal away her son and keep her alive in his heart even when she's dead."

"Stop talking about my wife!" Seth exploded.

"I won't deny I've never known that kind of passion," Rosie went on. "But *I* know the other half of what makes a family. It's commitment. It's holding on through thick and thin. It's surviving through freezing winters and burning summers and sick children and not enough food in the pantry. That's what it is. Commitment like that is plenty to make a marriage, and I'm going to find myself a husband no matter what you think, Mr. Seth Hunter!"

"Good luck to the man who hooks up with the likes of you!" he roared, his mouth just inches from hers.

She swallowed and blinked. To his utter dismay, her brown eyes filled with tears. She gulped. "I'll . . . I'll just go and see if Sheena found her pickles. Excuse me."

Rosie swung away, her palm cupping the bump beneath her bonnet. Seth watched her go, a slender twig of a woman with hair like a river, dark coffee eyes that glowed when she laughed, and enough spunk to survive the worst life had to offer. It occurred to him as he went back to his plate of salt pork that Rosie Mills would probably make some man a pretty good wife.

CHAPTER 3

AS ROSIE stood inside the stagecoach station watching Sheena and Jimmy count their purchases, she fought the lump in her throat. Once again, she had to confess she had stepped out on her own instead of turning to her heavenly Father for direction. In setting off for Kansas with Seth Hunter, she had been willful, selfish, and headstrong. To the best of her knowledge, she hadn't offered up a single prayer for guidance before climbing onto that mule wagon bound for the prairie. And now she would have to suffer the consequences.

Seth Hunter was a hard man. An angry man. A bitter man. He didn't want tenderness or compassion. And he certainly didn't seem to like anyone standing up to him. Unfortunately, his new hired hand was everything he found intolerable.

Rosie had always assumed a girl who had spent her life in a place like the Christian Home for Orphans and Foundlings ought to be meek, contrite, humble. Instead, she fought a constant battle with her willful nature.

Precisely because she had grown up in the Home, she had learned to rely on her wits and to trust her instinct. On an impulse, she could devise a game that would transform toddlers' wails into giggles. She could create meals when there was nothing in the kitchen pantry but a bag of bug-infested beans and a few withered carrots. She contrived ways to keep the orphans warm during blizzards. She improvised a pull-rope swinging fan to keep the kitchen cool in summer. If a townsman gave the Home a sack of old, half-rotten potatoes, Rosie had the children cut out the eyes, plant them in the kitchen garden, and grow a bumper crop. If a church donated an extra quilt, she cut apart the patches and used them to mend the holes in every child's clothing.

If Rosie had an idea, she acted on it. More often than not, her ideas were good ones. But sometimes . . . sometimes the consequences were disastrous.

"It's me, Father," she prayed as she leaned against the rough plank wall of the stagecoach station. "It's always me first, isn't it? You must be so tired of my willful stubbornness. Every day I do nothing but rely on myself. *I'll* climb the oak tree. *I'll* whack Jack Cornwall on the head. *I'll* go to Kansas with Seth Hunter. *I'll* find a man to marry me."

She shook her head in dismay. Why couldn't she remember to pray before she acted—instead of after?

"Father, forgive me," she murmured. "I do so want to have a home and a family. Help me to leave it up to you—"

"Rosie?" Sheena's green eyes studied her. "Are you muttering to yourself, then?"

"No, no—"

"Seth's just told us the knock on your head has been troubling you. He's fretting about you, he is."

"About me?"

"Aye, and now I hear you muttering to yourself. Perhaps we'd better try to find a doctor so he can have a look at your head."

"No, really, Sheena. I'm fine."

"You're certain? I'm sure I saw you—"

"I was praying."

The woman's green eyes widened. "First you pray in an oak tree. Now in the stagecoach station?"

"Our Father is with us everywhere."

"That he is, and a good thing, too. All the same, I wouldn't go talking to him just anywhere. People might wonder at it, you know." Sheena handed Rosie a wrapped bundle. "Now then, here's a gift for you from Jimmy and me. We want to see you started off right in your new life."

Rosie stared at the package in her hands. No one had ever given her anything new. Ever. Not in her whole life.

"Well, don't just stand there throwing sheep's eyes at the thing," Sheena said. "Open it."

Swallowing hard, Rosie unfolded the rough white cheesecloth. "A skillet! Cast iron. Oh, Sheena, it's beautiful."

"Jimmy traded one of his knives for it. He makes the best knives in all Kansas, he does."

"Mr. O'Toole!" Clutching the heavy skillet to her chest, Rosie danced across the room and flung an arm around the tall, gaunt man. "Thank you. Thank you so much!"

"Now then—" he began, but he stopped when she planted a big kiss on his cheek.

"A skillet! I wish I could show this to Mrs. Jameson. She wouldn't believe how beautiful it is! And so big. I'll bet a person could fry fifteen eggs in this skillet. If the kitchen at the Christian Home had a skillet like this one . . . You know, the skillet we have now is so thin at the bottom . . . everything burns . . . and the other has a hole in it . . . Why don't I send this one to Mrs. Jameson and the children? Would you mind if I gave it away?" She glanced at Jimmy. A look of confusion in his green eyes, he shook his head.

"Oh, thank you! Mr. Holloway, will there be a stagecoach or a wagon passing through here on its way to Kansas City?"

"Only ten or fifteen a day," the stationmaster said. He was eyeing the O'Toole children, who had filtered into the building and were peering into his cases—sticky fingers, lips, and noses pressed against the glass. "What is it you want with a stagecoach back to Kansas City, Missy? Ain't that where you folks just come from?"

Rosie set the iron pan on the countertop. "Mr. Holloway, will you please send this skillet by stagecoach to the Christian Home for Orphans and Foundlings? I've never been able to give anyone a gift. Tell them it's from me: Rosenbloom Cotton Mills."

The stationmaster scowled at her. "What kind of a dumb-fool name is that?"

"It's a beautiful name. It's the name my mother gave me."

"That ain't no name. It's a place. In Illinois, to be exact. I order my stockings from Rosenbloom Cotton Mills. Look here."

He reached into his glass case and brought out a pair of cotton stockings the exact shade of gray as the one Rosie had been put into as a baby. He tunneled his hand down to the toe and pulled out a scrap of white paper.

"See there, it's right on the label: *Rosenbloom Cotton Mills*. They make stockings, underwear, and gloves. I've been ordering from Rosenbloom Mills for fifteen years." He shooed the children away from his cases, and they scampered outside. "Now what's your real name, Missy? I don't know nobody in their right mind who would give a skillet as good as this one to a passel of worthless urchins. Half of them is of indecent birth."

"But Mr. Holloway—"

"It ain't right even to look at them devils—born to loose women and not worth the food that's fed 'em. Even God don't want nothing to do with the likes of foundlings. Ain't you read what the Good Book says? The book of Deuteronomy: 'A bastard shall not enter into the congregation of the Lord; even to his tenth generation shall he not enter into the congregation of the Lord.'"

Rosie caught her breath. "No . . . the children . . . we—"

"Who are you, anyhow?" Holloway went on. "The way I see it, anyone who goes by an alias is hiding something."

Her heart hammering, Rosie touched the small pouch she wore

on a string around her neck. The toe of the stocking . . . and inside it, the square of neatly printed paper. *Rosenbloom Cotton Mills*. For years, she had convinced herself her mother had written out that beautiful name for her newborn baby. Hadn't she tucked the tiny child into the stocking so her daughter would be safe and warm? Hadn't she cherished the child she had been forced to leave behind? Didn't the silent, long-lost mother mourn for her daughter every day—wondering where she was, praying for her safety, aching to hold her again, just as her child ached to be held?

The image Rosie had denied all her life burst into her thoughts with the force of an exploding bullet. She had been conceived by accident. Born unwanted. Stuffed into a sock. Abandoned on a stack of moldy hay in a livery stable. Expected to die.

The name was not a precious gift. It was a stocking label.

"You gone deaf, girl?" the stationmaster spoke up. "If you want me to send this skillet to Kansas City, you'd better give me your true name."

"Rose Mills," Seth said, stepping up to the counter and jabbing a finger into the man's chest. "That's who she is, and it's as good a name as yours or mine. Now send that skillet to the Christian Home like she said, or I'll see that nobody the other side of Bluestem Creek ever stops at your station again."

"You look here, Mister—"

"Now then, Seth." Jimmy O'Toole put an arm around his friend's shoulder. "Sheena's got her pickles, and the *brablins* are already climbing onto the wagon. Let's be on our way, shall we?"

"The sooner the better." Seth gave the stationmaster a final poke. Dropping his hat on his head, he grabbed Rosie's arm. "Let's go."

She barely had time to lift the hem of her skirt as Seth propelled her out the door onto the rickety front porch. She half ran to keep up with his long stride, and Jimmy hurried his wife along behind them.

"By herrings, that Holloway is a wicked fellow," Sheena puffed. "I hope it gets there. The skillet, I mean."

"It will."

When they reached the wagon, Jimmy helped Sheena climb aboard. As he pushed his wife from behind, the three oldest O'Toole children pulled on their mother's arms. Sheena couldn't hold back a giggle at her family's arduous effort, but Seth was in no mood to join the fun. He swept Rosie off her feet and tossed her over the side of the wagon like a sack of seed. Climbing onto the front, he flicked the leather reins. As the wagon began to roll, Jimmy gave his wife a final shove. Then he scampered around to the other side and climbed aboard.

"Whoa, Seth!" Sheena called, thumping him on the back. "You've nearly gone off hot-foot without my Jimmy! What's got you so scalded?"

"Holloway. The man doesn't deserve the privilege of running a station. Someone ought to take away his post office commission."

"Aye, he charges double what the merchants get in Kansas City," Sheena said. "Two dollars for a gallon of molasses. Seventy-five cents a pound for butter. Did you see his eggs? Sixty cents a dozen. Sure the man ought to be strung up for highway robbery."

"He'll charge what the market can bear," Jimmy said. "Holloway's got a good location, so he does. Hardly a soul can make it from Fort Riley to Kansas City without stopping at his station."

"Of course, if *we* had a better crossing at Bluestem Creek," Sheena suggested, "we could cut off Holloway and his high prices. We could—"

"Now you've done it." Jimmy shook his head at Seth. "Her blather won't let up for hours. 'If you would only put in a ferry, Jimmy. If you'd just build a bridge, Jimmy.' Seth, why don't you give my wife an answer, and see if you can put a stop to her ballyragging."

As the adults talked on, Rosie leaned her head against a keg of seed and shut her eyes. She couldn't make herself care whether some Kansas creek had a ferry or a bridge. She didn't even mind that Mr. Holloway overcharged for molasses and butter. Her head throbbed where she'd hit it, but the pain was nothing compared to that in her heart.

Rosenbloom Cotton Mills, that beautiful name. It wasn't hers. It belonged to a factory that made underwear. No mother had loved her newborn baby and tenderly laid her in a warm, safe place until she could be discovered by someone who had the means to care for her. Rosie had been abandoned. Cast away. Unwanted.

She fought the tears that welled in her closed eyes. The stationmaster's rebuff rang in her ears. *Even God don't want nothing to do with the likes of foundlings. Ain't you read what the Good Book says? The book of Deuteronomy. A bastard shall not enter into the congregation of the Lord—* Rosie forced the memory to stop. She couldn't believe such a thing was really in the Bible. No matter what Mr. Holloway said, she had to believe God loved her. Thanks to his mercy, she had been found. Taken in by the Christian Home. Fed. Clothed. Taught to read and do arithmetic and sew. Given honest work to keep her hands busy.

But nobody had ever wanted her. Her mother hadn't wanted her. She hadn't been chosen by any of the families who looked over the children for adoption. She hadn't been picked by any of the young men who came courting the older girls at the Home.

Even now. Seth Hunter didn't want her. Though he had come to her defense against Mr. Holloway, he had made it clear that Rosie was a bother to him. Annoying. Afflicting. Agitating. He hadn't wanted to take her to his homestead in Kansas. And he didn't like her spending time with his son.

Stay out of my life, was the message his blue eyes conveyed. *Keep away from me and those I love. I don't want you.*

"Sheena's right," Seth was saying as Rosie struggled to keep her tears from spilling down her cheeks. "If we had a better crossing at Bluestem Creek, we could cut Holloway right off the trail. The only reason people stop at his station on Walnut Creek is because they can't cross the Bluestem until they get almost up to the springs."

"So why don't you build a bridge, Seth?" Sheena asked. "It would bring you closer to our place, as well—just across the creek instead of half a day's travel upstream and back down again. Sure the stagecoaches would love it. And the military, too. Can you imagine? A straight stretch from Laski's Station to LeBlanc's Mill. It would cut off almost a full day's travel. Maybe you could charge a toll, Seth. Make enough money to pay for the bridge—and a little extra to save besides."

"You want fifteen stagecoaches a day passing across our property, Sheena?" Jimmy asked. "You want settlers stopping and begging you for eggs and milk? You want them slipping into our fields and picking our corn? You want soldiers poking around in your kitchen garden to see if they can find a spare spud for their stew? You want to be cooking for thirty at dinnertime instead of seven? I say let Holloway have the lot of them, and bad luck to them every one."

"And what if a fire burns our fields like it did poor Rustemeyer to the north, Mr. Contrary O'Toole?" Sheena hurled back. "What if a cyclone comes along and blows away our house? Did you ever think about that? Sure we could use the money then, couldn't we? What if we have a drought? What if—"

"What if St. Patrick drives all the snakes back into Ireland? What if all our spuds turn into gold nuggets? By all the goats in Kerry, woman, I'll not have fifty *spalpeens* a day traipsing across my homestead. I don't care how much you want a bridge, I'll not build it!"

"Then I will," Seth said. "I'll build it just downstream from my house, over near the barn. Jimmy, with your permission, I'll clear a path from the main trail across the corner of your land to that spot on the Bluestem where folks cross in a dry month. Nobody would come near your house, but I'll let them stop at mine for water and feed. You know it would do the both of us good to have a bridge."

"That Jack Cornwall would get to you quicker if he had a nice, straight road to ride down," Jimmy said.

"And you and I would be closer to each other in case we need help. It would even tie in Rolf Rustemeyer—"

"That *German?*"

"Yes, and you're Irish, LeBlanc's French, and Laski's Polish. Why not build a bridge to connect us? At harvesttime it would shorten your trip to Topeka, and I could get to the mill twice as fast." He paused. "*And* we'd cut off Holloway."

Sheena laughed. "There you have it! Cut off the scoundrel and his pickle-hoarding little wife."

"You'd cut off Salvatore Rippeto, too," Jimmy said. "Or did you forget about our Italian neighbor?"

"Sure, he and Carlotta would thank us kindly for such a thing. That poor woman's got so many wee ones she can barely keep her eye on them—not to mention tending all the travelers."

"Aye, build your bridge then," Jimmy said. "I knew it would come to this one day. Civilization. Before you can count to ten, the preacher will be dropping by to tie up our Sundays with his crawthumping. And then somebody will get the elegant notion to put in a mercantile. And a saloon. And a schoolhouse. In no time, there'll be lawyers and doctors and all manner of scalawags swarming us."

"And St. Patrick will drive all the snakes back into Ireland," Sheena said. "To tell God's truth, Jimmy O'Toole, you are the sourest man that ever lived. There's not a chance in all the world that Seth Hunter's little dugout will become the next Topeka."

"Dugout?" Rosie said, coming suddenly alert.

"Sure and what else did you expect?" Sheena asked. "A white clapboard with roses and morning glories twining the front porch? You're on your way to the prairie, my girl."

Rosie sank back against the seed keg and shut her eyes. The prairie. No bridge. No mercantile. No church. No school. Not even a house.

Unwanted, unneeded, unloved, the girl with no name was on her way to live in a hole in the dirt of the barren, windswept prairie.

"It makes me think of ironing," Rosie said to Sheena.

Seth frowned. What was she on about now? Ever since they'd left Holloway's Station on Walnut Creek, Rosie had been uncharacteristically quiet. No songs. No whistling competitions. No riddles. No long, drawn-out fairy tales about princesses and ogres. At first, it had been a blessed relief. Seth thought he'd had enough silliness to last a lifetime.

But then the O'Toole children began to whine and fidget. Sheena complained about the heat. Jimmy complained about Sheena. The whole cacophony was regularly punctuated by Chipper announcing he wanted his Gram and Gramps, and he didn't want to go live with "no Yankee."

Seth had almost rejoiced when he heard Rosie's voice from the back of the wagon. "I don't know what I expected," she said, and everyone grew quiet. "But this certainly isn't like anything I ever imagined."

"What are you talking about, lass?" Sheena had asked.

"The prairie," Rosie had said. And then she made her comment about ironing. No doubt this was going to turn into a riddle game or something, Seth mused. At least the sound of her voice had calmed the children. Even Chipper seemed to be listening to what Rosie would say.

"Ironing," she repeated. "You know how it is when you do the laundry? You start with a shirt fresh off the clothesline, and it's as rumpled and wrinkled as Missouri is full of hollows, hills, creekbeds, and bluffs. Then you begin to iron. The wrinkles smooth out, and the rumples flatten down. The hills vanish. The streambeds stretch out straight and smooth. And it's the prairie."

Sheena laughed. "What do you think of it then? Do you like this pressed down, flat land, Rosie?"

The young woman sat silently for a moment. "I think the prairie is the ugliest thing I've ever seen."

Seth swung around. "Ugly?"

She turned her big chocolate eyes on him. "Ugly. Boring, too. It's flat and dry and all but bare of trees. There's nothing to stop the wind. The water is so sleepy it makes hardly a sound. And the grass—it seems to go on forever like an endless pale-green-and-yellow sea. I know God created the prairie, but I can honestly say I've never seen anything so ugly in all my life."

Seth stiffened. "You call soil as thick and rich as chocolate cake ugly? You call a sky that stretches from one horizon to the other like a big blue bowl ugly? Miss Mills, you don't know a thing about ugly."

He glared at her. The prairie was his home, his certainty, his hope. The prairie was the source of his faith. In his lifetime, Seth had known enough pain to turn him away from God—a father who walked out on him, a war that tore his country apart, a best friend blown to bits by a cannonball, a wife whose parents despised him, a love who died in the bloom of her life. But the prairie refused to let Seth's bitterness and doubt claim his soul. The prairie was proof of a future, proof of heaven, proof of God himself.

"You call this ugly?" he asked, bending over the side of the wagon and snapping off a bunch of long-stemmed red blossoms. "This is Indian paintbrush. See these pink-and-yellow flowers? Goat's rue. Those little white flowers? Pussy's-toes. The purple ones? Bird's-foot violets." He reached down and plucked another handful of tiny blue flowers. "Blue-eyed grass. And here's yellow-star grass."

He tossed the wildflower bouquet into Rosie's arms. She caught it and clutched it with both hands. Her brown eyes were wide, as though she feared he might put her out of the wagon any moment and abandon her on the ugly, boring prairie.

Seth had half a mind to do just that. On the other hand, for some reason he couldn't explain, he wanted Rose Mills to see what this land meant to him. He wanted her to understand that it was his life.

"It's not just an endless sea of yellow and green. Right from this wagon seat I can count seven different kinds of grass. There's prairie dropseed over there and two kinds of broomsedge along the trail. See that patch of light green? That's Elliott's broomsedge. It'll be a brown orange come fall. This other kind looks almost the same, but it's not. The leaves on the seed stalks are broader, and they'll turn bright orange."

"There's little bluestem," Jimmy chimed in. "It's a sort of blue-green, so it is. And you see that stand of purple-stemmed grass over there, Miss Mills? That's big bluestem. By mid-August, the seed heads will divide into three parts."

"They look just like turkey tracks, so they do," Will O'Toole said. "I see silverbeard bluestem, Papa. Look down, Rosie, just by the wagon wheel. Silverbeard is very short. Do you see it?"

Holding tight to her bouquet, she nodded. "I never imagined—"

"I see Indian grass!" eight-year-old Erinn piped up. "Look just over there! It's so tall. Taller than me."

"And there's switchgrass!" Will said.

"I see sideoats grama," little Colleen pointed out.

As the children began exclaiming over the grass and flowers, Sheena patted her bonnet. "Sure, you've not said a word to Rosie about the animals, Seth Hunter. The prairie is teeming with animals, so it is. Deer, antelope, jackrabbits, prairie chickens, wolves—"

"Don't forget buffalo," Will cut in. "Sometimes we see them crossing the prairie by the thousands, so we do."

"And grizzly bears," Colleen added, touching Rosie's arm. "Sure, they like to follow the buffalo herds and eat up the weak shaggies. You'll want to beware of grizzly bears."

"She should beware of snakes, too," Erinn said. "You'll want to look out for copperheads, Rosie. If a copperhead bites you, well . . . you're done for."

Will squared his shoulders. "But there's lots and lots of other good snakes. We've ribbon snakes and garter snakes and bull snakes, not to mention prairie ringnecks and prairie king snakes—"

"All right, all right!" Rosie exclaimed, holding up her hands in surrender. "There does seem to be more to it than I thought. Just . . . just give me time."

"You've got six months," Seth said. "When I take you back to Kansas City after the harvest, you can tell me then if you still think our prairie is ugly and boring."

Rosie was smelling the bundle of wildflowers, but he could read the pain written in her eyes. She didn't want to go back to Kansas City. As unappealing as she found the prairie, she considered her old life a far worse prospect.

Chances were good she would find herself some farmer and marry him. Then her husband could put up with her songs and whistling and chatter. It sure would be quiet when autumn rolled around. Nice and quiet.

"There's Rippeto's Station!" Will shouted. "I see it! I see it!"

Sheena patted Rosie's arm. "Here's where we part ways. After a good night's sleep—"

"Good night's sleep?" Jimmy snorted. "With Carlotta's *brablins* hollering their lungs out?"

"Tomorrow morning," Sheena continued, "our Jimmy will put all the O'Tooles on the wagon we left at Rippeto's. Then we'll set off down the western bank of the Bluestem. You and Seth and the boy will travel down the eastern bank. Sure we'll see each other's wagons almost the whole twelve miles, but there's no way to cross."

"Until Seth builds his elegant bridge," Jimmy said, "and paves the way for Jack Cornwall and every other scoundrel from New York to California."

"*Whisht*, Jimmy," Sheena said softly. "Aye, Rosie, you're almost there. By tomorrow you'll have what you've always dreamed of. Home. A beautiful home."

Seth gave the reins a flick. "Six months," he said. "And the only home she'll have is the barn."

CHAPTER 4

BEFORE heading east to Kansas City with Seth Hunter, the O'Toole family had stored their wagon in Salvatore Rippeto's barn. Now loaded down with the seeds and farming equipment they had purchased, the wagon rattled across Bluestem Creek. Sheena and her children waved good-bye, and Rosie was never so sorry to see anyone go. As Seth turned his own wagon south, she felt more alone than she had in all her life. Not only was she lonely, she was concerned at what the day might bring. And she was tired.

The night at the Rippetos' had seemed as endless as Jimmy had predicted. Carlotta regularly shouted at one or the other of her ten children—evidently the only means she knew to control them. Salvatore hammered in his loft until well after dark. Four stagecoach passengers stretched out on the floor and snored loudly enough to raise the roof. Two military men talked for hours on the porch. And in the darkness, little Chipper sobbed.

It had been all Rosie could do to keep from creeping over to the grieving child and taking him in her arms. But she remembered his father's stern command to keep away. She was to provide for the boy's needs and nothing more. But wasn't compassion a need? Didn't a child have a right to comfort and love?

"We'll be at my place a little after noon," Seth said as he guided his mules downstream. It was clear to Rosie that the man kept his focus on himself and his own interests—and not on those around him. "Most of this land's unclaimed, though it was surveyed before the war. We'll pass Rolf Rustemeyer's place in a few hours. He's the fellow just north of me. German. Can't understand a word he says."

Rosie studied the man on the bench beside her. The nearer they drew to his homestead, the more civil Seth became. His blue eyes shone in the early morning sunlight. His dark hair lifted and feathered beneath his hatband. Rosie thought she even detected the hint of a smile at one corner of his mouth.

But the change in Seth's demeanor hardly made a difference to her. All she could see was how coldly he behaved toward his son. He gave no heed to the little boy's tears. He never laid a hand on the child or whispered even the slightest word of comfort. His indifference toward his son infuriated Rosie, and she began to wish she had whacked Seth on the head instead of Jack Cornwall.

"Rustemeyer's been working on his claim a lot longer than I have," Seth said, oblivious to the fact that she was attempting to bore holes through him with her glare. "He's been looking after my place while I've been away. I think I'll see if he has a notion to help me build the bridge."

"You just told me you couldn't understand him," Rosie said.

Seth glanced at her, one eyebrow arching a little at her retort. "Not much. It's all *ja* and *ach* and *nein*. But we manage."

"Does he have any children Chipper could play with?"

"Rolf's not married."

"Well then, Chipper, you'll just have to help your father build that bridge so you can walk over to the O'Tooles' house to play." Rosie bent down and kissed the little boy's hot, damp forehead. "Who do you like best of all the O'Tooles? I thought Erinn was very pretty with her long red braids. Do you like her?"

"Will," Chipper said softly. "I like Will best."

"I like him, too. Did you hear him going on about the snakes? I'll bet you and Will could have a fine time out by the creek. He can teach you all about the prairie, and you can teach him some games. What's your favorite game? Hopscotch?"

"Tag."

As the hours passed, Rosie did her best to draw out the little boy—and to ignore his father. She had come to the conclusion that Seth Hunter had kidnapped his son in the vain hope of recapturing a part of his dead wife. But he had no inclination to love Chipper for the special person he was. To Seth, the boy was a prize. A trophy. He would kill Jack Cornwall for the right to keep that trophy. But he had no idea how to truly cherish such a treasure.

Chipper had stopped crying and was beginning to catalog all his favorite foods when the wagon rolled to a stop. Rosie looked up to find Seth setting the brake and climbing down from the bench. In the distance, a blond giant of a man waved from his plow.

"Rustemeyer!" Seth called. "Good morning."

"*Guten Morgen*, Hunter! How you are?"

"Pretty good, and you? We've just come from Rippeto's."

"*Ja*, Rippeto. *Sehr gut*."

Curious, Rosie slipped down to the ground and started after Seth across the newly tilled field. Rolf Rustemeyer was no taller than Seth, but he had been built like a granite bluff. His thighs looked like two tree trunks. His hands, great slabs of ham, gripped the wooden plow handles. His hair hung to his shoulders in thick golden waves. When he smiled, his grin spread from ear to ear.

"Ah, Hunter, You have *Frau!* Vife, *ja?*"

Seth swung around. Seeing Rosie behind him, his eyes darkened. "Wife? No. She's going to work for me. Work."

"*Sehr schön!* Beautiful, *ja?* Pretty."

Rosie stopped. She stared up at the hulk of a man, her heart pounding. Unmarried. Hardworking. Friendly. *And* he thought she was beautiful. Had she just met her future husband?

"Name?" he asked. When Rosie said nothing, he placed a hand on the rock slab of his chest. "*Ich bin* Rolf Rustemeyer."

"I'm Rosie," she said. "Rosenbloom Cot . . . uh . . ."

"Rose Mills," Seth finished when she faltered. "She's come to look after my boy. Clean a little. Cook."

"Ah, *die Köchin!*" Rolf rattled off a long string of unintelligible words as he gestured toward his land and the ramshackle dugout in the distance. Then he finished with a grand smile. "*Ja?*"

"I don't know what you said!" Seth shouted, as though talking louder might somehow make Rolf understand. "I . . . want . . . to . . . build . . . a . . . bridge! Will . . . you . . . help . . . me?"

Rolf frowned. "*Helfen?*"

"What?"

"*Ach!*" He turned to Rosie. "*Sprechen Sie Deutsch,* Fräulein Mills?"

"A bridge," she said. "Over water. Bridge."

"Britsch? *Über dem Wasser?*"

Rosie looked at Seth. He looked at her. "This puts me in mind of the time Tommy Warburton came to live at the Home," she said. "He was as deaf as a fence post, poor little fellow. We had to draw pictures and point to things just to try to make him understand." She paused. "Look here, Mr. Rustemeyer. A bridge."

Hiking up her skirt a little, Rosie knelt to the ground. She drew her fingers through the soft, rich dirt. "This is the creek. The water."

"*Das Wasser?*" Rolf asked.

"*Das Wasser.*" She set a pebble by the stream. "This is you, Mr. Rustemeyer. And this pebble is Mr. Hunter. Over here across the *Wasser* is O'Toole. *Ja?*"

"*Ja!* Bluestem!" He was grinning like a coyote that had just gotten into the chicken coop. "*Ja, ja, ja!*"

Rosie picked up a stick and broke it in half. Then she laid it across the line she had drawn. "Bridge. To go across, see? Across the *Wasser.*"

"*Eine Brücke!*"

"*Ja!*" Rosie said. "*Eine Brücke!*"

"*Sehr gut!*" Then Rustemeyer rattled off another string of German that seemed to indicate he understood the idea very well. And he liked it.

Rosie glanced at Seth. "What's he saying?"

"Your guess is as good as mine."

She studied the big German. "Come to Mr. Hunter's house. Tomorrow. Build the *Brücke*."

"*Am Morgen früh? Ich kann nicht. Ich habe eine Kuh die krank ist.*"

"I don't know if he'll come," Rosie said.

"I'd say it's doubtful."

She shrugged her shoulders and turned back toward the wagon. Suddenly from behind, Rolf Rustemeyer grabbed her arm and swung her around. Rosie clapped a hand over her mouth, her breath in her throat.

"Fräulein, very pretty!" he said, falling to the ground on one knee and sweeping his frayed straw hat from his head. "Beautiful."

Before Rosie could suck air into her lungs, Rolf Rustemeyer planted a firm kiss on the back of her hand. She jumped back, bumping into Seth.

"Oh, my!" she gasped as Seth caught her shoulders. "Gracious, what are you doing, Mr. Rustemeyer? What's he doing?"

"Looks to me like he's courting." Seth stepped up to the kneeling German and lifted him by one suspender. "Listen, Rustemeyer, she's mine. Understand? The fräulein belongs to me."

"*Für* vork, *ja?*"

Seth paused. "That's right. She works for me. I brought her all the way from Kansas City. You leave her be."

"*Ja, ja.*" Rustemeyer nodded as Seth took Rosie's arm and started back across the field. "Goot-bye, fräulein! Beautiful!"

Seth helped Rosie onto the wagon beside Chipper. As she arranged her skirts, she took a peek at Rustemeyer from under the brim of her bonnet. The German wasn't bad to look at, though he did need a haircut and a wash. He was a hard worker. He seemed kind enough. And he thought she was beautiful.

As Seth started the mules, Rosie brushed a hand across her cheek. Her skin felt hot. Her mouth was dry. She thought she might be sick.

Beautiful? Nobody had ever said a word about how Rosie Mills looked—one way or the other. When she happened to catch her reflection in a window, she saw nothing but two big brown eyes, a tall gawky body, and the same blue dress she had worn for three years. Beautiful?

"Rustemeyer ought to learn some English," Seth said in a clipped voice. "And if you ask me, he needs to take a bath more than once a year."

Rosie felt a grin tug at her lips. For some odd reason, the big German's attentions to her had irked Seth. Of course, if she found someone to marry right away, she wouldn't be able to look after Chipper. Maybe that was what bothered him.

"Mr. Hunter," she said. When he turned his head, his eyes shone as bright blue as the sky. Her heart stumbled over a beat, but she lifted her chin. "I'll have you remember the war is over, and Mr. Lincoln freed the slaves."

"What's that supposed to mean?"

"It means I don't belong to you, Mr. Hunter. Not my arms for the working. Not my words for the speaking." She paused. "And not my heart for the courting."

Seth searched the trail for the first sign of his house. He had always liked that view—the roof coming into sight, and then the wall, his cows, the chickens, the fence, and finally his barn. For some reason, his pulse was pounding like a marching band. He couldn't wait to show off his place. And it wasn't just his son whose eyes would shine.

He glanced at the woman on the bench beside him. Ever since their encounter with Rustemeyer, Rosie had ridden in silence, her head held high and her eyes scanning the horizon. *Pretty*, the German had called her. *Beautiful*.

Seth gave a snort and studied the woman a little harder. Truth to tell, Rosie Mills wasn't half bad to look at. For one thing, she had those big brown eyes. In her eyes, a man could read everything she felt. Happiness, anger, fear, sorrow—her emotions were as obvious as the sun in the sky.

When Rosie was happy, her joy was about as hard to keep from catching as a case of hiccups. Anger flashed like lightning from those eyes of hers. And sorrow—Seth didn't know when he'd ever seen such pain as that written on her face when Holloway badmouthed her background. No matter that Rosie Mills was stubborn and willful and a lot more jabbery than Seth liked, nobody deserved the kind of abuse she'd taken from the stationmaster.

But pretty? Her nose was straight enough. Her cheekbones stood out high and sharp. Of course, a month or two of good food might fix that. And her mouth . . . her mouth . . . Rosie's lips—

"There it is!" she cried, turning those big chocolate eyes on him. "I see a roof! Is it your house?"

Seth cleared his throat, glad she had diverted his attention. "That's it. I built it myself."

As the mules pulled the wagon the last hundred yards, he couldn't deny the pride of ownership he felt. He had dug every inch of soil out of the ground with his own two hands. He had cut the blocks of prairie sod and laid them one atop the other to build the half-wall that fronted his dugout. He had chopped two of the scarce trees on his land and split them into boards. He had laid out his slanted wooden roof and covered it with more sod. And there it was. Perfect.

As he sat gazing on his dream, his future, Rosie stared in silence. Finally, she turned to him. Her brown eyes were luminous.

"Oh my," she whispered. "You live in a cave."

"I don't wanna live in no hole in the ground with no stinkin' Yankee," Chipper announced. "I wanna go back and live with Gram and Gramps."

Seth stared at the two of them, his face rigid. He couldn't believe what he was hearing. His farm—the labor of his hands, the legacy he would leave behind him—

"This is it, like it or not," he snapped. "This is where we stay."

Rosie stared at the dugout, her face as pale as winter prairie grass. "Home," she whispered.

Never in her life had Rosie seen anything quite so forlorn, so unwelcoming, so dispiriting as the cave in the ground Seth Hunter called home. Truth to tell, it was more like a three-sided cutaway into a low hillock than a house. As she walked up to the door, she noted that he had sided the front of the soddy with long planks. He had installed four long windows—though they had only oiled paper for panes—and a semblance of a front porch with an overhanging roof. The house itself was tucked into the hill, its roofline even with the ground. In fact, should anyone want to, he could drive a wagon right up the hill and over the sodded roof of the house without a pause.

Rosie let out a breath. This was no Kansas City cottage. There was nothing even to lend an air of beauty. No white paint. No pink-flowered curtains. No brick walkways. No picket fences. No roses or daffodils or tulips. It was . . . a burrow.

"I bought a stove from a fellow upstream who couldn't prove up his claim," Seth said, lifting the wooden bar across the front door. "He sold it cheap. You'd better light it if we're to have any supper tonight."

Rosie swallowed and stepped around a chicken on her way toward the door. Chipper sidled up against her, one thumb stuck securely in his mouth. Taking his free hand, she gave the little boy the bravest smile she could muster. "Your father built this," she whispered. "This is a prairie house."

"Looks more like a mole's house to me."

"You—!" Seth swung on the child, his finger outstretched. "I'll have you know my place is twice as big as Rustemeyer's, and I've got a better stove and a bigger bed than O'Toole—" He caught himself. "Just get your hide in here and start peeling spuds."

Rosie stood just outside the doorway. She easily read the hurt that ran beneath Seth's anger. And she understood it. He had built this house. It was his pride. His only possession.

Dear Father, she prayed silently, bowing her head under the open sky. *Please help me to see the beauty in this place. I know you can make good of all my willful mistakes. I'm almost sure you wanted me to stay back at the Home, but here I am with Seth Hunter—and I don't know why, nor what I'm to do for you. Oh, Father, please make a godly plan of my terrible mistake. Please bring joy and peace—*

"Are you coming inside?" Seth called, leaning one shoulder against the frame of his door.

Rosie breathed a quick "Amen" and hurried toward the house. As she brushed past Seth, she looked up into his eyes. They were as hard and blue as ice, and she suddenly knew she must do all in her power to soften them.

Not just his eyes, a voice spoke inside her. *Soften his heart.*

"I'm going to check on my cows," he said. "I'll bring in some meat from the smokehouse."

He started out, but she caught his arm. "Wait, Mr. Hunter. Please . . . will you show me around?"

"I thought you knew how to light a stove."

"I do. But . . . this is your home. You built it. Please, I'd like you to show it to me."

He looked down at her, his jaw tight. She saw a flicker of some emotion cross his face. And then he stroked a hand down the door.

"Walnut," he said. "You won't find a harder wood in these parts. Took me three days to build."

"And the hinges?" Rosie said. "They're leather. They look strong."

"Deer hide."

"I can't imagine anything that could break down such a sturdy door."

She gave him a bright smile as she walked inside. But there, her heart sank further. Darkness shadowed the cavernous room. A filmy cobweb stretched across one corner. A dank, musty smell mingled with wood smoke permeated the air, and the few pieces of furniture stood around on the uneven dirt floor like lonely soldiers.

"Here's the stove," Seth said, striding across the room. His head nearly touched the low ceiling. "I've only had it a couple of weeks. I reckon it could use a good cleaning."

Rosie swallowed at the sight of the large sooty stove with its rusted pipe and blackened burner lids. Half afraid of what she might find, she gingerly opened the oven door. A brown mouse lifted its head, gave a loud squeak, and jumped out at her feet. Rosie gasped and leapt backward as the mouse fled across the floor with Chipper racing after it.

"Mr. Hunter," she said, setting her hands on her hips. "Have you ever used this stove?"

He took off his hat and scratched the back of his neck. "Well, uh, not exactly. I figured I'd get Sheena over here one of these days to teach me how to work it."

Rosie brushed off her hands. If there was anything she knew, it was cooking and cleaning. Maybe God could use her to set up this household—if only for little Chipper's sake. In fact, the more she looked around the place, the easier it was to imagine what she could do with it. Scrub the table. Air out the mattress. Polish the stove.

"I built this table out of pine," Seth was saying. He stroked his hand down the three smooth boards of the long trestle table. "And the chairs. If you know anything about caning . . . "

"I do," Rosie said, studying the four seatless chairs. Obviously, Seth had been using a set of stumps assembled around the table for his perch. Those would have to go.

"And here's the bed." He cupped the ball on top of the foot post. "It's got a straw mattress. No bugs."

Rosie inspected the frame. To her surprise, the bed revealed skilled craftsmanship—its joints solid, its pegs tight, and its posts carefully carved, sanded, and polished. Curious, she returned to the table. It, too, displayed even planing and careful joinery. The chairs—though they lacked seats—stood level and rigid. And in the center of each chair's back a design of flowers and scrolls had been carved.

"You did this work?" she asked, straightening. "You built these things?"

Seth shrugged. "My uncle taught me carpentry. I always liked working with my hands." Before she could marvel aloud at the handiwork, he turned away. "See what you can do about that stove, Miss Mills. I'll be back in a few minutes with some meat."

"Eggs, too, please!" she called after him. "If you have any."

As he disappeared through the door, Rosie let out a breath. "Well, Chipper," she said softly. "Here we are at home. How do you like it?"

"I hate it." He picked up a potato from the basket at his feet and hurled it across the room. "Hate it, hate it, hate it!"

Rosie gathered the little boy in her arms and held him tightly as he began to sob. Never mind what Seth Hunter wanted, she thought. This child needed love—and she intended to see that he got it. If not from his father, then from her.

Seth decided Rosenbloom Cotton Mills's real name should have been Twister. The skinny little gal was a regular cyclone around the house. Declaring the stove too filthy to use, its chimney blocked with creosote and its ash pit jammed, she fixed a lunch of cold smoked venison. She boiled greens on an open fire, along with a few potatoes and some coffee. After lunch she broke down the stove, dragged it out the front door piece by piece, and began to scrub and polish.

While Chipper wandered the creek bank picking up kindling, Rosie scoured every pot and pan in the house. She hauled the mattress outside and threw it on top of a spice bush to air. Then she toted the sheets and bedding down to the creek and washed them in the cold water—declaring that she would do it again with hot water after she had the stove put back together.

By the time evening rolled around, she had reassembled most of the stove and all of the bed. Along the way, she had managed enough chitchat to wear out any man's eardrums. "Don't you have a broom, Mr. Hunter? Never mind, I'll make one tomorrow. I'm so glad you have a well. I thought sure I'd be obliged to make that trip to the creek five times a day. You need some new paper in your windows, Mr. Hunter. These oiled panes are all fly speckled. We had real glass panes at the Home, but I don't see how a person could ever bring glass out here to the prairie. It would shatter the first time the wagon hit a bump, wouldn't it? Don't throw those ashes away! I'll want to make lye for the soap. Have you seen any beehives around here, Mr. Hunter?"

As he went back and forth from the house to the barn, Seth couldn't help but marvel at his new employee. While he cleaned the cow stalls and checked on his chickens, the little brown-eyed twister sashayed around like there was no tomorrow. By the time she banged two pots together to call him to supper, he had to admit bringing Rosie Mills from Kansas City might not have been such a bad idea. The delicious aroma drifting through the front door of his house made his stomach groan in anticipation.

Seth washed his hands and face in the pot of warm water Rosie had set on the front porch. Still dripping, he walked inside to find the long table spread with wilted poke salad boiled with chunks of salt pork, fried sweet potatoes, and a mountain of steaming scrambled eggs. Seated on a stump at the table, his hair combed and his cheeks scrubbed, Chipper regarded the feast with wide blue eyes. Slowly, half unbelieving, Seth walked across the room and stared. He hadn't eaten a meal like this in . . . in years.

"Did you wash up, Mr. Hunter?" Rosie asked, breezing into the house carrying a plate piled high with turnovers. "I put a bowl of hot water—" She stopped and looked Seth up and down, breathless, as though the sight of a wet man had cast a spell over her. "I see you found it."

He raked a hand back through his damp hair. "Where did this come from? All this food?"

"Here and there." Coming out of her trance, she set the turnovers on the table. "You have a wealth of greens right outside the door. Poke, dock, plantain. I found some dried apples in the cellar. I hope you don't mind—"

"No, no. It's fine. Use anything you want. I'll make sure we always have fresh meat. Rabbits and quail, if nothing better. Anything in the smokehouse is yours. I dug a cellar when I moved out here late last summer. It still has a few things I managed to winter over."

"There'll be twice as much next spring," she said, sitting on a stump across from Chipper. "You'll hardly believe how good I am at pickling and canning. My cheeses and sausages are wonderful—though at the Home we never seemed to have enough to go around. Everyone says my—" She stopped and clapped a hand over her mouth. "I'm boasting. You'd better pray quickly, Mr. Hunter."

She stretched out her hands to him and Chipper and bowed her head. Thrown off-kilter by her action, Seth cleared his throat. Across the table, the boy slipped one hand into Rosie's, but he firmly tucked his free hand into his lap. Deciding the whole business of holding hands was for children, Seth propped his elbows on the table and closed his eyes.

How long had it been since he had prayed? During the war, maybe. A battle. Cannonballs bursting all around. A prayer for preservation. A cry for safety. Nothing more. He couldn't remember the last time he had spoken with God. Or listened. After all, God had allowed the Cornwalls to banish him from their property, allowed his best friend to be killed, allowed Mary to die.

"Are you going to pray before the supper gets cold, Mr. Hunter?" Rosie asked, slipping her hand into his. "At this rate, the turnovers won't be worth feeding to the chickens."

Seth glanced at her. Then he looked down at their clasped hands—his large and hard, hers much softer. An ache started up inside his chest. He couldn't speak. Could hardly move.

"Dear Father," Rosie said softly, "I thank you so much for our safe journey across the prairie. Thank you for this beautiful home Mr. Hunter has built. Thank you for providing us with this fine supper—surely more than we can even eat. In the name of Jesus Christ I pray. Amen."

Rosie gave Seth's hand a gentle squeeze. Then she picked up her spoon and began to dish out the scrambled eggs. "I have never, never in my whole entire life felt so happy," she said. When she looked up at him, Seth saw that a streak of stove blacking smudged her cheek and a puff of white flour dusted the end of her nose. Unaware, she gave him a warm smile.

"Have you ever been this happy, Mr. Hunter?" she asked.

Scooping up a spoonful of greens, Seth couldn't bring himself to answer. He felt a strange tickle at the back of his throat. And he had the terrible feeling he was going to cry.

CHAPTER 5

ROSIE had been happy at supper. But when she saw where she was to spend her summer nights, her spirits flagged. The barn smelled to high heaven. What little hay was left over from winter had grown stiff and moldy. Three milk cows and the mules used the barn for shelter. The chickens roosted in its rafters. And as she climbed the rickety ladder into the loft, Rosie gasped and stiffened in shock. On the moonlit barn floor below her, a five-foot-long blacksnake slithered out from under a tuft of loose hay and disappeared behind a wagon wheel.

"Don't worry about that fellow," Seth called up. "He's not poisonous. He keeps the barn cleaned up for me—eats mice."

Wonderful, Rosie thought. *How comforting*.

"Are you all right up there?" Seth asked.

Rosie looked over the edge of the shaky platform. "What about grizzly bears?"

"We don't see them around much. They follow the buffalo."

"Wolves?"

"Same." He shoved his hands into his pockets. "Would you like to keep my rifle on hand?"

Rosie shook her head. She could cook and clean and can and pickle—but she didn't have a clue how to shoot a gun. Seth glanced around the barn before looking up at her again.

"Well, then," he said, "good night, Miss Mills."

"Wait, Mr. Hunter!" she called out. "Please send my bonnet back to the Home. It's to go to Lizzy Jackson—after I die, I mean."

"Die?"

"Just see that it goes to Lizzy. She's wanted it ever so long, though Cilla gave it to me instead. I'd like Lizzy to have it."

Seth shook his head. "You're not going to die in the barn tonight, Miss Mills."

"Tomorrow you might put a bolt on the door."

"I can do that."

"Thank you, Mr. Hunter." Rosie drew back from the edge of the loft, but through the chinks in the floor she could see Seth staring up at where she'd been standing. She thought he had half a mind to allow her to sleep in the house—though she wouldn't do it. Such a thing would be improper. No, she would just make do in the barn, with the mice and the snakes. . . .

Seth finally left, and the absence of the lantern plunged the barn into darkness. Fortunately, through the open planks in the roof, Rosie could see the stars. They reminded her of how big God was, how powerful, and how very loving. The knowledge that a God who had created such beauty loved Rosie Mills—loved her enough to die for her—sent a wash of warm peace drifting through her. In spite of her fears, she curled up on the hay and pulled a threadbare quilt over her knees.

Seth woke with the sudden sense that something had gone wrong. He grabbed his rifle and sat up in bed. On the floor, the pallet beside the big bed was empty. The door hung ajar, admitting a draft from the night breeze.

Chipper? Confound it, the boy had run off. Or maybe Jack Cornwall had come in the cover of darkness and stolen the child away! Seth stepped into his boots, pulled on his shirt, and hitched his suspenders over his shoulders. Which would be worse? If Cornwall had taken Chipper, Seth would have no choice but to follow his enemy until he had tracked him down. This time, their confrontation would be bloody. Maybe even fatal.

But if Chipper was wandering around alone on the prairie, no telling what kind of critters he'd run into. True, wolves and bears followed the buffalo, but they kept a close watch on their whole territories. A straying child would be easy prey—weak, frightened, defenseless. . . .

His heart tight in his chest, Seth hurried outside. The moon was high overhead, a brilliant white coin. Chipper could see well enough in this light to travel a long way. And he'd been exploring the creek all afternoon. Bluestem Creek was tricky, even when it ran low.

A cold sweat dampening his shirt, Seth dashed toward the barn. He would have to wake Rosie. Two searching would be better than one. If Cornwall had kidnapped Chipper . . . if anything happened to the boy . . . his son—

"He's a very good man." Rosie's soft voice drifted down from the loft as Seth stepped into the barn. "He drove his wagon all the way to Missouri to get you because he loves you so much."

"He don't love me," a gruff little voice countered. "He don't even know me."

Chipper! Seth sagged against the barn door frame and let out a deep breath. The boy was in the loft with Rosie.

"He hasn't had time to get to know you, sweetie," she said. "And after all, you do keep calling him an old Yankee. I'm sure he doesn't think that's very polite."

"I don't care what he thinks. He's a rotten, mean, good-for-nothin' Yankee."

"I see." Rosie was silent for a moment. "By the way, Chipper, exactly what is a Yankee?"

"A bad man. Evil. Gramps used to tell me if I was naughty,

he'd turn me over to the Yankees, an' they'd string me up by my thumbnails."

"Oh, my!"

"They're ugly monsters with big yellow teeth an' hair all over."

"I don't think your father has yellow teeth . . . although he does seem to have a lot of hair."

"An' they come up behind you and *grab* you!"

"Oooh. Yankees do all that?"

"He grabbed me, didn't he? Probably tomorrow he's gonna string me up by my thumbnails." His voice went quavery. "I'm sorry I stole that piece of strawberry pie off the windowsill, Rosie. Gram switched me good for it, an' I figured that was enough. But then that Yankee came an' took me away—"

Chipper broke into sobs. From the barn floor, Seth could hear Rosie's soothing words of comfort and reassurance. He sat on the crossbar of a sawhorse, unwilling to interrupt—even though he sensed it was wrong to eavesdrop. All the same, the boy's words had stunned him. Chipper thought of his father as a monster? He believed he'd been taken away from his grandparents as a punishment for stealing a piece of pie?

"Let me tell you about Yankees," Rosie said to the little boy. "They're not such bad folks, really—once you get to know them. In fact, they believe in some very good things. Yankees believe that all people ought to be free."

"Even slaves?"

"Slaves are people, too, aren't they? They're just like us, only a different color."

"They're black."

"Yes, they are. Apples can be red or yellow or green—but they're all still apples. Each color is just as good as the other. Slaves are people even though they're black. Indians are people even though they're brown. And you and I are people even though we're white. Yankees believe no person should be able to own any other person. Your papa fought in a war to see that everybody—no matter what color their skin—could be free to walk around, do as they please, and live exactly as they like."

"That ain't true! If my papa wanted me to be free, why did he take me away from Gram and Gramps?"

Seth clenched his jaw, waiting for the reply. It was a good question—and it revealed more wisdom than he expected from a child as young as his son.

"Your papa loves you more than you can ever imagine, Chipper," Rosie whispered, and Seth felt a shiver run down his spine at the caress in her words. "God loves us so much we can't understand it. And your papa loves you in the very same way. He wants only the best for you. He knew your mama had gone to heaven—the woman he treasured most in all the world—and he figured you needed someone big and strong to look after you. Who better to look after a little boy than the papa who loves him most?"

"That Yankee loved my mama?"

"Sure he did. Just as much as you loved her." She paused a moment. "Tell me about your mama, Chipper. Tell me everything you remember."

"Mmm. She was pretty. She had yellow hair. Big long curls of it."

Seth smiled, remembering Mary and her curls. That hair had been her pride and joy. It was all her mother could do to make her wear her bonnet. As often as she could, Mary would whip it off and flounce her curls around. To the young farmhand she had set her cap on, she had looked like a porcelain doll—gorgeous, expensive, and untouchable. Until that day in the barn when she had stood on tiptoe and kissed him.

"Mama liked to cuddle me in the rockin' chair," Chipper said. "She used to sing, too, but . . . but I don't want to sing those songs now."

"Did she read stories?"

"Naw. Mama didn't like to read. She said readin' was borin';

school was borin'; hard work was borin'. Dancin' was fun. She liked to dance."

Seth had never known the motherly side of Mary. The thought of her holding a baby and rocking . . . singing . . . But he had watched her dance. *Oh, Mary.* How the young men would stare when Mary Cornwall whirled across the floor.

"Mama liked to go to town to buy things," Chipper said. "An' she would take me along. We would walk down the boardwalk together sayin' hello to all the men an' ladies. I used to like to watch her get dressed. She had pretty clothes—lots an' lots of dresses an' petticoats. She would stand in front of the mirror an' turn around an' around. I would help her get her hems straight."

"I'll bet that was fun," Rosie whispered.

"Uh huh. But when she got sick, she wouldn't rock me or sing. She just lay in bed gettin' skinny an' yellow an' . . . an' Gram would cry in the parlor . . . an' Gramps would run me out of the room. Until one day they called me in where she was lying still an' cold—"

"Chipper!" Seth called, cutting into words he couldn't bear to hear. "Chipper, are you in here?"

Silence fell over the barn. A small voice whispered. "He's gonna whip me."

"Chipper is up here with me," Rosie called down. "We were just having a little visit."

"That's enough jabbering, boy," Seth said. "Get on back to the house. If you keep us up all night, nobody will be fit to work in the morning."

"Yes, sir," Chipper said softly.

In the moonlight, his white shirt moved down the ladder. The child jumped barefoot onto the dirt floor and started past his father. Just as Chipper scampered out the door, Seth reached out and nabbed him.

"No more midnight journeys, young man," he said, lifting him high. He could feel the child trembling in his arms. "You hear me?"

Blue eyes that matched his own stared back at him. "Yes, sir. Please don't whip me, sir."

"I don't hold to whippings. My papa gave me enough of those to last two boys a lifetime. But if you pull this again, I won't like it, hear? Now get on back to bed."

He set the child on his feet, and Chipper hurtled out the barn door like a wolf was after him. Seth shoved his hands down into his pockets and looked up into the loft. He could just make out a pale face and a pair of dark, luminous eyes.

"I thought I told you not to baby him, Miss Mills," he said. "I don't want him getting attached to you."

"But he *is* a baby, Mr. Hunter."

"He's five years old."

"A mere child. He needs comfort. Who's going to give it to him?"

"Not you."

"Then who?" She crept to the edge of the loft and set her bare feet on the first rung of the ladder. "Why won't you comfort him, Mr. Hunter? Why must you always brush him aside?"

"I came and got him, didn't I? That ought to show him I care what happens to him."

"But every time he mentions his mother, you shout at him."

"I do not shout!"

"Yes, you do!" she insisted. "Chipper will live with the pain of his mother's loss until someone lets him cry it out. Do you want that for your son? Do you want him to live with the same open wound that tears at your own heart? Both of you loved Mary—"

"You be quiet about my wife!" Seth started toward the ladder. He had half a mind to climb up there and clamp a hand over Rosie Mills's blabbering mouth. What right did she have to talk about Mary? What did she know of the love . . . the pain . . . the loss . . . ?

"I won't be quiet," she said defiantly. "'Like as a father pitieth his children, so the Lord pitieth them that fear Him.' Where is your compassion, Mr. Hunter? Where is your pity? Why can't you treat your child as a son ought to be treated—with love?"

"I'll treat him the way I think he ought to be treated. Who are you to tell me how to look after my son? What do you know about it, anyway? What makes you an expert?"

The figure on the loft ladder sagged. "You're right," she whispered. "I'm sorry, Mr. Hunter. Please forgive me. I don't know a thing about families."

Uncomfortable at her sudden silence, Seth shifted from one foot to the other. "I didn't mean it that way."

"I never had a mother." The words were barely audible. "Never knew parents of my own. You and Mr. Holloway are right—"

"Don't lump me together with him."

"I won't interfere again. You must be whatever sort of father to Chipper you want to be. You must be the sort of father you had—"

"No," Seth cut in. He would never be like that man. He stopped himself from blurting out the truth about his own childhood. "Leave Chipper to me. I'll look after him."

"Yes," she said softly. "You do that."

Seth turned to the barn door. "And if he comes here again, send him straight back to the house."

As he stepped out into the moonlight, he could hear Rosie's voice. "Yes, sir," she said in the same resigned tone his son had used. "Whatever you say, Mr. Hunter."

Rolf Rustemeyer did not show up to build the bridge the following morning. Rosie kept one eye on the trail as she fried eggs and salt pork over a fire she built outside. She could see nothing but pale green grass stretching endlessly to the horizon. A jackrabbit bounded across the road, but that was all. No Rolf.

Sometime in the night Rosie had concocted a drama in which the big blond German rode up on his mule and carried her off to his homestead—like King Arthur and Guinevere, or Prince Charming and Cinderella. Rosie had read those stories over and over to the children at the Christian Home. Fortunately, Mrs. Jameson had permitted the fairy tale book a place with the copies of the Bible, *The Pilgrim's Progress*, Dante's *Divine Comedy*, and Milton's *Paradise Lost*. What Rosie wouldn't have given for a Sir Lancelot. Or even a Frog Prince.

Instead, she spent the morning putting the rest of the stove back together and searching for kindling along the creek bank. When she discovered an old willow tree about a mile downstream, she asked Seth to cut some branches for her so she could weave seats for the chairs. Chipper followed her everywhere, but Rosie made a point to give kind yet brief responses to his thousand questions.

After lunch, Seth sent Chipper off with a burlap bag to gather dried buffalo and cow chips for the fire. Rosie didn't like the idea of the little boy wandering alone across the burning prairie, but she kept her mouth shut. What did she know about being a parent, she reminded herself. Seth continued his plowing, even through the worst of the heat. And Rosie made up her mind to work just as hard as father and son.

She took down the tattered window paper and tacked up the gauzy cheesecloth in which her skillet had been wrapped. This screen let in scant light, but it kept the flies and mosquitoes outside where they belonged. Then she fashioned a broom by shaving a sapling into fine splints and binding it with a rawhide thong. She swept the pounded dirt floor of wood chips, food scraps, and other evidences of bachelor habitation. Small piles of rodent droppings made her wish that the household included a cat.

By dinnertime, Rosie had cleaned the chimneys on all the lamps and nailed up shelves for the pots and pans. Then she had cooked a big supper of corn bread and stew. Chunks of squirrel meat swam with potatoes, wild onions, and beans in a rich broth that made even little, sunburned Chipper perk up.

When Seth walked into the soddy and spotted the table with its steaming cauldron, golden brown corn bread, and bouquet of wildflowers, his blue eyes lit up like a summer afternoon. "Miss Mills," he said as he sat down. "I'm beginning to believe I made a wise choice in bringing you out here. You're as fine a cook as any I've known."

Rosie flushed as though he had called her Helen of Troy. Her hands shook as she poured fresh milk into his mug. No one had ever said Rosie was fine at anything. She knew she was a good cook by the way everybody at the Home ate and ate—and then asked for seconds. She knew her cherry pies were delicious because she had tasted them herself. But "as fine a cook as any I've known" was the biggest compliment she'd ever received. It was even better than Rolf Rustemeyer calling her beautiful. After all, any number of women could be called beautiful. But to be the finest cook a man had ever known . . .

"There's a gooseberry bush upstream aways," Seth said. "We'll have pawpaws and chokeberries, too."

"I do make good pies," Rosie said, and quickly realized how vain her words sounded. "What I mean to say is—"

"I'm sure you do. I'll look forward to tasting them." He glanced at his son. "And Chipper, at this house you can eat all the pie you want."

The little boy's blue eyes darted up in surprise. "Really? Really, truly?"

Rosie could hardly believe her ears as she sat down across from the little boy who had been too astounded to glower and label his father a Yankee. Seth nodded, and one corner of his mouth turned up in the hint of an actual smile.

"And now," he said, "shall we bless the food?"

The shout that echoed from the barn many days later sent Seth's heart straight into his throat. He dropped his seed planter in the furrow and took off running. Chipper jumped up and spilled a bowl of potato peelings on the ground as he raced after his father. Seth had just hurtled the low fence that ran around the barn when he heard the cry again.

"Oh, my! Oh, my!"

"Rosie?" Forgetting her formal name, he burst through the door. "Rosie, what's wrong?"

"Grain sacks!" she exclaimed. "Piles and piles of them!"

Seth stopped, breathing hard. "Grain sacks?"

Chipper skidded to a halt beside him. "What happened, Rosie?"

"Just look what I've found!" Rosie grabbed a bundle of empty flour sacks and hugged them tightly. "It's a treasure. Better than gold! Better than diamonds! There must be fifty of them. Maybe a hundred! I was searching for eggs because the hens seem to be roosting anywhere—and I think you'd better build a coop, Mr. Hunter—but anyway I came across this mound covered by canvas here at the back of the barn. Straw was scattered everywhere and the cobwebs were thick, so I almost went right past it. Then something whispered to me to lift up the corner of the canvas. So I did, of course. Believe me, I've learned to obey those messages I get from the good Lord above. At first I couldn't believe my eyes, but then I took my skirt and began to dust—"

"Miss Mills, what are you jabbering about?" Seth exploded.

"Grain sacks! Look at them all. When I dusted them off, I realized what I'd found. These bales are all white and stamped 'Hunter,' but these others are printed with flowers and stripes and . . . and here's a check and a plaid . . . blue and yellow and green . . . oh my, is this an actual paisley print—"

"Miss Mills!" Half fearing she'd lost her mind, Seth grabbed Rosie's shoulders. "They're grain sacks."

"I know! Aren't they beautiful? Oh, Mr. Hunter, what do you mean to do with them?"

"The ones with my name will go to the mill in the fall. The

others are extras. I got them off that fellow who went bust. He sold the whole batch to me for fifty cents, and I figured if I had a bumper crop some year—"

"Might I use a few of them, Mr. Hunter?" she broke in, her lips moist and her brown eyes glowing.

What could he say? "Use as many as you want."

"Oh, Mr. Hunter!" She threw her arms around his chest. "Thank you!"

For an instant, shock rippled through Seth. The woman smelled so sweet . . . of fresh air . . . lemongrass . . . wild pinks. Her cheek was warm and downy against his neck and her eyelashes soft, so soft, on his skin. In his arms she felt small, slender, fragile. And real. Soft and feminine and very real. She pressed against him in the briefest of hugs, and then she whirled away.

"Catch, Chipper!" she sang out and tossed the little boy a bundle of grain sacks. "We'll have curtains! A rug! Pillows!"

He giggled and flung the bundle back at Rosie. "Your turn!"

"Mr. Hunter!" She swung around and tossed it to Seth. "You'll have a new shirt by Sunday! Checks or stripes? Blue or brown?"

"Well, blue is nice enough, I reckon," he said, watching in amazement as she pulled open the bale and began tossing sacks into the air. "But I think you should—"

"Pink roses for a tablecloth. Morning glories in the windows. Cherries for a kitchen towel." And then she began to sing as she took Chipper by his chubby little hands and danced him around and around the barn.

> "Shout! Shout! We're gaining ground!
> Oh Halley, Hallelujah!
> The love of God is coming down!
> Oh Halley, Hallelujah!"

Seth stared at the woman and the little boy spinning in giddy circles over the joy of finding a few empty grain sacks. Laughing,

Rosie picked up a sack and tied it around Chipper's shoulders like a cape. She tucked another into her skirt to form an apron. Then she draped a third across Seth's arm, linked his elbow, and swung him into a jig.

"The devil's dead and I am glad.
Oh Halley, Hallelujah!
The devil's dead and I am glad.
Oh Halley, Hallelujah!"

Seth was surprised at how easily his feet slipped into the once-familiar steps of the dance. How many years had it been since he had danced? But there was no time to reminisce. His little twister was circling him around the barn, kicking up her heels, and waving grain sacks like patriotic flags as she belted out the song.

"The devil's dead and gone to hell.
Oh Halley, Hallelujah!
I hope he's there for quite a spell.
Oh Halley, Hallelujah!"

Seth joined in, unable to hold back his favorite verse.

"My uncle had an old red hound.
Oh Halley, Hallelujah!
He chased the rabbits round and round.
Oh Halley, Hallelujah!"

Rosie sashayed him across the barn while Chipper skipped and hopped around them like a squirrel. When the song faltered into la-da-das, Rosie grabbed a handful of hay and threw it up into the air. Dancing away from Seth, she twirled amid the falling stems as they settled on her bonnet and skirt. He stepped back to watch her, but she took his hand again and pulled him into the dance.

"You'll settle down no more to roam.
Oh Halley, Hallelujah!
Grain sacks will make your house a home.
Oh Halley, Hallelujah!"

"Red and yellow, green and blue. Oh Halley, Hallelujah!" Chipper shouted from the third rung of the loft ladder. "I like Rosie 'cause she is nice. Oh Halley, Hallelujah!"

"Oh, Chipper, that's a good one!" Rosie sank onto the floor laughing. "I can't dance another step!"

A shadow blocked the door. "Fräulein Mills? Hunter?"

Seth swung around. "Rustemeyer."

"*Guten Morgen.*" The man stared at the hay-covered woman who sat gasping on the barn floor. "How you are?"

"Uh, we were just . . . Miss Mills found some grain sacks." Seth jerked the flowered bag from his arm. "We were dancing."

"*Der Tanz.*"

"I'm going to sew curtains," Rosie sang out, rising and attempting to brush off her skirt. "I'll braid a rug."

"*Ja?*"

Rosie glanced at Seth. He watched in wonder as the young woman's cheeks colored. Then she shrugged her shoulders and, if his eyes weren't deceiving him in the dim light, she winked at him. "Excuse me, please. I was searching for eggs."

Slipping between the two men, Rosie practically ran out of the barn. Chipper studied the situation for a moment, then he took off after her. Seth crossed his arms over his chest.

"What do you want, Rustemeyer?"

"*Die Brücke?*" the German said. He pulled a stem of hay from Seth's collar. "Britsch?"

"The bridge," Seth said. "You came to build?"

"*Ja, ja.*" He glanced out the window at the young woman carrying a basket of eggs toward the soddy. "Fräulein Mills. Beautiful."

Seth gave a grunt and started toward his tool chest. As a matter of fact, Fräulein Mills was beautiful. Especially when she was dancing in the hay. Or laughing like a bell. Or throwing her arms around a man's chest. *Oh Halley, Hallelujah!*

CHAPTER 6

ROSIE felt so excited about the grain sacks that she forgot to daydream about becoming Rolf Rustemeyer's wife. While the two men walked down to the creek to survey for the new bridge, she and Chipper quickly hoed the little garden Seth had planted just outside the house. It was a good spot, and she hoped late summer would bring an abundance of healthy vegetables.

Rosie dug grass sprouts and weeds from among the emerging onions, turnips, potatoes, beans, and corn. Chipper picked cutworms, potato beetles, and harlequin bugs until he had filled the bib pocket of his overalls. While Rosie hauled water from the well to the garden, he smashed the pests under a big stone.

Gardening done, Rosie sent Chipper off to collect buffalo and cow chips while she settled down in the soddy with the grain sacks. By lunchtime she had hemmed four curtains of pale green fabric printed with blue morning glories, dark green vines, and curling tendrils. She made rods from peeled branches and hung the curtains so they stirred in the breeze at each window.

After lunch with the men, she fashioned a tablecloth of pale periwinkle blue stripes and a matching straw-stuffed cushion for each of the cane seats she had woven earlier that week. Her fingers were sore from stitching, but she had promised Seth a shirt by Sunday. The man certainly did need one. Though he washed his face and hands at every meal, he never took off the only shirt he had, and it was in dire need of a wash. Chipper needed new clothes, too. Of course, Rosie herself had only the one dress, but she managed to wash it now and again, hang it up in the night air, and wear it again by morning.

Determined to fulfill her promise to her employer, she selected a pair of grain sacks that had been dyed a beautiful sky blue—the exact color of Seth's eyes. As she slit the sides of the sacks, Rosie thought about those blue eyes. When Seth had laughed that morning in the barn, his eyes had lit up and begun to sparkle. They fairly glowed against the deep tan of his face—as though they were lit from inside with a hot blue fire. Rosie felt her stomach do an odd little flip-flop at the mere memory of the way Seth Hunter had looked at her as they danced.

She wished she could say it had been a look of fascination, intrigue, or maybe even admiration. But Seth probably thought his hired hand was a little touched in the head, the way she had been so silly about finding the grain sacks. Rosie didn't care. After all, the first chance she had, she was going to ask Rolf Rustemeyer to marry her, and she felt pretty sure he would say yes. He thought she was beautiful.

She draped the grain sacks over one shoulder and set out from the house toward the creek to find Seth and take his measurements. As she tramped down to the water's edge, an odd thought occurred to her. She had met Rolf Rustemeyer three times now: the other day on his land, earlier that morning in the barn, and at lunchtime. What color were his eyes?

A pontoon bridge. Perfect. The bridge would drop when the creek ran low—as it did right now. It would rise when the creek ran high. Seth's infantry unit had built and crossed a hundred pontoon bridges during the war. He knew the bridge across the Bluestem would need to support the weight of heavy wagons and be stable enough to keep travelers from toppling into the water. The construction would require strong cables, two or three flat-bottom skiffs, wood planks for the walkway, and secure piers on each bank. But how to explain the structure to Rolf Rustemeyer?

Seth rubbed a hand around the back of his neck as he studied the big German. Maybe the thing to do was call on Rosie. At lunch, she had managed to teach the fellow the English words for meat, potatoes, and bread. She could get a few facts across to him by pointing things out with her hands or drawing pictures in the dirt.

On the other hand, Seth wasn't crazy about the way Rustemeyer ogled Rosie. The man had no manners. He followed her around like a big, shaggy dog. When she set out the lunch, he would have wagged his tail if he'd had one. And he ate like he hadn't had a decent meal in two years. He probably hadn't. Most bachelor farmers had a hard time tending to both crops and housekeeping. Like every unmarried male homesteader other than Seth, the German would be eager to find himself a wife. Though isolation and language barriers had kept him from the few social gatherings on the prairie, Rustemeyer wouldn't overlook an unmarried female living so close at hand.

No, Seth thought he'd better try to explain the pontoon bridge to the German without Rosie's help. After all, she belonged to *him*. No, that wasn't quite right. She worked for him. And the more she worked around the house, the better he liked having her here. No doubt about it, Rosie could cook. Clean, too. The garden looked good. Chipper stayed busy. Even the floor—

"Fräulein Mills!" Rolf hollered, waving one of his big beefy paws. "How you are?"

Seth glanced up to see Rosie coming down the creek bank, her skirt dancing around her ankles and a smile lighting up her face. She was toting some blue grain sacks over one shoulder. As she approached, Rolf nudged Seth.

"Pretty, *ja?*"

"What is it with you?" Seth said, his voice more irritated than he liked. "Look, Rustemeyer, the fräulein works here. Understand? She works for me."

"*Ja*. Not vife."

"No, she's not my wife."

"*Gut. Sehr gut.*" The German grinned broadly. "*Ich bin glücklich.*"

Seth gave a grunt. "Whatever that means."

"Hello, Mr. Rustemeyer," Rosie said as she stepped up to the two men. When she looked at Seth, he could see a pair of pink spots on her cheeks. "Mr. Hunter, I've come to borrow your shirt for a moment. I need to make a pattern."

Seth glanced at Rustemeyer, who was scanning Rosie up and down. He wished she would get on back to the house. "Maybe tonight, Miss Mills. We're busy right now."

"But I promised you a shirt by Sunday. If I wait to measure until tonight, I'll never get it done. Tomorrow I'll be baking bread, and the next day I'll be making soap, and the day after that I mean to hunt for strawberries. With the gardening and cleaning and gathering chips and such, I barely have time to sit down for a moment. You need a new shirt so badly, Mr. Hunter, and this blue color I've found will make your eyes . . . your eyes . . ."

The pink spots on her cheeks blossomed into red roses. Seth couldn't hide the grin that tickled the corners of his mouth. So, Miss Mills wasn't all housekeeping and chores. Her eyelashes fluttered down, and she cleared her throat.

"This fabric is a very nice shade of blue," she said, lifting her chin. "It will hide the dirt well, and that shirt you're wearing is so dirty it could walk around on its own. Now take it off and let me measure it. As soon as you're wearing the new one, I'll give the other a wash and you can have it back—if it doesn't fall to shreds at the first touch of soap and water."

"All right, you can have it. While I get out of it, see if you can explain a pontoon bridge to Rustemeyer."

"You'll have to explain it to me first."

Briefly, Seth outlined his proposal for the bridge. He had two skiffs himself—one he'd bought off the farmer who went bust—and he suspected Rustemeyer had a third. They could braid regular rope into heavy cable, build piers out of stone and mortar, and add the plank walkway last. With hard work, the construction shouldn't take too long.

"Think you can get that through his head?" he concluded, jabbing a thumb in the direction of the curious German.

"All you have to do is draw him a picture, Mr. Hunter." Rosie turned away and knelt to the ground. She began to sketch. "Here's the bridge. *Brücke*. Here's the water. *Wasser. Ja?*"

"*Sie sprechen Deutsch!*"

Rustemeyer squatted down next to Rosie and gazed at her with those big puppy-dog eyes of his. Seth had the urge to topple him straight into the creek.

"You must learn better English," Rosie said. "Now you and Mr. Hunter are going to build a pontoon bridge. Floating on the water, see? The small boats will float. The water can go up and down, but the wagons can still cross over the bridge."

With some gratification, Seth watched Rustemeyer shaking his shaggy blond head. Not even Rosie could make the big hound dog understand. Seth dropped his suspenders and pulled his shirt over his head. When his eyes emerged, he saw that Rosie was walking down to the creek. In one hand she held a stone. In the other, she carried a leaf.

"The stone sinks," she told the German. "You see? It goes under the water. But the leaf floats on top of the water. The bridge must float. Like the leaf. *Float*."

"Float? *Nein. Ich verstehe nicht*."

"Oh, he doesn't understand, Mr. Hunt—" Rosie caught her breath as Seth tossed her his shirt. Her focus dropped to his bare chest, then darted quickly back to his eyes. The flush on her cheeks spread down her neck, and she hugged his shirt as though it were some kind of shield.

"Excuse me," she muttered. Turning away quickly, she hurried to the spot where she had laid the blue fabric. "I'll just measure this now."

"You do that," Seth said.

He rubbed a hand across his bare chest and gave Rustemeyer a victorious smirk. *See if you can make her blush*, he wanted to crow. *Go ahead and kneel at her feet. Kiss her on the hand. Tell her she's pretty. Trail her around the house. I don't notice her turning pink when you look at her, you ol' shaggy dog.*

"The bridge is going to float, Rustemeyer," he shouted. He had the feeling if he could just talk loud and slow enough, the German would understand. "A . . . pontoon . . . bridge. Like . . . like boats."

"Boat? *Das Boot! Ah, die Schiffbrücke! Ja, ja!*" Rustemeyer splashed out into the creek, spread his long arms wide, and indicated with his hands how the pontoons would float.

"*Ja*," Seth said. "That's right. You got the idea."

Excited now, Rustemeyer began a long discourse in German. He pointed at his farm, gestured toward the creek, and formed his hands into circles and parallel lines. As he talked, he strode back and forth in the water. He drew marks on the bank and set stones in little piles. After a while, Seth gave up trying to make sense of it and wandered over to where Rosie was working on the new shirt.

"I think Rustemeyer understands about the bridge," he said, hunkering down beside her. "It could be tricky getting the cables across the stream. It would be nice to have O'Toole's help. Even so, I don't reckon it'll take us long to build it, once we gather enough lumber."

"I haven't seen many trees around here." Rosie was laying out his shirt as a pattern on the blue cloth. She kept her attention squarely on the fabric. "You may have quite a time getting boards."

"I bought a big load of lumber off that fellow who went bust. It's stacked out behind the barn. There's enough for the bridge and a good start on the house I plan to build after I've proved up my claim. I built my barn from that wood. Most folks around here don't have frame barns, you know."

"It's a very nice barn."

"You been sleeping OK out there?" He wished he could entice her to look at him. He liked the way it flustered her to see him without his shirt. "That blacksnake hasn't bothered you, has he?"

"Not a bit."

"You reckon I ought to invite the O'Tooles over after we get the bridge built?"

"That would be nice. Chipper's been lonely."

"Maybe we could have a dance in the barn." He paused and leaned toward her. "Like this morning."

Rosie bit her lip but kept her attention on her work. "I've never been to a real dance," she said softly as she began to cut the fabric. "I wouldn't know how to fix things up right."

Seth sat, stretched out his legs, and plucked a stem of grass. He hadn't enjoyed talking with a woman this much since . . . well, he didn't know when. Mary had always been the one causing him to stumble over his words. The way she had batted her eyes and flounced around him had left him all but dumbfounded. Truth to tell, he had felt like a puppet around her—always ready at her beck and call, always subject to her whims. And Mary Cornwall had had a lot of whims.

But with skinny little Rosie—this brown-eyed twister—he was the boss. He could make her laugh. Make her blush. Make her mad. Look at her now, furiously cutting away on that shirt. All day long he had been thinking about the way Rosie had flung her arms around him. He had liked that. Liked it a lot.

"I reckon a barn dance might be fun, Miss Mills," he said, chewing on the grass stem. "Come late spring everybody's working so hard that a break would be good. Maybe you and Sheena could plan the party. What do you think about that?"

Rosie nodded and kept cutting. "Who would come? Everybody's so spread out."

"The O'Tooles, of course. Casimir Laski's a nice fellow. His family could visit. They'd have to stay the night. And then there's LeBlanc. He's the French fellow who owns the mill. He's got a passel of pretty daughters. I'm sure they'd love to dance."

Rosie stopped her cutting. She was silent for a moment. Then she flipped Seth's shirt into his arms and stood. "I certainly hope you won't forget to invite Mr. Rustemeyer," she said, looking straight into his eyes. "I'm sure he would be more than welcome by the women at the dance. And by the way, he appears to be miles ahead of you in building the bridge."

Before Seth could stand, Rosie was striding away with the scraps of fabric fluttering in her hands.

"*Auf Wiedersehen*, Fräulein Mills!" Rustemeyer called to her from the heap of stones he was gathering to build a piling.

She swung around and waved. "*Auf Wiedersehen!*" Before she turned again, she gave Seth a curt nod. "Good day, Mr. Hunter."

Rosie knelt by the window at the back of the barn loft and laid her forehead on her folded hands. Though several days had passed since her encounter with Seth by the creek, she still felt terrible inside. Her sewing had been far from perfect. Yesterday she had spilled a pot of peeled potatoes across the floor and had to haul water from the well to wash them all. And this morning she had scorched her skirt on the coals of the outside fire. It was her only skirt, and she had been vainly musing about whether Seth had noticed how it showed off her small waist. Now all he would see was the ruffle of charred holes peppered across the hem.

Consequences. Oh my, but she deserved consequences. She had

been so silly with Seth. Dancing in the barn. Ordering him to strip off his shirt. Flaunting Mr. Rustemeyer at him as though the German were a serious beau.

"Father," she prayed softly, squeezing her eyes tight to keep from crying. "I've been willful again. You've allowed me to come out to this wilderness for a much higher purpose than grain sacks and barn dancing, and I think I'm beginning to see what it is. It's Chipper, isn't it?"

She stopped, opened her eyes, and looked up at the sky as if she could read the answer in it. Clouds like scraps of white lace floated across the blue. From the window, Rosie could see the two men working below. The bridge would cross the stream some distance beyond the barn, and they were gathering stones from the fields nearby. Seth was hammering, while Rolf Rustemeyer set stones in place, his huge arms bulging with the effort.

"I think you've put me here for Chipper," Rosie said, squeezing her eyes shut again so she could concentrate. "Father, what do you want me to do for that precious child? He doesn't love Seth. His mother is gone, but I'm not allowed to take her place. I wouldn't even know how to be a mother, and Seth won't act as a father should. He won't so much as touch Chipper. I don't see how they're ever going to become a family, Father. By rights, there should be a mama and a papa and their little boy, all together and all happy. But things don't always go right, do they?"

Rosie thought about her own birth as she clasped the little stocking-toe pouch she still wore around her neck. No, things didn't always go right. Why had God sent her to help Chipper and his father learn to love each other? She didn't know anything about families—as Seth had rightly reminded her. If she angered him too much, he might tell Rolf Rustemeyer about her past. Then the German would probably never agree to marry her.

"Oh, Father!" she whispered. "I don't want to go back to the

Home. I want to build a family out here on the prairie. I want a husband. I want a house of my own. I want children—"

She cut off her words. Willful. She was so willful!

"I surrender," she said out loud. "Whatever you want, Father, I'll do. Wherever you send me, I'll go. Even if it's back to the Home. Please show me how to help Chipper. And please . . . please . . . keep my thoughts from Seth Hunter's blue eyes . . . his black hair . . . broad chest—"

"Rosie! Rosie, where are you? Where's Chipper?"

At Seth's shout, Rosie jerked upright and leaned out of the window. She could see the tall man racing up the slope toward the soddy, his shirttail hanging out and his hat tumbling from his head. Rustemeyer pounded paces behind, long blond hair flying.

"Fräulein!" he bellowed. "*Achtung!*"

"Rosie! Rosie!" Jimmy O'Toole, pant legs sopping wet, came huffing after the German.

"I'm here!" Rosie shouted down from the barn window. "Has something happened to Chipper?"

She tore across the loft and skidded down the rickety ladder. Just as she landed on the floor, Seth burst into the barn. "Rosie, where's Chipper? Have you seen him? He's not in the house!"

"I sent him for buffalo chips."

"When?"

"Hours ago. After lunch. What's wrong, Seth? Is Chipper hurt? Jimmy, what are you doing here?"

"We've had a message from Casimir Laski," Jimmy said. "He wrote us that he's had a letter from his brother in Topeka. The brother said a man's been asking in all the businesses around Topeka if anyone knows of a Jimmy O'Toole or a Seth Hunter. It must be that *sherral* who tried to shoot our Seth in Kansas City. He's still after the boy."

"Jack Cornwall," Seth spat.

"Are you sure?" Rosie asked, her spine prickling at the sound of the name.

"Who else could it be?" Seth took Rosie's shoulders. "Can you remember which direction Chipper went? Did he follow the creek? Or did he head out onto the prairie?"

"He went upstream toward Mr. Rustemeyer's farm."

"Come on, Jimmy. Rustemeyer, you stay here and look after Rosie. If Cornwall comes around, shoot him."

"I can't go, Seth!" Jimmy broke in as Seth began trying to explain the situation to the German. "What about Sheena and the *brablins?* I must wade back over the creek and see that they're all right."

"I'm going with you," Rosie said to Seth. "I won't sit about waiting for word of Chipper when I have two strong legs to search for him myself."

She tied her bonnet ribbons as she ran from the barn. Seth quickly caught up with her. They hurried down to the creek and began to follow it north toward Rolf Rustemeyer's farm. The German had vanished, Rosie realized.

"Did the message say Jack Cornwall has already come out to the prairie?" Rosie asked. "Does he know where you live?"

"I'm not sure. But he'll find out soon enough." Seth paused and looked at her. "If he's taken Chipper, I'll kill him."

Rosie shook her head. *No,* her heart cried out. *No!*

"Footprints!" he said, grabbing her arm. "He went this way. Chipper! Chipper!"

Doing her best to match Seth's long-legged stride, Rosie crossed a fallen log and skirted a cottonwood tree that had sent long roots into the water. She felt sick inside. Seth would shoot Jack Cornwall. Or Jack Cornwall would shoot Seth. Either way Chipper would be the loser. The child would suffer the most.

And which of the two selfish men cared about the boy himself? Neither. He was the trophy. The prize.

"Chipper!" Rosie cried out. "Chipper, where are you, sweetheart?"

"Confound it, I've lost the prints."

"There they are. Just ahead." Rosie brushed a tear from her cheek. "Jack Cornwall won't hurt him. You must remember that. Chipper may be frightened, but at least with his uncle he'll be safe."

"Safe?" Seth barked. "What are you talking about? Chipper belongs to me!"

"*Belongs* to you?"

"He's mine. Cornwall has no right to him."

"Why do you want him? Why do you even care?"

"He's my son!" Seth stopped running and swung around to face Rosie, his blue eyes crackling. "He's all I have."

"You can't *have* people, Mr. Hunter. Chipper doesn't belong to you. He's God's child. If you truly love your son, you'll care first about his safety."

"Stop preaching at me, woman! You don't know anything about true love. You don't know anything about families."

"And you do?"

"Better than you!"

"And how is that? You treat the child like a hired hand. Fetch the water. Pick up buffalo chips. Eat your supper. Go to bed. A father should be . . . he should—"

"What? What should a father do, Miss Know-it-all?"

Rosie drew back at the venom in his voice. "You had a father. What was he like?"

"It's not your business what my father was like. And it's not your business how I see fit to bring up my son. You don't know anything about me or my son. You don't have a father, so don't—"

"God is our father, and what better example could there be? He's loving and kind, tenderhearted and patient. You must learn to know your son, Mr. Hunter. He needs your love so desperately!"

Rosie realized she had grabbed Seth's shirtsleeves in her fists. She unclenched them and stepped back. Then she stumbled up the creek bank and climbed onto the flat prairie. Pushing through the tall grass, she searched for the trail.

Dear God, she must never shout at Seth again! The look on his face! How dare she be so brash? He would turn her out of his household and send her back to the Home in Kansas City. And she would deserve his rejection. She had no right to tell him how to raise his son. She must learn to stop caring so deeply about people. God had given Chipper to Seth—not to her! She must let go. *Let go.*

"Hi, Rosie. What are you doin' out here?"

At the familiar voice, she whirled around. Not twenty feet behind her, Chipper trundled along dragging the burlap sack filled with dried buffalo droppings. He stopped and gave her a grin.

"Are you huntin' wild strawberries, Rosie?" he called.

"Chipper!" Rosie raced toward him. "Oh, Chipper, honey. There you are! We've been searching all over for you."

He laughed as she swept him up in her arms. "Rosie, you're so funny! You're not a thing like my mama was. You're silly!"

"I *am* silly, Chipper. You're right about that. But I do know that your papa—"

"Miss Mills, listen, I—" Seth emerged over the rise and stopped. "Chipper!"

"Rosie's dancin' again," the boy said. "See, she's swingin' me around an' around."

Seth's face darkened. "Miss Mills, I want you to take my son back to the house immediately. I'm going to scout around my land for any signs of Cornwall. Chipper, from now on, don't go anywhere without me or Miss Mills around. You hear?"

"Yes, sir." The child's blue eyes lost their joy. "I was just pickin' chips. Rosie told me to."

"That's fine. You're . . . you're a good boy to do as you're told. Now go on home."

"Yes, sir."

Chipper stepped into the shelter of Rosie's skirts. She glanced down at the child; then she looked at his father. In the child she recognized the fear and distrust of a hunted animal—a baby rabbit or a kitten when confronted by a ferocious dog.

In the father she saw something entirely different. Seth was a man bound by ropes. Constrained by iron bands. Held by a leash too strong to snap. If he could break free, what would he do? Rush to the child and beat him? Hurl Rosie to the ground to break her impudent spirit? Chastise them both for their failure to conform to his will?

No, that wasn't what Rosie saw in Seth at all. To her amazement, what she sensed was the man's intense desire to run to his son and gather him in his arms. A need to laugh with relief. A need to weep away the fear of losing something priceless.

Stunned, Rosie stood for a moment, staring at Seth and trying to pray away the chains that shackled him. But he didn't escape. Instead, he turned stiffly and began walking down the trail toward Rustemeyer's farm. Going to check his land. Going to find Jack Cornwall. Going to do all the things he thought a father ought to do and none of the things his soul cried out for.

"Come, Chipper," Rosie whispered, taking up the burlap sack. "Let's go back to the house. And along the way, I will think of a plan."

"What sort of a plan, Rosie?"

"A plan to unlock your papa's heart."

CHAPTER 7

THE MINUTE Rosie and Chipper disappeared around a bend in the trail, Seth sank onto a rock and buried his face in his hands. Chipper was safe! When that little dark head had come into view, it had been all Seth could do to keep from shouting hallelujah. Like a child at Christmas, he had longed to grab the little boy—his precious gift—and squeeze him tight.

Like a child—that's how he had felt. He had wanted to act like a little boy himself, and he knew he could never display such behavior. Not in front of his son. Not in front of Rosie.

Despite what she said about him, Seth *did* know how to be a father. Or at least how *not* to be a father. He would never whip his son with a leather belt or a stripped tree limb until the child's tender flesh tore. He would never hurl abuses: "Stupid boy," "Idiot," "Can't you do anything right?"

No, Seth would treat his own son with respect. Decency. He would expect hard work, and in return he would provide shelter, food, clothing. He would see that his son learned how to read and write. Most important, he would never abandon the boy. Never.

Seth raked a hand through his hair and looked up at the setting sun. From the time he was ten years old, he had grown up without a father. The man who had given him life simply walked away one day and left his wife and children to fend for themselves. A penniless woman. Four little boys. Fatherless.

"No," Seth said, standing. He had lost his own wife. Chipper had lost a mother. But as long as Seth lived, the boy would have a father. A good father.

What did Miss Rosenbloom Cotton Mills know about it anyway? Named after a stocking label. Abandoned in a livery stable. Raised in an orphanage. What right did she have telling him how a father ought to act?

Seth stuffed his hat down on his head. Now that he'd calmed down a little, he needed to get back to his house. He didn't like the idea of leaving Chipper. If Jack Cornwall got his hands on the boy, he'd whisk him back to Missouri before Seth could stop him.

And Rosie. He didn't want to leave her alone either. Not with Rustemeyer lurking around the place. That country bumpkin German might just figure out a way to tell Rosie he wanted to marry her. In spite of the way she shouted at Seth—in spite of her stubbornness, her bossiness, her irritating, audacious, and downright silly ways—he wasn't about to let Rustemeyer cart her off.

No sir.

As Rosie and Chipper came in sight of the soddy, Rolf Rustemeyer and the entire O'Toole clan rushed out to meet them. Sheena had convinced Jimmy to ferry her and every one of their redheaded children over Bluestem Creek in his flat-bottomed boat. Now they all swarmed the returning wanderers.

"Rosie, you've found Chipper!" Sheena exclaimed. "Glory be to God! The child is safe!"

"*Und* Hunter?" Rolf asked. "*Wo ist* Hunter?"

"Mr. Hunter is searching his land." Rosie handed Chipper over to little Will and his sister Erinn. "Stay near the house now, sweetheart. Don't let him run free, Erinn."

As the children scampered to play in the barren front yard, Sheena slipped her arm around Rosie. "I've a big pot of Irish stew on my stove at home," she said gently. "Sure you must all come for supper. Even the German. Jimmy, don't say a word about him not talking straight. Rustemeyer does the best he can, so he does. Rosie, do say you'll come. We must plan what to do if that *sherral* Cornwall turns up. And Jimmy's been doing some thinking about Seth's pontoon bridge. We have that flat-bottomed boat that'll be all but useless to us. Sure I do believe he'll be joining in the building of the bridge, won't you now, Jimmy?"

By the time Seth returned to the house, Sheena and Rosie had rounded up the children. Jimmy tried to invite Rolf to dinner, but the German couldn't understand his rapid speech and wild hand gestures. Finally it was left to Rosie, who pointed toward the O'Toole place across the creek and then to her stomach. At that, Rustemeyer nodded and started walking toward the creek.

Seth insisted that he didn't want to leave his house unguarded, but Jimmy convinced him of the need to discuss a plan. It took two trips in Jimmy's boat to ferry everyone across the water, but as the sun dipped into the prairie grass, the settlers were trekking the half mile to the O'Tooles' snug soddy.

"So what do you think of our Seth, now?" Sheena whispered while she and Rosie were setting the long table. "He's a hardworking man, is he not? And handsome. Have you ever seen a pair of eyes like that on a man?"

"Seth's eyes? Hmm. I think they're blue, aren't they?" Rosie gave a shrug and walked to the cupboard to fetch some spoons.

"You think! Sure, my Jimmy's green eyes put me in mind of the fair Emerald Isle. But I won't lie to you. That Seth Hunter can turn a woman's heart with one glance, so he can. Don't you think so, Rosie? Haven't you noticed?"

"I've noticed that eyes are not the only thing to a man. It's his heart that counts with me."

"And what man has a better heart than Seth Hunter? Will you tell me that, now?"

Rosie glanced out the window where the three farmers stood talking and smoking pipes. Moonlight brightened the swirls of white smoke that drifted around their heads. Seth was laughing about something, his head thrown back and his chuckle deep.

Rosie turned away. "I believe Rolf Rustemeyer has a good heart."

"The German!" Sheena squawked. "And what do you know of his heart?"

"I know he's a hard worker. He seems kind enough. He's very smart. Strong, too—you should see how hard he works on the pontoon bridge. And he doesn't shout at me."

"Shout? Does our Seth shout then? Surely not! It would take a mighty great lot of ballyragging to induce that sweet man to shout."

Rosie flushed. "I can't believe *any* amount of trouble would compel Mr. Rustemeyer to shout. He's very nice."

"Nice is he? And what does Mr. Rustemeyer say about all the hard work you've done stitching curtains and tablecloths? Has he paid you compliments? Does he approve of your labors?"

"I don't know—"

"What's his favorite food then? Does he like rabbit? Or does he prefer squirrel?"

"Well, I really don't—"

"How many children does he want? Does he believe in God? What plans has he made for his homestead?"

"I don't know!" Rosie said so loudly that the men turned from their conversation and looked at her. She grabbed the ladle and began to dish out the stew. "I don't know very much about him," she said to Sheena in a low voice. "He speaks German."

"That he does."

"But it makes no difference to me. If God allows it, and if Mr. Rustemeyer will have me, I'm going to marry him."

Sheena thunked a bowl down on the long table. "Now *that* I should like to see."

"I'm sure we'll be very happy together."

"As my dear mother always said, 'Marriages are all happy. It's having breakfast together that causes all the trouble.'"

Rosie cocked her hands on her hips. "You're just like Seth. You think I don't know how to make a good marriage. You think just because I was brought up at the Home, I'm ignorant of what it takes to be a good wife. That's not true, Sheena! I can sew and cook and wash as well as any woman. I know how to tend children. I would never let the pantry run bare or allow my little ones to run around with holes in their socks. And I can be kind to a husband, too. Even though I sometimes shout—"

"*You* shout? I thought it was Seth doing all the shouting."

Rosie flushed. "Sometimes . . . sometimes we shout at each other."

"Do you now? Well, that's a good beginning." Sheena slipped her arm around Rosie's stiff shoulder. "Aye, lass, shouting shows you have feelings—and you're not afraid to show them to each other. Sharing what's in your heart gives life its purpose. It's what makes marriage a godly gift. Marriage is much more than darning socks and keeping the pantry stocked, so it is. It's the two of you together, through thick and thin."

"I can go through thick and thin with Mr. Rustemeyer. With any man, for that matter—as long as he's kind and hardworking."

"And what will you say to Rustemeyer when one of your wee ones comes down with the diphtheria? Or cholera? Will you cry on the German's shoulder then? Will you pour out your heart to his listening ear? And in the long cold days of winter when the snow is piled against the door so nobody can go outside for a week at a time—what will you talk about to Rustemeyer then?"

Rosie gave the stew a stir. "I could teach him how to speak English."

"Perhaps. And then you might learn that he loves none of the things you love, he believes in nothing you've given your heart to, he shares none of your dreams." Sheena let out a deep sigh. "God

Almighty tells us that when two marry, they become one flesh. I cannot explain how that is, Rosie. But you must believe me when I tell you 'tis true. Why not set your heart on a man who needs you as Seth needs you? He's a man you could love with a fire that would carry you through every cold, dark night. Why not love him?"

Rosie studied the men as they stood talking outside under the stars. Thin as a fence post, Jimmy was speaking animatedly about the pontoon bridge. Rolf Rustemeyer took a deep draw on his pipe and stared up at the moon. Seth—tall, straight-backed, and handsome—glanced into the house for a moment and looked at Rosie. Then he turned away.

"Sheena," Rosie said softly, taking her friend's hand. "A long time ago, Seth became one flesh with his first wife. I don't believe that bond has ever broken, and I know I don't have the power to sever it. Look at me, Sheena. I'm skinny, I'm a foundling, and I'm afraid that sometimes I'm very . . . very silly. Seth's blue eyes don't look on me with honor or passion or love. I'm nothing to him. I'm as bad as one of those cutworms—a pest that has invaded his well-ordered life. Sheena, please try to understand. If I'm to have a marriage at all, it will have to be with a man who has no more notion of love than I do. A man like Rustemeyer."

Sheena's green eyes sparkled in her round face. "Aye," she said. "You have no notion of love. And that is why, when your brown eyes meet with Seth Hunter's blue ones, the two of you turn into a pair of *googeens*. Sure the feeling between you is thick enough to cut with a knife."

"It is not!"

"I'll hold you, it is. But never mind. Marry the German, Rosie. Gaze all winter long into his eyes." She paused. "What color are Rustemeyer's eyes, by the way?"

Rosie swallowed. "Brown."

"Are they, now? Well, that's very nice, I'm sure." Sheena walked to the door. "Come inside, all of you, and leave your planning until tomorrow. Sure you'll never plow a field by turning it over in your mind. Jimmy, please send Erinn after the rest of the *brablins*. Put out your pipe, Seth. There's a good man. And Mr. Rustemeyer, take a chair. That's right. Well, glory be to God. Rosie, have you noticed what a fine pair of eyes Mr. Rustemeyer has? They're gray, so they are. As gray as iron."

Seth straightened in his chair and listened to the sound in the distance. A dull rumble. He glanced across the room. Rosie and Sheena were in one corner putting the littlest ones to bed. Chipper was telling riddles with the other children. Jimmy had gone out to check his stock, and Rustemeyer had fallen asleep by the stove.

Seth stood and walked to the door. He stepped outside and sniffed the heavy air.

"Miss Mills," he called. Rosie lifted her head, and their eyes met. "Storm's coming. We'd better get home."

Without a moment's hesitation, she rose and took Chipper's hand. "Come on, sweetheart. Bedtime."

Sheena woke Rustemeyer while Rosie tugged on her bonnet and pulled Chipper's hat over his brow. Seth checked the sky again. The storm was a long way off but moving fast. Like a hundred snakes' tongues, lightning flickered across the black sky. A strong breeze skittered over the tops of the grass, infusing the air with the sweet scent of cool rain. Wings outstretched, an owl drifted over the face of the moon.

By the time Seth and the others had said their good-byes and hurried down the half-mile trail to Bluestem Creek, the lightning had crept closer. Wind pulled at Seth's hat and whipped Rosie's skirt against her legs. Thunder rolled like a drum across the prairie. Chipper began to cry.

"Water's rough," Seth said. "We'll have to be careful with the boat. Rustemeyer, help Miss Mills."

For some reason, the big German had no trouble understanding the request. As Seth lifted Chipper in his arms, Rustemeyer swept Rosie off her feet and set her in the bottom of Jimmy O'Toole's boat. She let out a shriek of surprise and clapped her hands over her bonnet. Too late. The scrap of threadbare fabric whipped off her head and sailed across the creek.

"My bonnet!" she cried. "I've lost my bonnet!"

Rustemeyer began to speak in German, but Rosie was insistent.

"I don't know what you're saying! My bonnet blew away!"

Seth set Chipper in the boat and pushed off toward the other bank. Within moments, they were across. "Go fetch the lady's bonnet," he said to Rolf. "Her hat. Go . . . and . . . get . . . it!"

"*Aber der Sturm!*"

"Forget the storm. Get the bonnet. It's her only one."

As they climbed out onto the bank, rain began to patter across the parched ground. "Let's run for the house!" Seth said against Rosie's ear.

Throwing one arm around Chipper, he lifted the boy to his hip. He circled Rosie with his free arm, and they began to run into the mounting wind. Grass whipped at their legs. Blowing dust stung their skin. Rosie's hair pulled loose from its pins and billowed to her waist, a whirling, tossing sheet of silk.

"What about Rolf? I wish he hadn't gone after my bonnet!"

"He'll be fine." Seth said the words with more confidence than he felt. Lightning cracked across the sky in hissing white bolts. Thunder shook the ground beneath their feet. Chipper's little arms squeezed tightly around Seth's neck, and he could feel that his own cheek was wet from the child's tears.

Holding Rosie close to protect her from the stinging rain, he raced down the muddy trail toward the vague outline of his soddy roof. They passed the barn. Ran through an open gate. Dashed across the yard. Releasing Rosie for a moment, Seth lifted the bolt across his door and shouldered it open.

"Dry the boy off by the stove," he told her. "I'm going to check on my cows."

As Seth splashed back across the yard, he could see Rustemeyer in the flashes of lightning. Empty-handed, the man was sprinting toward the soddy. So Rosie's bonnet had been lost. The only gift she'd ever had.

If Rustemeyer hadn't been so bound and determined to scoop Rosie up in his arms, her bonnet would never have blown away. Crazy German. No doubt he'd want to spend the night. And stay for one of Rosie's breakfasts. And build the bridge all day just so he could be near her.

Seth gave the barn door a kick. It swung open. Inside, his three cows turned their heads to give him sorrowful stares. Poor gals might as well have been standing outside for all the good that plank roof did them. Rain streamed down in miniature waterfalls. Two hens had huddled up in a pile of dry hay. A narrow cascade dribbled down the loft ladder.

Though it sometimes seeped in a heavy rain, there was a lot to be said for a sod roof, Seth thought as he made his way back to the house. It kept the interior cool in summer and warm in winter. A twister could blow right over it without disturbing the people huddled underneath. And a fire was hard put to burn the thing down.

He was feeling pretty good about his situation until he stepped into the soddy. Rosie was bent over the big bed tucking Chipper beneath the covers. Behind her, Rustemeyer stood gaping at the mass of shiny hair that fell from the top of Rosie's head to below her waist.

"Shut your trap, Rustemeyer," Seth growled as he brushed past the German on the way to the stove. "If you hadn't lost her bonnet, she wouldn't be in such a fix."

For some reason, Seth didn't like the idea that Rustemeyer knew about Rosie's hair. It had been a secret vision, something that Seth realized he had thought about more than once while lying alone in his bed at night. Rosie's long brown hair mesmerized him, ribbons and streamers of it draping around her shoulders and down her back. He had touched her hair—just that once—and he'd be switched if he would let Rustemeyer get his big paws into it.

"Better put up your hair," he said to her, and the words came out more harsh than he intended. "It's dripping on the floor."

She cast him a wounded look as she moved toward a chair at the table. "I'm sorry it bothers you. I don't have a bonnet now. I lost most of my pins."

Seth looked at Chipper. He hadn't intended his comment to sound as though he disapproved of her hair. Rosie's hair fascinated him, lured him. The little boy was staring out over the hem of the sheet, his blue eyes fastened on his father.

"I like Rosie's hair down," Chipper whispered. "It's pretty. Don't you think so?"

Seth turned to the stove and cleared his throat. "A woman ought to have a bonnet. It's not right to go bareheaded in front of strangers."

"We're not strangers. Rosie's our friend."

Seth nodded. "Yes, but a bonnet keeps the sun off."

"It's nighttime now." Chipper edged up on his elbows. "Rosie, I think your hair looks like maple syrup."

Across the room, the young woman laughed. "Wet and sticky?"

"Long and brown and flowing everywhere. I never saw such long hair. How many years did it take you to grow it?"

"All my life. I've never had reason to cut my hair before. But now that I've lost my bonnet and my pins—and since it bothers your father so much—"

"No," Seth cut in. He felt hot around the collar at the very idea that she might shear off those long, billowing tresses. Her hair was her glory, the essence of her beauty, the expression of her very soul. How could he tell her so without sounding like a sentimental fool?

"Leave your hair," he said, absently fiddling with the stove's warming oven, as though he might discover a bedtime snack or something hidden inside. "You can tie it up under one of those grain sacks."

"If it troubles you—"

"No, it's . . . it's fine." He faced her. She was holding the pile of her hair in her hands, looking down at it as though it was somehow separate from her. In the lamplight it shimmered—strands of gold, threads of copper, tendrils of bronze—as her fingers slipped into it. "The boy's right. You shouldn't cut it. It suits you."

At the admission of approval, Seth glanced at Rustemeyer. Though he couldn't comprehend the conversation, the German was studying the scene with great interest. Seth didn't like the way those puppy-dog eyes had fastened onto Rosie. Not at all.

Rustemeyer didn't deserve the gift of a look at Rosie's beautiful hair. He didn't know her the way Seth did. There were things about Rosie that made her different from other women. Special. The way she had danced with the grain sacks in the barn. The way she tilted her chin when she laughed. The way her arms felt when they slipped around Seth's chest. No, Rustemeyer didn't know Rosie, and Seth felt an unbidden urge to set his stamp on her. To somehow set her apart . . . to make her his.

But how? And why? Just to keep her away from Rustemeyer? A flash of possessiveness was no reason to toss his whole life into chaos. And admitting he wanted to keep Rosie Mills to himself would certainly create havoc. After all, he didn't really need her. Or want her. Did he?

"Are you warming up, Chipper?" Rosie was asking as she ruffled the boy's damp hair. "I don't want you to catch cold."

"I'm warm . . . and I'm so sleepy," Chipper whispered.

"That's good. I'm going out to the barn now, sweetie."

"Good night, Rosie."

"Wait a minute. You can't sleep in the barn," Seth said as she started for the door. "Rain's pouring through the roof. You'll get wet."

"I'm already wet."

"You won't sleep."

"I'll make my bed under the wagon where it's dry."

"But the snake—"

"I will not sleep in your house," she said firmly. "It's bad enough you find my hair shameful to look at. I won't have people saying evil things about me for staying in a house with two unmarried men."

Lifting the latch, she slipped out the door. Seth glanced at Chipper. The boy was staring at him, blue eyes accusing. Rolf Rustemeyer wore a grin of pity mixed with triumph. Seeing that, Seth made up his mind to follow Rosie. He threw open the door and stepped into the rain. She was hurrying ahead of him through the sheets of water, her feet splashing from puddle to puddle as she raced toward the barn. A bolt of lightning cracked like a whip across the prairie, and she paused, startled.

His heart hammering against his ribs, Seth used the moment to catch up with her. "Miss Mills."

She swung around. "Mr. Hunter? You should go back inside. You need to watch over Chipper. What if Jack Cornwall shows up?"

"Rustemeyer's with the boy." Breathing hard, Seth studied her damp face. Her features were lit by pale moonlight shining through the rain clouds. "We made a plan tonight, Jimmy and I. We're going to send word to all the coach stations along the trail. If anyone spots Cornwall, we'll have advance warning."

She nodded and looked at the barn. "Then I'd better go on. It's late."

"Wait. About . . . about your hair." He shifted from one foot to the other. It was bad enough to stand outside in such a downpour. Bad enough to force his presence on a woman who was clearly anxious to get away from him. And now that he had Rosie alone—all to himself—he didn't even know what to say.

"My hair?" she repeated.

"I . . . I just don't think a man like Rustemeyer ought to take on airs like he does."

"Airs?"

"The way he looks at you. As though he thinks he has a right to see your hair."

Seth rubbed a hand around the back of his neck. This wasn't coming off well at all. Rosie stared up at him, water running down her cheeks and dripping off the end of her nose.

"What I'm trying to say is that it's Rustemeyer that bothers me," Seth tried again. "Not your hair. Not that it's hanging down. Loose."

"I lost my bonnet."

"It wasn't your fault."

"He picked me up."

"He shouldn't have done that. It wasn't his place."

"Well, he didn't want me to get . . . wet." As she said the word, the humor of the situation lit up her brown eyes. Her mouth twitched. "I guess I'm wet anyway."

"Are you sure you won't sleep in the house?"

"No. I'll be fine." She gave him a smile. "Good night, Mr. Hunter."

"Good night, Miss Mills." As she turned to walk away, he caught her hand. "About your hair—"

"Yes?"

"Don't cut it. You could make a bonnet out of grain sacks. For the sun, I mean. Just to keep the heat off your face. Not because I don't like to see your hair down. I don't think it's shameful. That wasn't what I meant."

Rosie tilted her head to one side. "Mr. Hunter, are you trying to tell me that you like my hair?"

"I reckon it's not too bad." He cleared his throat. Though he was wet and shivering, he felt exactly like a chicken roasting on a skewer. With Mary Cornwall, conversation had been so different. She had giggled and teased and flirted around him until he could hardly think. Truth to tell, Mary hadn't thought much either. She was all air and light. A serious thought never crossed her brain. But Rosie demanded honesty. Those brown eyes confronted him with an expectation of truth. He squared his shoulders.

"Miss Mills, the fact is you have the prettiest hair I ever laid eyes on," he burst out. "The shame would be if you cut it off just because Rolf Rustemeyer was careless enough to lose your bonnet. If you like, you can sew yourself a new bonnet to keep off the sun and wind. But as far as I'm concerned, you can leave your hair loose from now until kingdom come. If the truth be known, you've prettied up my homestead a lot since you came. And I'm not just talking about the new curtains."

As he finished speaking, Seth realized he was still holding Rosie's hand. She was staring up at him, her eyes shining beneath the droplets beaded on the ends of her lashes. Before he could further embarrass himself, Seth loosed her hand and turned back toward the house. He knew his boots were slogging through mud, but for some reason he had the strangest sense that he was walking on air.

ROSIE woke under the wagon to find three chickens, a rooster, seven baby chicks, and a very wet puppy cuddled up beside her. A puppy? Where had it come from? She reached out to touch the ball of yellow fur, and the rooster let out a squawk. Feathers flew. The puppy yipped. The barn snake slithered from a clump of hay near Rosie's shoulder. At the unexpected sight of the black, shiny undulation, she sat up and banged her head against the axle—in the exact spot she had hit it the day she fell from the tree into Seth Hunter's arms.

"Ouch!" Clutching the bump and ruefully recalling the tumult of her life since that first moment with Seth, she straggled out from under the wagon. The puppy regarded her with sleepy eyes. Then it began to wag a short, stumpy tail. "Well, good morning to you, too. Where's your mama, little fella?"

The puppy waddled forward and pushed its wet black nose against Rosie's palm. She rubbed the soft fur, aware that the movement of sharp ribs beneath meant the creature hadn't been eating regularly. A bowl of fresh milk would help that.

"Come on, then," she said, hoisting the wiggly bundle into the crook of her arm. "You might as well join the rest of us misfits here on this forlorn prairie. You and I have no parents. Chipper has lost his mama. Seth doesn't have the first notion how to be a good father. And who knows what became of his folks? Not one of us understands how to make a family, so you might as well join in the muddle."

Rosie stepped out of the barn into a bright, hot morning. Steam rose from the plowed fields around the dugout. My, but the neat furrows were a beautiful sight! The promise of a bountiful harvest and a future of hope filled her heart with an unspeakable joy. She started for the soddy, but at the sound of regular pounding coming from the direction of the creek, she stopped. The bridge. Seth and Rolf were building the bridge. On a Sunday!

Picking up her skirts, Rosie marched down the bank toward the water's edge. "Mr. Hunter! Mr. Rustemeyer! Have you forgotten what day this is? It's Sunday!"

The two men stopped their hammering and gaped at her. For the first time that morning, Rosie realized how she must look. Her dress was damp, hemmed in mud, and stuck with bits of straw. Her hair hung in a long tangle past her waist. In between licking her cheek with a soft pink tongue, the little yellow puppy nipped at her chin with his tiny milk teeth.

"It's Sunday," she repeated, attempting to hold the puppy back.

"I told you there's no church around here." Seth set down his hammer. "Until we get this bridge built and cut a trail to the main road, the circuit preacher won't even come by."

"All the same—I think it's only right to honor the Sabbath. Sing. Read the Scriptures. Pray. Don't you agree?"

As Seth gazed at her, Rosie felt the heat rise in her cheeks. What was he staring at? Did she look so appalling in her muddy dress? Or was her long hair distracting him again? Maybe it was the puppy.

"He was sleeping with me this morning," she said, holding up the little ball of fluff. "Under the wagon."

Seth gave the dog a quick glance, then he focused on Rosie again. "Did you sleep all right? You look cold."

"I'm all right. But it's Sunday, Mr. Hunter. You really shouldn't be hammering, should you?"

"I can't see how it matters."

"Of course it matters. You're working. We are to honor the Sabbath and keep it holy."

"I'm building a bridge."

Rosie stroked her hand over the puppy's head as she studied the pile of lumber near the water's edge. Bridges linked people together. Bridges brought circuit preachers. Missionaries. Church builders. Building a bridge on the Sabbath might not be too great a sin in the eyes of the Lord. Still, it couldn't please him to ignore a holy day.

"I think we should turn our hearts to God," she insisted. "I think we should read the Bible."

In Seth's blue eyes, she recognized the flicker of anger. She knew what he was thinking. His skinny, mule-headed farmhand was contradicting him again. Being stubborn. Willful. He clenched his jaw, and she steeled herself against his wrath.

"All right," he said, slapping his hands on his thighs. "I reckon our angel of mercy has spoken. Rustemeyer, it's time for church."

"Was ist los?"

"Church." Seth pronounced the word loudly to the German as they followed Rosie toward the soddy. He didn't much like the idea of stopping their work on the bridge just to sit around reading and singing hymns all morning. The creek was running full after the rain the night before; the high water had prevented Jimmy O'Toole from crossing to help with construction. If they hoped to have the bridge built before the crushing heat of summer set in, they would need to work on it every day.

On the other hand, Seth was beginning to sense that Miss Rosenbloom Cotton Mills had a good head on her shoulders when it came to how things ought to be done around a homestead. Maybe she *was* a fatherless foundling who had grown up in an orphanage. But since she'd come out to the prairie, Seth had eaten three square meals a day, slept on clean sheets at night, and lived in a house with curtains at the windows, a cloth on the table, and flowers in a jug. More important, in Rosie's presence, Chipper's sullen attitude had begun to fade. If she thought it was right to pray before meals and sing on Sundays, who was Seth to argue?

"It's Sunday," he said to Rustemeyer. Then he pointed at heaven and folded his hands. "Time to pray. To God."

"*Gott. Ja, ja.*"

"We'll sit in the sunshine," Rosie said. "That way we can dry off."

As they approached the soddy, Chipper came dancing through the front door. He was wearing the nightshirt Rosie had sewn, and at the early hour his hair was still rumpled from sleep. "A puppy! Rosie, you have a puppy! Can I pet him? Can I hold him?"

Chuckling at the utter delight in the child's eyes, she handed over the pup. "He's hungry now. We must feed him some milk right away."

"What's his name? Where did you find him? Where did he come from?"

"God sent him to us. He's our gift from heaven. He has no mama, no papa, and no name. But he's a very special treasure all the same."

"Like you, Rosie!" Chipper said. Then he turned to his father. "He's just like her, isn't he?"

At the implications behind the question, Seth stiffened for a moment. Then he gave his son a deliberate grin. "Muddy and damp, you mean? With lots of tangled hair?"

"Not that!" Chipper said, breaking into a giggle. "I meant that the puppy has no mama or papa, and neither does Rosie."

"I reckon you're right." Seth rubbed a hand roughly between the puppy's two perky ears. "Miss Mills is wet, homeless . . . and a very special treasure. Our gift from heaven."

Rosie's mouth dropped open, and Seth couldn't resist giving her a wink as he sauntered toward the soddy. But inside the darkened room, he could hear his heart hammering in his chest. Now why had he gone and done that? Why did the opportunity to tease and disconcert her give him such amusement? Why couldn't he keep his focus on practical matters—instead of on Rosie's long brown hair and warm smile? What was happening to him?

Last night Seth had followed her into the pouring rain like some lovesick fool. He had held her hand. He had told her he liked her hair. It was pretty, he had said. She was pretty. Now he had all but admitted she had become special to him. How could such foolishness have come about? He felt half dizzy inside. Light-headed. Off balance.

He had to put a stop to this, or she would get ideas. Wrong ideas. Carrying the heavy, black, leather-bound Bible his mother had given him, Seth strode back outside. He arranged himself on a big stump near the woodpile and spread the book open across one knee. Rosie crouched on a log, draping her skirts out to dry in the sunshine. Rustemeyer sat down near her. Chipper stroked the puppy as it lapped at a saucer of milk.

"All right," Seth began, determined to take control—of himself and the entire situation. "We'll start at the beginning. Genesis."

"Deuteronomy," Rosie said. "Please."

Seth frowned. "That's a bunch of laws and rules, isn't it? I think we should start at the beginning—the way a book ought to be read."

"But Mr. Holloway said there's a verse about . . . about foundlings." Her voice was small, wounded. "He told me I'm not supposed to go to church. It's forbidden . . . for people like me."

"What's wrong with you, Rosie?" Chipper asked. "Why shouldn't you go to church?"

"Whoever my mama and papa were, I don't expect they were married to each other. God likes for people to marry each other before they have babies, Chipper. He wants . . . families." She swallowed, and Seth thought his heart was going to tear open at the pain written so visibly in her brown eyes. "You know, I've been to church all my life, but now I wonder if I've done wrong. Maybe . . . maybe God hates the sight of people like me in his house. Mr. Hunter, would you find that verse? It's in Deuteronomy. I want to know what it says. I want to try to understand."

Seth scratched his head. It couldn't be right to talk about touchy subjects like illegitimacy with children around. Could it? And Rustemeyer was getting restless. The German didn't understand a word of the conversation. He kept glancing in the direction of the unfinished bridge. Worst of all, Seth couldn't even remember where Deuteronomy was situated in the Bible.

"Maybe we should just read a psalm and be done with it," he said. "My mama used to read them to us kids all the time after Papa went off and . . . when she was feeling lonely. Or sad."

"Deuteronomy," Rosie repeated. "Please, Mr. Hunter."

What could he say to those brown eyes? Seth flipped around through the pages until he found the book. It was near the beginning of the Bible—almost like starting in Genesis.

The first batch of chapters had to do with the Israelites wandering in the desert. He bypassed that part as too boring. Then came the Ten Commandments. Those had been hanging on the wall in the house where Seth grew up. The neat sampler sewn by his mother had stated God's laws in bold black cross-stitch. And Seth had watched his father methodically break every one of them. He elected to skip over that part of Deuteronomy, too.

"All right, chapter six," he said. "Maybe Holloway's verse is in here. 'And thou shalt love the Lord thy God with all thine heart, and with all thy soul, and with all thy might. And these words, which I command thee this day, shall be in thine heart: And thou shalt teach them diligently unto thy children, and shalt talk of them when thou sittest in thine house, and when thou walkest by the way, and when thou liest down, and when thou risest up.' That sounds good enough to me. OK, who wants to pray?"

Rosie blinked. "But that's not the part about the foundlings."

"It's about children. It says to love God and teach your children about the Bible."

"It's not what Mr. Holloway was talking about."

"All right, all right." Seth lifted his hat and raked a hand through his hair. To tell the truth, he didn't really want to find the part about the foundlings. It might upset Rosie. Seth couldn't stand the thought of her eyes filling with tears the way they had in Holloway's station. Fact is, if the Bible made Rosie cry, Seth would be tempted to chuck the book in the creek. Though he believed in God—Jesus' death on the cross, the resurrection, and all that—he'd never seen much good come of religion in his own life.

After his papa had run off, Seth used to pray every day for God to bring the man back. But he never did come back. Seth had longed for a father—a good, strong father—more than anything in the world. But all his praying hadn't done a lick of good.

"You know there are an awful lot of verses in here," he told Rosie as he flipped through the pages. "Chances of finding that particular one are mighty slim."

"I'm praying for you to find it," Rosie said. "The Lord will lead you there."

Seth shrugged in resignation. "Here's something about the church. Chapter 12. 'But unto the place which the Lord your God shall choose . . . thither thou shalt come. . . . And there ye shall eat before the Lord your God, and ye shall rejoice in all that ye put your hand unto, ye and your households, wherein the Lord thy God hath blessed thee.' Sounds to me like God wants everybody to go to church—and even have a good time eating and rejoicing. OK, *now* who wants to pray?"

"Keep reading," Rosie said. "You haven't found it yet."

Seth turned through passage after passage about which animals to eat, what to do about murder, and who ought to marry whom. Just when he was ready to shut the book and get back to the bridge, his eye fell on Deuteronomy 23:2. He read it silently. Read it again. Finally, he looked up at Rosie.

"Go on," she whispered.

"'A bastard shall not enter into the congregation of the Lord; even to his tenth generation shall he not enter into the congregation of the Lord.' I don't believe that," he exploded. "What's a child got to do with how his parents behave? It's not right to blame a child for what his father did. You can't hold innocent children accountable for their ancestors' sins and failures. That's a bunch of bunk."

He dropped the Bible to the ground. "Enough," he went on. "We've got to get to work on the bridge. Pray, Rustemeyer. Do it in German. I don't care to understand it anyhow."

Rustemeyer stared at Seth. "*Was ist los?*" he asked, gesturing angrily at the fallen book.

"You're not supposed to throw the Bible in the mud," Chipper said. "Only a nasty ol' Yankee would do that."

"What do you know?" Seth snapped, his own father's harsh voice echoing in his head. "What do you know about anything?"

Chipper shrank into himself and buried his face in the puppy's fur. Rosie sat forlornly on the log, her shoulders sagging, her focus on her lap. Rustemeyer glowered.

"So much for Deuteronomy," Seth barked, standing. "So much for the whole worthless Bible. So much for religion and church and a God who doesn't love people for who they are and not what they came from."

Hot, frustrated, confused, he stomped off toward the bridge. At least building was something he knew how to do.

On the first day of June, Rosie, Chipper, the new puppy, and the entire O'Toole clan gathered to watch Seth drive the last nail into the pontoon bridge that spanned Bluestem Creek. He, Rolf Rustemeyer, and Jimmy had worked on the project every minute that they weren't plowing, planting, or hoeing. Rosie had used her own spare minutes to sew a flowered scarf that would hold back her hair. But they didn't have another Bible study, even though two Sundays passed during the building of the bridge.

Rosie could hardly see the point in forming a group to worship God. The preacher at the church in Kansas City had said that wherever two or three believers were gathered in Christ's name, he was there among them. But now Rosie knew that God didn't want her—an illegitimate child—to worship in a gathering of his believers. As far as she could understand the verse in Deuteronomy, it would be just plain wrong for her to bring them all together again like a small church. Her very presence would defile the gathering.

Since that Sunday morning after the rain, nothing had gone particularly well around the homestead. The harmony had been spoiled. To Rosie, it felt like Satan had used the moment of discord to jump right in and throw everything out of kilter. Seth was so angry about the verse in Deuteronomy he had stopped praying at mealtimes. Chipper crept around like a lost lamb. He seemed half fearful that Jack Cornwall would jump out from behind a bush and grab him—and half hoping he would. It was hard to tell what Rolf Rustemeyer was thinking.

If Rosie and Seth had begun to build a bridge toward accepting and understanding each other, it too had been destroyed the morning of Deuteronomy. Rosie felt that her stubborn insistence on observing the Sabbath had led Seth to reject God—and Seth in turn had rejected her. He worked day and night, and he hardly gave her a second glance. There were no more long midnight conversations, no more teasing compliments, no more dances in the barn. For some reason, Seth's disinterest in her hurt almost as much as the discovery that God didn't want her to set foot inside his church.

"Casimir Laski sent us a message this afternoon," Sheena O'Toole whispered to Rosie as the two women led everyone who had observed the ceremonial pounding of the last nail across the new bridge for a celebratory evening meal at Seth's soddy. "Jack Cornwall has been spotted around the Red Vermillion River, so he has. Word is he's been asking the whereabouts of the Hunter and O'Toole homesteads. He's working his way closer to us, Rosie. Sure, you and Seth must keep a sharp eye on the wee one. First thing you know, that *sherral* will kidnap the boy and ride hotfoot back to Missouri."

Stopping in the front yard, Rosie dipped a spoon into the large black cauldron that hung on a tripod over the outdoor fire. The stew she had made that morning looked delicious, and it smelled even better. With fresh greens from the prairie, wild onions and carrots, and the very last of the stored potatoes, the concoction would fill hungry stomachs well. Best of all, Sheena had whipped up a batch of Irish dumplings, which floated in the broth like puffy white pillows.

Rustemeyer, who had ridden over for the celebration, leaned across Rosie's shoulder. "Fery goot," he said. "Schmells fery goot."

"Thank you, Mr. Rustemeyer. I'm glad you think so," Rosie replied. She had grown accustomed to Rolf's awkward attempts at speaking English. He reminded her of the toddlers at the Home—the way they stumbled over words and put sentences together in funny combinations.

"You are velcome." He executed a neat bow, which sent Sheena into a fit of giggles. Ignoring her, the German picked up a stack of bowls. "I helpen you, fräulein. *Mit der Suppe*."

"With . . . the . . . soup," she pronounced carefully.

"Vit . . . dee . . . zoop."

"All right." Rosie looked up into the German's gray eyes as she ladled the bowl full of stew. Rolf had spent a great deal of time at Seth's homestead in the past weeks, and Rosie was accustomed to his presence. In fact, she hardly noticed him. He worked hard. He was cheerful. He treated Chipper kindly. And he ate like a hungry horse.

But other than creating a need to calculate extra portions into her meals, Rolf had been invisible to Rosie. She had been so busy setting up the household, weeding the kitchen garden, baking, washing, ironing, and sewing that she hadn't given a second thought to her plan to marry the big blond German. Now she realized she had only five months to make it happen. She ought to start paying him some heed.

"You did a good job on the bridge," she said, handing Rolf a bowl. "Good work."

"*Ja, ja.*" He smiled. "You are velcome."

She didn't think he had understood. Oh well, he certainly fit every item on her list for an ideal marriage partner: strong, honest, hardworking, kind. Rolf was a good man. He didn't disturb her the way Seth did. He never teased or argued. He never complimented or criticized. He never said anything at all. He just happily went about his work, pausing only to devour grizzly bear-sized portions of whatever she put on the table. Rolf was the perfect mate.

Seth, on the other hand, was complicated, intelligent, edgy, and a demanding perfectionist. When he looked at Rosie, the blood in her temples began to pound, and her heart jumped into her throat. If he inadvertently brushed her hand, strange fiery tingles raced straight up her arm. She found herself listening for his whistle at dawn when he came across the yard to milk the cows. And at night, when he walked her to the barn to light her path with the lantern, she searched for things to say just so she could hear his deep voice.

Truth to tell, Seth Hunter had become a constant presence in her thoughts. He made her feel nervous. Challenged. Alive. Very much alive. She couldn't understand what it meant. Her feelings about him reminded her of the stories she had read to the children at the Home—stories about princes and princesses falling in love.

"Love?" she said out loud. The very thought of that word in connection with Seth Hunter threw her for a loop.

Rolf handed her another empty bowl to fill. "Lof," he repeated. "*Was ist* lof?"

"Love? Oh, it's nothing." She swallowed hard and waved away the word. "Some people think it has to do with marriage. Husbands and wives. People have a wedding, you see. They marry. They live together and have children. Getting married is—"

"What are you talking to Rustemeyer about?" Seth demanded.

He had approached the fire so quietly Rosie hadn't heard him. When she turned toward Seth's voice, she saw that his blue eyes were blazing, and the muscles in his jaw flickered with tension. Behind him, a group of travelers—six mounted horsemen—were talking with Jimmy O'Toole some distance from the soddy.

"Who are those men?" Rosie asked. "Where did they come from? Is Jack Cornwall among them?"

"No. They're all right. Casimir Laski sent them from his station. They were hoping we had finished building the bridge so they could cut a few miles off their trip. They're cattlemen on their way to Salina to pick up five hundred head and drive them to Kansas City." Seth eyed the stew. "Do you have enough to feed them?"

"Of course."

"Good. Rustemeyer, see to their horses." At the man's blank look, Seth leaned closer and said loudly. "*Horses.*"

"You won't make him understand by shouting," Rosie said. She pointed at the lead rider's horse. "Help, please."

"*Ja, ja.*" Rustemeyer gave Rosie a warm smile and headed off in the direction of the visitors. She watched him go, and she felt happy that with each new word he learned he was fitting in better with prairie society.

"Mr. Rustemeyer is doing very well with his English, don't you—"

"I don't want you to marry that man," Seth cut in, his voice hard. "You hear me, Miss Mills? Rosie?"

At his use of her first name, she glanced at him in surprise. "And why not? I can marry whoever I want to."

"No, you can't. Not him."

"Rolf is a good person. He's kind. He's hardworking." She stirred the stew for a moment. "Do you think he wouldn't have me? If he knew . . . about Deuteronomy, I mean?"

"It doesn't have anything to do with Deuteronomy."

"Then what? Why wouldn't he—"

"It's not you. It's . . . well, it *is* you. You're . . . you're . . . you're mine. My worker, I mean. I brought you from Kansas City, didn't I? You're sleeping in my barn. Eating my food. I need you. Need you around the house. You do good work. Chipper likes you. I won't have you going off to marry Rustemeyer."

Rosie stared at Seth. The tips of his ears had gone bright red, and she could see a little vein jumping in his forehead. What on earth had upset him so? The thought of her marrying Rolf Rustemeyer had him fairly steaming. But why? Did he dislike the German so much? Or did he consider Rosie his own personal servant over whom he had absolute power? Or did his concern have something to do with Chipper? Or was there something . . . something else . . . behind it?

Slowly she turned back to the stew and set the lid on the cauldron. The feel of Seth's eyes on the back of her neck set her skin prickling. She took three deep breaths, and then she straightened.

"You don't understand," she said evenly. "You don't understand me at all."

"I do understand. You think you have to hook onto some man in order for your life to have any meaning. You think your mama rejected you, and you think God rejected you. So the only way you're going to have a future is if you latch onto a husband. Anybody will do. You don't think enough of yourself to believe that you could matter to another person."

"I don't matter to anyone."

"You matter." He shifted from one foot to the other. "You matter to Chipper."

"You told me not to matter to him. You don't want me to mean anything in his life. And now you expect me to give up the hope of marriage and a family for a five-year-old child? A child whose father plainly told me to keep my distance from the boy?"

"Arguing again, are you?" Sheena said, taking the ladle from Rosie's hand. "Well now, that's a good sign, so it is. But if the pair of you stand around ballyragging all evening, we'll none of us have any supper. So come along, and put this nonsense behind you for the time being. You can go at it again later. In private."

Sheena gave Seth an exaggerated wink, and Rosie wished she could crawl into a hole. When she glanced around she saw that Jimmy O'Toole, the five O'Toole children, Chipper, Rolf Rustemeyer, and the new visitors were all arranged in a circle, holding their bowls of stew and staring at her and Seth. Even the puppy had squatted near the fire to see what would happen.

Seth cleared his throat and grabbed his bowl. "Welcome to our guests," he said. "Thanks to Mrs. O'Toole and Miss Mills for the supper. Thanks to Jimmy and Rolf for their help building the bridge. Let's eat."

"Let's pray first," Rosie cut in, brushing past Seth. "It's only right. I'll do it."

Before she could cower in the presence of so many guests, she stepped into the middle of the circle and bowed her head. She hadn't prayed in a very long time. Not since the Deuteronomy Sunday. But all that time, she had felt such an aching emptiness inside her heart. Now, though the words seemed difficult to form, she knew it was right to honor this special event with a prayer.

"Dear Father," she began. Her next breath caught in the back of her throat. Father. *Father!* God was her father. Of course. She had believed it for years. She had stated it so boldly: *But as many as received him, to them gave he power to become the sons of God.*

Rosenbloom Cotton Mills was not illegitimate. God himself had made her his own child. *And because ye are sons, God hath sent forth the Spirit of his Son into your hearts, crying, Abba, Father.*

"Dear Father," she repeated. But the sudden knowledge of his redeeming love, his unconditional acceptance, his constant grace filled her heart. Overwhelmed her. As a joint heir with Christ, she could walk into any church with her heart full of the assurance of her heavenly Father's eternal, unchangeable welcome.

As tears spilled down her cheeks, Rosie turned away and ran sobbing into the twilight.

CHAPTER 9

ROSIE? Rosie, where are you?" Sheena's lilting voice called out.

Rosie blotted her cheeks with the hem of her skirt. "I'm over here, Sheena. On the big stone near the willow tree."

"I see you now!" Puffing a little from her run, the Irishwoman lifted her skirts and clambered down the bank. "You gave us quite a scare, running off the way you did in the middle of your prayer. Sure, Seth wanted to come after you, and Rolf, too. It was all I could do to hold Chipper back. Even my Jimmy was set to hotfoot it across the prairie in search of you. You've earned yourself quite a gaggle of lovesick men, so you have."

"Oh, Sheena." Rosie scooted over on the flat stone to make room for her friend. "Don't be silly. For all Seth has tried to accept me, he finds me as frustrating and irritating as a goat-head burr."

"Aye, you've gotten under his skin, so you have. I'll warrant the man's in love."

"Sheena! Please don't tease me." Rosie swallowed. "Anyway, I've seen the error of my thoughts in that direction. I've been looking at Seth in a human way—instead of as God sees him. Tonight—just now—my Father spoke to me, Sheena."

"Spoke to you? Glory be, but you're a strange wee thing, Rosie Mills. God in heaven spoke directly to you? I can't credit it."

"Then you've never experienced it." Rosie briefly explained

about the Deuteronomy Sunday and its outcome. Then she told Sheena how the moment she had called her heavenly Father by name, the meaning of the cryptic verse had become crystal clear. "When you pray, Sheena, you mustn't do all the talking. You've got to listen, too. Listen to what he's telling you."

"But how can you be sure it's God speaking—and not some little imp of the devil inside your head?"

"That's easy enough. Everything God says is true. He can't lie. Satan is the father of lies, and he finds great joy in distorting the truth. He confuses us and fills our heads with doubt and despair. But if I take what I believe God has said to me and hold it up to the Bible, it should reflect his Word. In fact, when I hear my Father's voice, it most often comes in words straight out of the Scriptures."

Sheena sat for a moment, pondering. "I don't know that I've ever listened to God, Rosie. But I'll try. Truly I will. And I'm thankful you've seen that scrap of Deuteronomy clear to its rightful meaning."

"My greatest flaw is taking the reins of my own life and trying to guide myself. When I do, everything gets twisted, and I go off on the wrong path."

"Do you believe God's path led you out here to the prairie?"

"I don't know. But I'm certain he can bring a blessing from it if I continually give myself to him."

"Do you plan to ask God which man he wants you to marry, Rosie?"

"I can't think about marriage, Sheena. When I do, I get so confused. I can't see God at all. I just see myself and . . . and someone else."

"Seth Hunter?"

Rosie twisted her hands together in her lap. "It should be Rolf."

"Well now, you've certainly set every man's heart aflutter with your shenanigans tonight. What do you mean to do about it,

Rosie? Which one will you have? Will it be Rolf Rustemeyer? Or Seth Hunter? Or will you wait for some other man to come along?"

For a long time, Rosie sat in silence, turning the questions over and over in her mind. Finally she laid her hand across Sheena's. "I only know one thing. I'm going to try to stop listening to my own heart and start listening to God. He knows the plans he has for me. If I care enough to follow him, I'll find the right path."

"You're a good girl. Seth would do well to put his past behind him and look to his future."

"He is thinking of his future. He cares so deeply about Chipper. He told me he didn't want me to marry Rolf because he knows Chipper needs me right now."

Sheena let out a squawk. "By all the goats in Kerry, girl, it's not Chipper that needs you! It's Seth himself, so it is."

"I don't see why. I've hardly done a thing but sew him a blue shirt and put three meals a day on his table." Rosie searched her mind, trying to make sense of the messages she had read again and again in Seth's blue eyes. Yes, he did seem to need her. Every time he caught her eye he seemed to be saying, *Don't go. Don't leave me.*

"It's the prairie," she said finally. "If Seth needs me at all, it's because he understands that I can make a difference in his life out here. If I can keep the kitchen garden growing, keep Chipper healthy, keep the clothes and the bedding washed and mended, then his days will be easier. He spoke once about all the dangers he faces. Wind. Hail. Prairie fires. Plagues of insects. Cyclones. I should find a way to help . . . help Seth through all that. Whether he knows it or not, he does need me, Sheena. God can use me in his life."

Sheena gave a little chuckle and shook her head. "I'll warrant the good Lord can use you in Seth's life—one way or another." Standing, she gave a stretch. "Now, my sweet lass, we'd better get back to the soddy, or they'll send a search party after the both of us, so they will."

Filled with a new sense of mission, Rosie lifted her eyes to the heavens. God had given her five months—five months to do his will on the prairie. If her Father wanted her to have a husband, he would provide one. Until then, she must set about to do his will as a single woman in possession of a strong back, willing hands, and the determination to provide for the well-being of her employer.

Seth was pacing by the campfire when Rosie and Sheena emerged arm in arm into the circle of light. His relief at seeing the younger woman was so great, he had to fight himself to keep from letting out a whoop of joy and swinging her up into his arms. Instead, he stopped his pacing and set his hands loosely on his hips as Chipper and the other children swarmed around her. Even the puppy, whom she and Chipper had named Stubby, danced in delight, tugging on the hem of Rosie's skirt and yipping in the excitement of the moment.

"Rosie's been talking to God again, so she has," Sheena declared to the gathered company. She accepted the rough willow chair offered by one of the visiting cattlemen. "Our Rosie talks to God—*and* she listens when he talks back to her."

The cowboy laughed. "Maybe we should build her a shrine or somethin'."

"Make light of it if you will," Sheena went on, "but to Rosie every place on earth is a shrine. God talks to her anywhere."

"Quite a little saint, is she?" The man took off his tall-crowned Stetson and surveyed the slender woman. Then he looked at Seth. "Your wife?"

"She works for me. Takes care of my son."

The man let out a slow whistle. "I'd keep a sharp lookout if I was you, my friend. A man gets lonely on the trail, and she's a mighty purty little thing. Can she cook?"

"Fery goot cook," Rolf Rustemeyer said. "Fräulein Mills *ist* fery goot cook. Maken fresch bread, potato, egg, chicken. *Ist* goot *für* eaten—breakfascht, lunsch, zupper."

"What's he talkin' about?" the cowboy asked Seth. "Is he French or somethin'?"

"German." Seth struggled with the urge to tell the men to keep their eyes off Rosie and their thoughts to themselves—she wasn't free for the looking. But she *was* free. She had kept her heart pure. No man had claimed her. He shoved his hands into his pockets and started toward her.

At that moment, the cowboy stepped in front of him. "Ma'am, that was a real fine supper you fixed," he said to Rosie. "As fine a supper as I've ate in many a month."

Rosie had been carrying Chipper on one hip. Now she let him slide to the ground. "Thank you, sir," she said, her face lighting up. "They were Sheena's dumplings."

"I'd be much obliged if you'd allow me and my men to pay you for the meal. What would you say to fifty cents?"

"Fifty cents!" Rosie gasped.

"*Per,*" the man added proudly. "Pay up, fellers."

"Now just a minute." Seth held up a hand. "We don't take money for food. This is my homestead, not a boarding house. If we have extra, we share it."

"Well, sir, that's mighty generous of you. Mighty generous. If you feel thataway, why we'll just bed down over in your barn for the night. Awful late to be hitting the trail again."

Seth's spine prickled. "The barn's off limits. Head over the bridge to LeBlanc's mill. He's got a bunkhouse all set up, and his wife serves breakfast. If you start out now, you'll be there by midnight."

"Midnight! C'mon, now. If you don't want us in your barn, we'll put our bedrolls down by the crick."

Seth crossed his arms over his chest. He wasn't about to allow six lonely cowboys to sleep within half a mile of Rosie Mills—let alone as nearby as the creek. "Now listen here—"

"Sure, you gentlemen can stay in my barn," Jimmy O'Toole said, laying a hand on Seth's shoulder. "It's dry enough if you can stand the smell."

The cowboys eyed each other. Finally their leader turned back to Seth. "Say, farmer, by any chance do you know a feller by the name of Hunter?"

"What's it to you?"

"Just curious. We been hearing about this Hunter rascal all the way from Topeka. Seems he once took a woman against her will and used her most cruel. Then he run off and left her alone and in a delicate condition. More'n five years later, he showed up and kidnapped the child the poor woman had borned before she died a terrible death. There's been talk of puttin' a bounty on the scalawag's head."

"Is that so?" Seth stared hard at the man, his blood boiling in his veins. "Where'd you come by such a farfetched story as that?"

"Folks talkin' about it everywhere. There's a feller by the name of Cornwall huntin' for the missin' boy. It's him as is thinkin' of a bounty. They say if he puts one on Hunter's head, it'll be for a hundred dollars."

Seth wanted to laugh out loud. Jack Cornwall didn't have a hundred dollars to save his yellow-bellied soul. The war had stripped him of house and farm—his only means of livelihood. He'd be hard-pressed to come up with ten dollars, let alone a hundred.

"A hundred dollars could make a lot of folks sit up and listen," the cowboy went on. "You ever heard of this Hunter feller around these parts?"

"I mind my own business," Seth said. "But I can tell you one thing. Before I'd set off chasing any man for a bounty, I'd take a close look at Jack Cornwall's hundred-dollar reward."

"*Jack* Cornwall, is it?" The cowboy gave his cronies a grin. "Well now, I reckon you know more about this matter than we do."

"Bad news travels fast."

The man laughed. "Shore enough! I guess we'll be crossin' that bridge of yours then. Keep us in mind if you hear of Hunter. We'd be the first in line to ride out in search of a hundred-dollar bounty. If we don't get to Salina purty quick, we're gonna be flat broke."

"You'll need at least two dollars apiece tonight," Rosie said. Seth watched in amazement as she approached the cowboys. Head held high and shoulders squared, she confronted them. "If you want to cross the Bluestem Creek, you have to pay the bridge toll."

"Bridge toll!"

"You don't think that bridge built itself, do you? Lumber doesn't come cheap and easy out here on the prairie. Unless you men intend to ride all the way up the Bluestem to the shallow crossing at Salvatore Rippeto's station, you'll have to pay the toll."

"But that's twelve dollars!"

"Twelve dollars exactly," Rosie agreed. "We crossed plenty of bridges ourselves on the way here, and it's a fair price." She stuck out her hand, and the six cowboys dug around in their pockets for the silver coins. Grumbling, the men handed over their money and then shuffled off toward their horses.

As the cowboys rode away, Rosie took off her scarf, shook out her long hair, and tied the coins into the scrap of cloth. "I will take it upon myself to keep the money safe," she said.

Rolf Rustemeyer—who evidently had comprehended the nature of the transaction—burst out into a deep, hearty chuckle. Sheena gave her a hug as the children cheered. Even Jimmy clapped her on the back.

From a distance, Seth listened as the cowboys' horses clattered across the new pontoon bridge. He was glad he had put a heavy bolt on the barn door. Glad he had begun to shingle the roof. Glad the puppy always slept beside Rosie. But he had a bad feeling that his efforts might not be enough to keep her safe.

Swallowing hard, he fought the strong urge that welled up

inside him. He wanted to protect Rosie. Shelter her. Care for her. It was different from the way he had felt about Mary Cornwall, who had lived so near her ever-vigilant papa. This feeling toward Rosie was stronger, and it filled his chest with an ache so powerful he could hardly suppress it.

But he didn't want to care so deeply about Rosie Mills! Didn't want to care about *any* woman. He had vowed never to fall into that trap again. Throughout his youth, all he'd ever wanted was a family. When he was grown, he hoped for a wife, children, a home. He wanted to be father and husband. He was sure he could do a better job of it than his own father had.

With Mary Cornwall he had tried. He had gone into that marriage with all the hopes and dreams a man could carry. And look what it had brought him. Anger, banishment, loss. He had a son who didn't love him. His brother-in-law had become an enemy who planned to kill him. Chances were that before the summer was out Seth would have a bounty on his head. And his wife—the wife with whom he had planned to spend his years—was dead.

Seth studied Rosie as she cleaned up from the supper, her hair flowing around her like a long silk cape. Beautiful. Rosie Mills was beautiful. But if he allowed himself to care about her—to commit his future to her—he might lose her. Just the way he'd lost Mary.

No. He wouldn't do that. Hardening his heart, Seth made up his mind. He would train his focus on his work. He would try as hard as he could to be the kind of father he thought Chipper needed. And . . . yes, he would encourage Rolf Rustemeyer to make Rosie his wife.

June brought such excitement, such joy, that Rosie knew she had done well in turning her heart toward her Father. Overriding everything hung the anticipation of the dance celebrating the new bridge. Rosie and Sheena took on the project with all the enthusiasm their blossoming friendship brought. It was hardly more than a twenty-minute walk from one soddy to the other, and they were constantly back and forth—talking, planning, even doing chores together.

Seth had decided to shingle the barn completely, and with each passing day Rosie's home became more snug and secure. She hung a curtain in the loft window and set a stool beside her mattress. She even made herself a pillow. Stubby slept at her feet, and at the slightest disturbance, he barked with all the ferocity of a wolf—albeit a very young, slightly yappy wolf.

The barn had been chosen as the site of the dance. Rosie scrubbed the rough plank walls top to bottom, and she and Chipper kept the stalls cleaned and filled with freshly mown hay. Even if it rained on the momentous afternoon, the barn could hold almost everyone invited to the party.

Sheena's list seemed to grow by the day. The Polish family, Casimir Laski and his wife, would come. Salvatore Rippeto had sent word that he and his wife and all their children were planning to attend. LeBlanc and his reputedly beautiful daughters were coming. They were said to be sewing new dresses expressly for the event.

Even Holloway and his wife—as community neighbors—had been invited. They hadn't responded to the invitation. Rumor had it they were angry about the bridge that had effectively cut their station off from the flow of traffic down the main road from Topeka to Salina. But Rolf Rustemeyer would be at the dance and so would all the O'Tooles, as well as a collection of homesteaders from around the area. With music and dancing and wonderful food, the celebration promised to be the highlight of the prairie summer.

As if all this weren't enough to keep her busy, Rosie had discovered a new source of activity: toll-taking.

"Here comes a party bound for the west," she told Sheena one afternoon as they stood in Seth's yard stirring soil-based pigment into the vat of milk paint they had made. They had decided to paint the barn a deep red. "Is it three wagons? Or four?"

"Three. That's nine dollars."

Rosie laughed and set down her paddle. "I never thought tending a bridge could be so rewarding. Did you know I've started taking goods in trade, too? Several travelers didn't have cash to pay the toll. Rather than make them travel all the way to Holloway or Rippeto, I accepted other things. Tea. Flour. Buffalo skins. Blankets. I've put everything in a big chest that I found in the barn."

Sheena studied the wagons as they rolled slowly toward the bridge. "Does Seth know?" she asked. "About the trade goods, I mean?"

Rosie chewed on her lower lip for a moment. She didn't like to do anything without Seth's approval. He hadn't seemed too happy about the toll-taking in the first place. He never asked where she put the money or what she planned to do with it. In fact, he more or less ignored the bridge and the growing stream of travelers who crossed it each day. There could be no question he would object to taking away the hard-earned goods the settlers brought with them in order to establish their new homes.

All the same, Rosie knew if she let one wagon or stagecoach cross without paying, word would spread, and nobody would want to pay. There were plenty who could afford it—cowboys with their pockets stuffed full of earnings from their latest trail ride, miners heading back east from the gold fields of California, peddlers and politicians, fur traders. All travelers knew they would have to pay ferry and bridge tolls. It was an accepted part of the journey. But Rosie had no doubt Seth would despise the notion of taking goods from settlers. On the other hand, how could it be right to turn poor travelers away just because they couldn't produce a silver dollar or two?

"I haven't told him," she admitted to Sheena. "I don't think he'd like it much."

"You might ask his opinion on the matter, Rosie. What's the harm in it?"

"Seth doesn't . . . he doesn't exactly talk to me anymore, Sheena. Ever since that night when I ran away to the creek to talk to God, Seth has been angry with me. Not exactly angry. He just doesn't seem to know I'm here. He never looks at me. He barely speaks."

"By herrings, I don't believe it. Seth doesn't speak to you? Why not?"

"I don't know. I suppose he's upset that I left the company that night. Maybe he's upset that I charged those cowboys a toll. Maybe it has something to do with Rolf Rustemeyer. I don't know. Seth and I can't seem to talk to each other without a squabble. We had been arguing just before I ran off that night. Remember? Seth was ordering me not to marry Rolf Rustemeyer, and I was telling him I could marry whoever I pleased. I didn't think it would make him so furious. But it did."

"He's jealous."

"No, Sheena. You're wrong there. Seth doesn't care for me. If he did, he would behave differently. You should see how he is with Chipper these days. He takes the boy with him everywhere he goes. They plow together, hoe together, even cut shingles together."

"Seth's afraid if he doesn't keep a close watch on his son, Jack Cornwall will kidnap the boy."

"That's part of it. But there's more, Sheena. Seth is trying hard to be a good father. It's a beautiful sight to watch the two of them together in the fields—though I must admit I can't see that it has bound them any tighter. Chipper holds back his heart."

"He must have learned that trick from his papa."

Rosie smiled. "Don't be so hard on Seth. He's a good man."

"Then why don't you tell him the truth about the trading you've been doing?"

"What difference can it make? I'm simply doing what I believe God has told me to do. I'm laying up provisions for Seth and Chipper. I'm taking care of them. Seeing to their welfare. If it comes in the form of silver dollars or extra blankets, what's the difference?"

Unwilling to hear Sheena's response, Rosie lifted a hand in greeting to the wagon team leader. He set the brake and climbed down. "Mornin', ma'am," he said.

"Welcome to Hunter's Station."

"Hunter's Station, is it?" Sheena murmured behind her. "Now isn't that a lovely how-do-ye-do?"

Rosie cast her a disapproving look. Then she turned back to the team leader. "Are you headed for Salina?"

"That's right, ma'am. Any news on the condition of the road that direction?"

"We had word this morning that it's dry and clear all the way to Salina. You'll have a delay at the Pawnee City ferry crossing. The town is right there at Fort Riley, you know, and I think a lot of the soldiers are leaving for home now that the war's over. They tell me it's a rope ferry, and it's been horribly backed up with traffic. The wait is several hours. Sometimes even a whole day. You'd do best to get there first thing in the morning. The ferry starts up at dawn."

"Much obliged to you, ma'am." The man smiled warmly beneath the walrus mustache that covered his upper lip. "Suppose we'll be able to find a place to spend the night in Junction City? My wife is coming near to her time—for the baby, you know. It's our first—and she sleeps better in a bed."

"There are two hotels. Good ones, I hear. The store is not too well stocked, but you can get flour and sugar. They're always low on coffee and soap, but they have plenty of cornmeal."

"Turns out we won't be needing all the coffee we brought. Didn't realize we could make the stuff just as easy out of chicory root."

"Oh, yes, and soap is simple enough, too."

"Soap? Is that right?" He scratched the top of his head. "Come to think of it, I don't recollect that we even brung any soap with us. We been traveling so long, we haven't given much thought to washing."

Rosie had sensed that fact right off. "You must take some of my potash with you." She started toward the barn with the man following. "Most of the time, I use lye to make my soap; you leech it from wood ashes. But these potash crystals are much more convenient. I just boiled down some lye to make them yesterday. Give the crystals to your wife, and see that they're kept well away from children. Any woman who has lived on the prairie can teach her how to use the potash to make soap. Sheena taught me. It's really not hard at all."

In the barn, she handed the man a crock containing half of her hard-earned supply of potash crystals. Truth to tell, it was a little painful to part with. The process of turning lye into potash was slow and smelly. But Rosie couldn't stand to think of that poor woman not even having a bar of soap to wash her new baby's clothes. The man cradled the crock like it was a treasure of gold.

"I don't have much to pay you with, ma'am," he said in a low voice. "We're trying to save what we've got for hotels and food. Would you take something in trade?"

"The potash is free. My gift for the new baby."

Again, the warm smile formed under the man's huge mustache. "I don't suppose you'd take some of my coffee in exchange for the bridge toll, would you?"

"Coffee . . ." Rosie pondered the offer for a moment. "A pound will do. One for each of the three wagons."

The grin grew wider. "You don't have any blankets for trade, do you, ma'am? We been colder at night than we expected."

"As a matter of fact, I do have blankets." Rosie could hardly believe her good fortune. She had more blankets than she knew what to do with in the big chest. But coffee—now that was a treasure hard to come by. Real coffee had a flavor that chicory couldn't match, and everyone at the barn dance would appreciate the unexpected pleasure.

She hauled two long planks from Seth's remaining lumber pile and laid them side by side across a pair of sawhorses. Then she opened the storage chest at the back of the barn and began to take out her trade goods. "I have five blankets," she said, laying them across the makeshift counter. "This one is really nice. Pure wool. I'd need more than coffee for it, though. I took this blanket in trade for the toll on seven wagons."

The man's eyes widened as Rosie took out a handmade quilt, a crock of pickles, and a small keg of nails. In a flash he left to fetch his wife from the wagon. Pretty soon, she and the travelers from the other wagons had gathered in the barn to look over the items. Even Sheena craned her neck to admire a little round mirror someone had traded in.

"Would you be willing to take a packet of needles for that ball of yarn?" the man's very pregnant wife asked. "I'd like to knit booties for the baby."

"Silver needles?" Rosie asked. You could never be too careful about this sort of thing. The woman nodded. Rosie smiled. "And let me tell you that coreopsis will make the most beautiful yellow dye. Be sure to gather the flower heads when they're in full bloom."

"What about blue? I was thinking of blue booties."

"Indigo—but it's not water soluble, so it's very hard to work with. I'd stick with yellow, if I were you. Do you like that knife, sir? I'd be willing to take an extra ax head you might have. Or a razor."

"Look, she has dried apples, Mama!" a child cried out.

"They're all the way from Pennsylvania," Rosie said. "Do you like apples? Here, take this one. Your mother can have a few more apples in trade for that half-pound of lard she seems so eager to be rid of."

"Oh, thank you kindly, ma'am. We haven't had apples for weeks. Can I take five?"

"Take seven. That way you can bake a pie. Or a big juicy cobbler. I've found children love cobbler, especially if you add just a pinch of—"

"Miss Mills." The icy voice gripped Rosie's stomach like a vise. She looked up to find Seth Hunter—hat in hand, sweat dampening his brow, hands planted on his hips—staring at her from the door of the barn. "Would you mind telling me what you're doing?"

CHAPTER 10

SETH could hardly believe his eyes. Right there in his barn stood Miss Rosenbloom Cotton Mills and fifteen complete strangers haggling over coffee, blankets, mirrors, and sewing needles. Where had she gotten all these things? Who were these people? What were they doing in *his* barn?

"Oh, hello, Mr. Hunter," Rosie called, giving him a wave. She smiled, but he could see that her face had paled at the sight of him. "We're just working out an exchange for the bridge toll." She dropped her voice. "And a few other things."

Seth crossed his arms and stared at the unexpected scene. Chipper skipped over to Rosie's side and gave Stubby a pat. The dog wagged his tail. "Where'd you get this stuff, Rosie?" the boy asked as she handed a man a knife and took a big iron soup ladle in trade. "This looks almost like a regular mercantile."

"That's a funny thought, Chipper," Rosie said, giving Seth a wary glance. "You know good and well this is just the barn. I keep a few things stored away in case somebody would rather trade than pay the toll."

"A few things! You gots *lots* of things. You even gots beads and shoes and a pair of scissors. What's in these cans?"

Seth stepped forward and lifted a tin. *Oysters!* Oysters were a luxury item only the rich could afford. How had she managed to get her hands on five tin cans of them? Beside the cans sat a ream of writing paper. And bullets. Rosie had a stack of ammunition that could keep Fort Riley in business for at least half a day. Where on earth had it all come from?

"If you had a post office here," the man with the huge mustache told Rosie, "you could set up your own store. Your prices are fair. You deal honest with folk. And you got good quality merchandise. All you need is a post office commission, and you'd pick up twice the trade."

"Oh, I wouldn't want to do that," Rosie said. "I have so much work to do around the house."

"Put your son to work doing chores."

"Chipper isn't my son. He belongs to—" Again she gave Seth a nervous glance. "He belongs to my employer."

"You mean you're a hired hand? Well, your boss would be smart to put you to running the mercantile and hire someone else to do the cleaning."

"That would never do," Rosie mumbled. "Really, we're very satisfied with things the way they are. This is all just for . . . just for the toll bridge."

As he passed, the man gave Seth a long look. "I'd think about that post office commission if I was you. She's got a good eye for business, that one. She could turn you a handsome profit."

Seth kept his focus trained on Rosie as the line of travelers wound out of his barn and back to their wagons. When she began to pack all her goods back into the chest, he decided it was high time to take up the differences between them. If she was going to work for him, she would have to do things his way. And the sooner he got her out of his homestead and married off to Rustemeyer the better.

Rosie Mills was trouble. Every time he looked at her, something twisted up inside him. A knot of pain formed in his stomach and began to torment him in a gently luring voice he found impossible to resist. *She's beautiful, isn't she? She's a good woman. Chipper adores her. She sure knows how to run a house.* No matter how hard Seth would try to silence the voice, it only grew louder. *Take the risk, Hunter. Reach out to her. Open your heart and let her heal you.*

"No," he said out loud.

"What?" Rosie swung around, her arms full of brightly colored wool blankets.

"I said no. You do not have my permission to do this."

"Do what? Take a few items in trade for the bridge toll? I can't see what harm it does, Mr. Hunter. You heard the man yourself. I'm fair and honest."

"No." He placed his hands palm-down on the makeshift counter. "I don't want you to do it."

"But trading helps everybody. The poor man had brought enough coffee to drown two armies, and he needed blankets for his wife." Rosie leaned across the counter and whispered conspiratorially. "She's going to have a baby. Their first."

Seth stared into her big brown eyes. Big warm chocolate eyes. A pang ran straight through his heart. That awful knot began in his stomach, and the voice began. *Kiss her, Hunter. Shut up and kiss that pretty woman.* He couldn't breathe.

"If you're worried I'm not taking in enough cash," she said, "I can assure you there's plenty. And it's well hidden, too. Is that the problem?"

"No," he managed. *No, the problem is you, Rosie Mills. You scare me. You make me want to hope again. You make me want to dream of things I was sure I had put away forever.*

"Don't think I'm hoarding all these goods for myself," she said. "No sir. I can promise you everything will be divided equally among the three men: you, Jimmy O'Toole, and Rolf Rustemeyer. Just say the word, and I'll split up the goods, and that'll be the end of it. But let me tell you, Mr. Hunter, that bridge you men built is as good as a gold mine. We've got floods of travelers coming across it every day—going both ways. Don't we, Sheena?"

"Aye, that we do," the Irishwoman called. She and Chipper were playing with the puppy.

"Settlers, cowboys, fur trappers, even some rich landowners from back east. They all stop by here—every one of them—and we make a trade. Well, how do you think I got those oysters? It was a Mr. Hercules Popadopolous. He's a Greek fellow who said he owns half of New York state. He gave me the oysters in trade for a large buffalo skin I had accepted from a trapper who had bartered it from an Indian. I told the Greek man it wasn't a fair trade, but he insisted mine was the first real buffalo hide he'd ever seen, and he was bound and determined to have it. And what do you think he did when I handed over the hide? He knelt down on the ground and kissed my hand just like I was a lady from the Middle Ages, and he was a knight in shining armor. I told you about that, didn't I, Sheena?"

"That you did," she called.

"Did you see the mirror?" Rosie went on. "It was given to me by a gentleman from Virginia—a Confederate general. He said he had lost everything in the war, and he was going to California to make his fortune in land speculation. But I don't think he really had lost everything, because you should have seen his carriage. And all the things in his trunk! The mirror was the least of it, let me tell you. He had gold chains and candlesticks and pieces of cut lead crystal. I warned him he might get robbed if he didn't watch out. He paid his toll in cash, but then he turned around right before he crossed the bridge and handed me that mirror. And do you know what he told me, Mr. Hunter?"

Seth swallowed. If he didn't say something soon, Rosie Mills would talk herself blue in the face. Worse, the more she talked and the harder he looked into her brown eyes, the crazier he felt. Crazy enough to kiss her. Crazy enough to just haul right off and ask her to marry him.

"No," he said. "No . . . I . . . I don't know what he told you, but

I do know that you'd better not be taking oysters and gold mirrors off single men, Miss Mills. It's not safe. You don't know the first thing about these fellows. They could be robbers, or confidence men, or worse."

Her face paled. "They seemed nice enough to me. They just stopped by to pay the bridge toll—like they would at any other town or station that had a creek."

"But this is not a town, Miss Mills. It's not even a station. This is a homestead. Do all these travelers know who lives here? Have you told them my name is Hunter?"

Rosie glanced at Sheena, and her pale face went even whiter.

"You'd better tell him," Sheena said.

Rosie knotted her fingers together and swallowed hard. "I did mention . . . that is, I have said on occasion . . . I more or less did say—"

"She calls it Hunter's Station," Sheena said, coming to her feet. "And what of it, Seth? This is your place, isn't it? What harm is she doing? Why are you acting the *sherral* about her trading? She's a good woman, and people like to do business with her. All she's done is—"

"Is spread the word from New York to California the exact location of my homestead!" Seth exploded, his fear overriding every need he felt to hold Rosie and bury his pain in her embrace. "Don't you see? Now everyone knows. *He* knows."

"Jack Cornwall?" Sheena said.

"Shh!" Seth cast a quick look at his son. Chipper was studying the three adults as Stubby attempted to nip off a mouthful of his hair. "Don't mention that man's name aloud."

"And why not? Chipper knows his uncle is searching for him. Don't you, boy?" Sheena held out a hand and pulled Chipper to his feet beside her. "But you live here now with your own good papa. Even if that Jack Cornwall came to fetch you, would you go with him? Would you go away and leave your own soft bed? Little

Stubby? My fine Will and all the other wee friends you've made? And Rosie? Would you leave her?"

Chipper stuck his hands in his pockets and eyed Sheena. Then he looked at his father. His blue eyes narrowed. "I might," he said.

"Would you then?" Sheena asked, her voice high. "To tell God's truth, I never would have thought it. And you such a fine boy. Such a good boy. Your papa needs you here, so he does. I can't think why you'd ever want to go away with that Jack Cornwall."

Chipper stuck out his chin. "Uncle Jack and me always make popcorn strings at Christmastime. He lifts me up high, and I hang the strings on the tree. And Uncle Jack gots a mouth harp that he plays when I'm sitting in his lap. When my mama died, Uncle Jack held me tight and we cried and cried. He loves me."

"Oh, but Chipper, your papa loves you too!"

Seth could hear the Irishwoman's voice, but he could stand the pain in his chest no longer. He felt as though his heart had been ripped away. Turning on his heel, he walked out of the barn. A razor-sharp lump formed in his throat. His eyes burned. If he could just make it back to his plow. Just bury everything in the rich prairie soil.

"Seth!" Rosie's hand slipped into his and pulled him up short.

He couldn't make himself look at her.

"Don't take what Chipper said as a rejection of you," she said softly. "Learn from it. Didn't you hear what he loves about his uncle? It's the touching! His uncle lifts him up to hang popcorn strings on the Christmas tree. His uncle lets him sit in his lap. And they cry together. Seth, please hear what your son is trying to tell you. If you want his love—and I know you do—you must touch him! Wrap your arms around him! Let him come into your heart!"

Seth clenched his fists. His own father had never behaved in such a way. Never held or touched him. How could it be right? Wouldn't the boy turn out weak? A sissy? Wouldn't he disrespect a father who showed tenderness of heart?

He could feel Rosie moving closer to him. Her hand slipped up his arm, and she leaned against him. "Please, Seth," she whispered. "You've built such a wall around yourself that no one can come inside. You won't let anyone care for you. You won't let anyone love you. Please, please don't shut us . . . shut him—Chipper—out of your life."

"I don't . . ." He struggled to express himself. "I don't understand . . . how . . . how to touch him."

"But it's so easy."

"No!" he exploded again, turning on her and taking her shoulders in his hands. "No, it's not easy. I can't . . . I've never . . . my father didn't . . . I can't do it."

"You can learn," she said, her brown eyes melting the edges of his frozen heart. "Ask God to teach you how to touch Chipper. Pray, Seth. Pray for the wisdom to win your son's love."

"Pray? You heard the verse from Deuteronomy. If God can shut his heart to a foundling child, what makes you think he'd listen to me? Why would I want to ask him anything?"

"No," Rosie said, laying her hands on his chest. "We read the Scripture all wrong that morning. I understand it now. Anyone who surrenders his heart to Christ becomes a child of the heavenly Father. I'm an heir to the kingdom of God, Seth! I can walk boldly before his throne—and I can call him my father . . . my daddy . . . my papa. He welcomes me, and he welcomes you, too. He'll teach you how to be a good father to Chipper. Ask him. Ask him!"

She laid her cheek on his shoulder for a moment; then she turned and pulled out of his arms. He watched her as she walked back to the barn, her long hair blowing in the early summer wind. *I love her.* His soul spoke the words, and he realized they were a prayer. *I love her, and I don't know what to do about it. Teach me. Teach me . . . my heavenly Father. Break down the wall and show me how to love my son. Guide my hands to touch him, hold him, draw him into my heart.*

Seth felt the tension slide out of his arms. His fists unknotted. The lump in his throat melted. Tears spilled down his cheeks. *And about Rosie, God. Tell me what to do about Rosie.*

The barn wore a coat of bright red paint. Chipper sported a new white shirt, a pair of sturdy canvas overalls, and a handsome haircut. Seth almost matched his son in his own starched white shirt, blue denim trousers, and carefully combed hair. Rosie could not have been more proud of her handiwork as the two stood side by side to greet the stream of guests driving over the new bridge for the party.

Seth had insisted Rosie make herself a dress from a bolt of blue gingham he had noticed in her storage chest. She had protested. After all, she had given a wagon's toll and an iron stew pot in exchange for that fabric. Surely it would bring a nice trade-in someday.

But Seth had told Rosie he was tired of that old skirt with the burned hem, and it was high time she had something new. As for the chest and Rosie's trading business, he reluctantly told her she could continue trading for bridge tolls as long as she kept a close eye out for trouble, especially trouble in the form of one Jack Cornwall. And she was no longer to refer to the barn as Hunter's Station. If it needed a name, she would have to come up with something else.

Pleased to have his permission, Rosie set to work sewing herself a new blue gingham dress. By the afternoon of the dance, she finished the hem and slipped on her creation. It was pretty. She couldn't deny it. The bodice had puffed sleeves, and the skirt billowed out from her waist to her ankles in a cloud of airy fabric.

If only she had a bonnet, she would feel like a queen. But as hard as she tried, she could not fashion a bonnet brim that would stand stiffly in place. Everything she attempted flopped down in her face, until she was forced to abandon the project and put her hair up in a high bun. Fortunately, she did have pins and a ribbon—having traded the gold mirror for them.

"Glory be but you're the vision of a lady!" Sheena exclaimed as she and Rosie carried trays of doughnuts from the cooking fire to the barn. "Has Seth laid eyes on you yet?"

Rosie shook her head. "No. He was in such a hurry to be out and about as the guests arrived. Before I dressed, he and Chipper went out to the bridge to welcome everyone. He's been looking forward to showing off the bridge. To tell you the truth, I think Seth is very proud of the work the men did and all the bridge has meant to our community."

"Community!" Sheena laughed. "Sure, you always think bigger than the rest of us, don't you, Rosie? We build a little pontoon bridge, and you turn it into a grand gold mine. Seth puts up a rickety barn, and you have it shingled, painted red, and transformed into a social hall before half the summer's passed. Two families live across a stretch of creek, and suddenly we're a community."

The sight that greeted the two women as they entered the crowded barn seemed to confirm Sheena's description. Ladies in their brightest dresses set out bowls of blackberries and fresh cream, strawberry pies, gooseberry pies, and raspberry cobblers. Salt pork boiled with greens and cabbage sent a delicious aroma around the barn, a fragrance that mingled with the scents of warm gingerbread and freshly baked biscuits. Rosie had never seen such a vast quantity of food. And to think it had all come from what she once considered a barren prairie.

"Fräulein Mills!" Rolf Rustemeyer swept off his hat and gave Rosie a low bow. "Ist fery goot party you maken."

"Thank you, Rolf. But you must remember Sheena fried all the doughnuts, and it took the two of us and all the children to paint the barn red."

"Ist fery goot barn," he agreed.

Rosie favored him with a radiant smile and went back to arranging the trays. Rolf tapped her shoulder. "Fräulein Mills, *bitte*. Vill you vit Rolf Rustemeyer *tanzen?*" He did a few polka steps across the floor. "*Der Tanz*. Fräulein vill vit me *tanzen?*"

"Dance?"

"*Ja*. Danz!" He waggled a finger back and forth between them. "You *und* me?"

Rosie looked up into his eager gray eyes. Rolf was such a good man. Such a kind man. Such a hard worker. He wanted to dance with her. Maybe he would ask her to marry him. Maybe even tonight, and then everything would be settled.

"I can't," she said quickly. "I don't know how to dance. I'm sorry, truly I am. But I grew up in an orphanage, you see, and we didn't have socials there. I can't dance."

Rolf frowned. "*Ja*, you danz. I zee you in barn vit Hunter. You danzen fery goot."

"Oh, that was just silliness. I had found the grain sacks, remember? I don't really know how to dance. Not properly."

Rolf snapped his suspender. "You not *freundlich* vit me? You not liken me?"

"Of course I'm your friend, Rolf. I like you very much."

"Danzen vit me. First danz."

Rosie let out an exasperated breath. "All right, I'll dance the first dance with you. But I'm warning you, my dancing is likely to turn your toes black and blue by morning." She paused, waiting for him to chuckle at the image she had created. Instead, he bowed with a flourish and strode away, his mission accomplished.

Oh Lord, how can I marry Rolf? Rosie prayed as she gazed down at the raspberry cobblers. *I can't talk to him. He doesn't understand me. We won't be able to laugh together. We won't even be able to pray together! Father, please don't make me marry Rolf.*

But even as she prayed the words, Rosie knew Rolf was her best option. Though her heart was filled with Seth, he kept her shut away. He lived behind a barricade of his own creation. If she were ever to build a family, she must find a willing man. Why not Rolf?

"Rosie, you look beautiful!" Chipper cried, spotting her from the door of the barn and making a mad dash to her side. "Your dress is all checkerdy! It gots puffs and buttons and everything. You look like a princess. Don't she look like a princess?"

He turned to his father, who had just stepped into the barn. At the sight of Rosie, Seth drew in a deep breath. He jammed his hands into his pockets. His blue eyes blinked, as if unsure of what they were seeing.

Rosie's heart began to hammer like a woodpecker on a fence post. Seth took a step toward her, and she swallowed hard. Was her hair still up? Had the bow drooped? Was her hem hanging straight? Had she remembered to button every button? Would he notice the little snag in her sleeve?

"Evening, Miss Mills," he said as he approached. "Chipper's right. You do look like a princess."

Rosie tried to smile, but she felt like her lips were stuck to her teeth. "Thank you."

"Is that the blue gingham I found in the storage chest?"

"Yes." She clamped a hand over the snag on her sleeve. "It might have been better used as curtains."

"It's perfect as a dress. It suits you."

He stopped and stared at her. Rosie felt a flush crawl up the back of her neck and settle in her cheeks. Never . . . never in all her life had she seen a man who looked as handsome as Seth Hunter did tonight—and he was staring at her!

"There's . . . lots of . . . of food." She tried to smile again.

"Your hair sure is pretty. I've never seen it like that. So high up on your head."

"Is my bow crooked?" She nervously fingered the scrap of blue ribbon. "I wasn't sure how it looked. I traded . . . traded the mirror. For the hairpins. And the ribbon."

Seth took another step forward. "Miss Mills . . . would you do me the honor of dancing the first dance tonight?"

"Yes!" She let out a rush of air. "Oh, yes, I'd love to."

"Until then," Seth said, tipping his hat.

"Until then," she replied, favoring him with a slight curtsy. "Excuse me." Feeling faint, Rosie walked out of the barn for some fresh air. She was being so silly! He had only asked her to dance. Just a simple request. *Will you dance the first dance with me tonight?*

The first dance? The significance of his words tumbled through her. She couldn't dance with Seth. She already had agreed to dance the first dance with Rolf Rustemeyer! This was terrible. She would have to tell Rolf she hadn't understood him. No, that would be a lie. She *had* understood. But she had forgotten Rolf as soon as Seth walked into the room. It was Seth who took her breath away. Seth who made her heart beat twice as fast. Seth Hunter.

Oh, what was the matter with her? Why did she feel this way? So mixed up. So anxious. All she wanted was to be near Seth and look into his blue eyes. Was this what he meant when he once told her how it felt to be in love?

Had Seth felt this way about Mary Cornwall? No wonder he couldn't abandon his wife's memory. Seth had been right that this . . . this incredible feeling must somehow be important in making a marriage work. There were two parts to it, weren't there? The lifetime commitment *and* this wonderful . . . frightening . . . amazing . . . feeling!

"Fräulein Mills?" Rolf touched her arm. "You are zick?"

"Sick . . . no . . . I'm all right. I just . . . oh Rolf, you're such a good man, such a very kind man, and I really do think I ought to marry you. But the trouble is with Seth, you see. I can't stop thinking about him and feeling so very odd inside when he looks at me. It wouldn't be at all right if I were your wife and yet I felt this way whenever I thought of Seth. Even though I know . . . I know very well . . . that he loves his wife, and he won't ever forget her . . . I can't make myself feel good about . . . What are you staring at?"

"*Die Musik!*" He grabbed her arm. "*Komm*, fräulein. Ve danzen, you *und* me!"

"But Rolf!" Rosie grabbed her skirts to keep from stepping on them as the big German whisked her back into the barn.

At the far end near the loft, a platform had been set up. A fiddle, a harmonica, an accordion, and a banjo had been assembled along with musicians who claimed to play them passably well—though this was a matter of opinion. As the music swelled through the barn, couples formed into squares and began to dance in time to the caller's directions.

> "All to your places
> And straighten up your faces.
> All join hands and circle eight.
> Ladies face out and gents face in
> And hold your holts and gone again."

The caller let out a loud whoop, and Rolf twirled Rosie around and around among the other dancers. Still dismayed at what she had done—agreeing to dance with two men—she could barely keep her feet untangled. She had never square danced in her life, and she didn't know which way to turn or where to go. Rolf didn't seem to care in the least. Laughing, he caught her around the waist and spun her once, twice, three times around the square in an awkward imitation of the other dancers.

Assembled around the barn, the elderly men clapped and stomped their feet in time with the rhythm. Young girls—LeBlanc's daughters, Rosie assumed—giggled in clumps of two and three as the young single farmers paused to chat with them. Wives cut cakes and poured lemonade or joined with their husbands in the dance. Wishing the song would end, Rosie searched the barn for Seth.

"Goot danzen," Rolf said as he galloped past her. "Ist fery fun, *ja?*"

Rosie grinned bravely and sashayed with him beneath a long arch of upstretched arms. If Seth saw what she had done, he could turn away from her forever. He would believe she had chosen Rolf over him. He might even think she wanted to marry Rolf, as she had so firmly told him.

But she didn't. She knew it—knew beyond the shadow of a doubt—that she could never marry Rolf Rustemeyer.

"You fery pretty!" Rolf half-shouted as he jigged around her. "I lof you!"

What? Rosie flushed in mortification. Had Rolf just announced that he loved her—in front of everyone? As she examined the faces of the other dancers, she realized no one had understood his meaning. But she knew. She knew!

Oh, where was Seth? Why didn't he step in and claim her? She had no more formed the thought in her mind when a man's firm arm slipped through hers. Linked at her elbow, he twirled her out of the square and away from the crowd.

"Seth," she began, breathing hard. "I must explain—"

But when she looked up, it wasn't Seth's blue eyes that met hers. A slow smile spread across the man's face as recognition dawned in hers. "Howdy, ma'am," he said. "Any idea where I might find Chipper tonight?"

Rosie caught her breath and jerked her arm away from his. The man was Jack Cornwall.

CHAPTER 11

"AREN'T you the little gal who whacked me on the head back in Kansas City?" Jack Cornwall asked.

Rosie couldn't speak. Fear had caught in her throat and blocked her urge to scream. She clutched the edge of the table behind her.

"Yeah, I'm sure you're the one. You were up in a dang tree. So, you and Hunter hooked up together, I hear. I hope he didn't play you for the fool the way he did my sister."

Rosie shook her head. She wanted to explain, wanted to shout for help, wanted to run away. But nothing happened. She merely stood staring at the man with her mouth hanging open and her knees locked beneath her.

"Where's my nephew?" Jack asked. A tall, raw-boned, rangy man, he studied her with a pair of eyes the color of hard, cold slate. Thick brown hair hung to the collar of his battered leather coat, and a sweat stain ran around the band of his hat. "I didn't see him playing out front with the other children. What have you done with him?"

Not with the other children? Rosie quickly searched the throng of dancers. Where was Chipper? And where was Seth? Why couldn't he see what was going on? Why didn't he come? Had Jack Cornwall done something to him?

"Listen, ma'am," the man said, "I really don't want to make a scene here. Truth is, I've spent the last four years fighting Yankees like Seth Hunter, and I'm a little tired. But I never have liked winding up on the losing end of things. So if you don't tell me where the boy is, I may have to get rough." At that, he reached out and took Rosie's arm in a firm grip.

"Wait . . . what are you—?"

"I'd hate to have to hold you as a hostage," he cut in. "After all, I don't know what you mean to Hunter. But you whacked me on the head and landed me in jail. He violated my sister and kidnapped my nephew. And the fact is—I don't really much care what becomes of either of you. I want the boy. Now tell me where he is."

"I-I-I don't—"

"Fräulein?" Rolf Rustemeyer stepped up beside her. "I danzen, *und* I not zee you no more. *Was ist* hoppened?"

Rosie let out a breath of relief. Rolf was a good three inches taller than Jack Cornwall and at least fifty pounds heavier. "Rolf, get Seth. You've got to find him. This man . . . this man—"

But her captor had released her and melted into the crowd of dancers before she could even make the German understand the problem. Frantic, she searched the room until she spotted Cornwall's dark hat as he left the barn. He was gone. Into the cover of night. Chipper was somewhere out there unprotected. And Seth. Where was Seth?

Grabbing her skirts, she brushed past Rolf. As she stepped into the throng, the big German caught her arm. "Fräulein, you danzen vit him? *Der* man vit *braunen* hat? I liken you. You maken goot zupper *und* breakfascht. You fery goot fräulein. Fery pretty. But you danzen vit him? Not goot. *Nein, nein, nein*—"

"Rolf, stop talking!" Rosie cried. "We have to find Chipper. That man with the brown hat wants to take him away. Where's Seth?"

"Hunter? You danzen vit Hunter now? But I vill danzen vit you."

"Oh, just move!" Rosie let out a cry of frustration and pushed him aside. Unwilling to cause panic in the crowd but terrified for Chipper, she elbowed her way among the dancers. "Excuse me, Miss Rippeto. Pardon me, Mr. Laski."

By the door, Jimmy O'Toole stood picking his teeth with the end of a hay stem. He spotted Rosie and straightened as she grabbed his arm. "Sure, you look as if you've seen the ghost of St. Peter himself," he said. "What's the matter now, Rosie?"

"Jack Cornwall is here!"

"Here?" He looked around. "In the barn?"

"He just left. He's after Chipper. Where's Seth?"

"I saw him walk out of the barn at the start of the first dance. He looked angry enough to chew nails, so he did."

"Where did he go?" She shook her head. "No, never mind about Seth. We have to find Chipper. Tell Sheena. Get some of the men together. Cornwall has threatened trouble."

Leaving Jimmy to round up help, Rosie dashed out of the barn. The children were playing prisoner's base in the light of lamps hung from the circle of wagons in the yard. Rosie grasped Will O'Toole by the shoulders and stopped him in his tracks.

"Will, where's Chipper?" she demanded.

"He's around here somewhere. He was playing with us a few minutes ago. What's wrong, Rosie?"

"I want you to help me find him. Now."

"But the game—"

"Never mind about the game. Find Chipper. Take him to your papa right away."

Her heart tight in her chest, Rosie raced toward the soddy. Three women stood tending the outdoor fire and trading gossip. They insisted they hadn't seen the little boy, but Rosie threw open the door and hurried into the house.

"Chipper? Are you in here, Chipper?" The soddy was empty. Fear clutching her stomach, Rosie fell to her knees. "Oh, Father, please help me find Chipper! Please don't let Jack Cornwall take him away. Chipper belongs to Seth. Seth needs him so much. Father, please show me how to find Chipper. And where is Seth?"

Seth sat on the flat rock by the willow tree and flipped a pebble into the creek. Things were about as good as they ever had been in his twenty-four years. He owned one hundred and sixty acres of fertile land. He had a house, a barn, two mules, three cows, a couple dozen chickens, even a dog. His crops had come up healthy and strong, their straight green rows promising him a stable future. Spring wheat, oats, sod corn, and barley should turn a decent profit come fall. The kitchen garden would provide lettuce, beans, cucumbers, tomatoes, and roasting ears for the table. The bridge had been a good idea, bringing toll money and opening the path to easier travel. All in all, things looked mighty fine.

And they looked terrible. Seth shook his head and tossed another stone into the gurgling water. Chipper didn't love his father. Didn't even call him "papa." In fact, the boy clearly preferred the puppy to his own flesh and blood. The dog could make Chipper's blue eyes light up with joy. Rosie could make the child laugh that bubbly chuckle that tore up Seth's insides. But in spite of all the time Seth had spent with his son, Chipper remained wary, his little heart carefully guarded against the man he had been warned never to trust. No matter what he tried, Seth couldn't seem to break down that sturdy wall.

And then there was the matter of Rosie herself. A few weeks ago, Rosie Mills had fallen into Seth's arms and knocked him flat. He'd never recovered. But Rosie seemed bound and determined to marry Rolf Rustemeyer. What did she see in that big German hound dog? Must be something pretty special. Though she had promised Seth the first dance, she had forgotten her pledge as easily as she had slipped into Rolf's embrace.

Seth hurled another pebble into the water. Why did he care? If Rosie married Rolf, she'd have a good life. With all those hearty meals under his belt, Rolf would sure be happy. And Chipper could visit them often. They'd probably have children of their own pretty soon, and Rosie would have everything she'd ever wanted: a home, a husband, a family. She had told him that was all there was to marriage, and it was more than enough for her.

Rosie didn't understand the kind of mixed-up, heart-stopping, breathtaking whirlwind that could tear through a person's soul. She didn't think that kind of love mattered. And she was right. It didn't. So why did Seth feel it every time he looked into her big brown eyes?

"Seth!" Rosie's voice startled him out of his reverie. "Seth Hunter, where are you?"

"Here," he called. "By the creek."

Rosie raced down the bank and nearly crashed into him. Stopping short, she took his hand and squeezed so tightly the blood stopped flowing through his fingers. "I've been looking all over for you!" she said. "He's here. He's right here. And Chipper's missing. I can't find him. I don't know where he—"

"Who's here?"

"Jack Cornwall."

"No!" Seth jumped to his feet. "Where is he? Did you bring the rifle?"

"Seth, you can't fix this with violence. That's not the way. You have to find Chipper. You have to get to him before Cornwall does."

"Wasn't he with the other children?" Seth was running through the darkness now, careless of snagging branches and roots that caught at his feet. As Rosie lagged behind, he grabbed her hand and hauled her along so he could keep pumping her with questions. "Is Jimmy searching for Chipper? What about Casimir and

Salvatore? They brought their horses, didn't they? Have you checked the soddy?"

He could hear Rosie sobbing as she tried to answer. By her despairing response he knew her message must be true. Jack Cornwall had found his enemy. He would take Chipper. Possibly he already had. Unless Cornwall was stopped, Seth would lose his only son.

As the thought tore through him like a knife, he dropped Rosie's hand and raced ahead. At the barn, the dance was breaking up. Women called frantically for their children to round them up and hold them close. Men were standing in clusters, forming search parties. When Seth got to the barn, Jimmy stepped out into the circle of light.

"No one can find the boy around here, Seth," he said. "We haven't seen any sign of Cornwall either."

"What do the children say?" Seth asked.

"They thought your son was playing with them, so they did. Erinn told her mother that when the music started up, she saw Chipper wander away from the others. But she lost track of him in the midst of their game." Jimmy held up a lantern. "We're going out in groups of three and four, Seth. Some of us will take the road to LeBlanc's Mill, and the rest will head for Laski's Station. Sure Cornwall can't have gotten far."

Seth agreed to the plan, and he watched as the men rode off into the darkness. The women bustled their children into the wagons. Seth went from child to child, asking what each one remembered about the evening. Chipper had wandered away. But where?

"Why would he have left the others in the middle of a game?" Seth asked Rosie when she appeared at his elbow. "The music and dancing had just started up. Where would he have gone?"

"You went down to the creek at the same time," Rosie said. "Maybe he followed you. Why did you leave?"

Seth rubbed a hand around the back of his neck. He could see that the question in her brown eyes was an honest one. "I wanted to think," he said finally.

"In the middle of a barn dance? Seth, you're the host. You should have stayed among the company. If you had been there, Jack Cornwall wouldn't have been nearly so bold. The first thing I knew, he had me by the arm and was asking all about Chipper."

"The first thing *I* knew, you were dancing with Rolf Rustemeyer. Why didn't you ask your beau for help with Cornwall?"

Rosie's cheeks flushed a brighter pink. "Rolf didn't have any idea who that man was. He doesn't speak English well enough to understand."

"He must have spoken well enough to ask you to dance." Seth spat the words and turned away from her. Rosie didn't deserve his wrath, even though she was chastising him for not being in the barn when Cornwall appeared. She blamed him for Chipper's disappearance.

And he blamed himself. He had known good and well that Cornwall was lurking. Searching for him. Intending to steal the boy. Why had Seth relaxed his guard for a minute?

Self-loathing tore at his gut. He could almost hear his father's words provoking him. *How could you be so stupid? You're no good. . . .*

"No!" Seth shouted as he ran down the path toward the creek. *I'm better than that. I'm better than you were. I'd never walk out on my family. I'd never abandon my son. I love my son. I love Chipper!*

"God!" He stumbled over a tree root and fell to his knees. Clutching handfuls of the moist, reedy river grass, he shook his head. "God, please help me find him. Show me where he is!"

He climbed to his feet again and continued down the creek bank, peering into the darkness, calling his son's name. In all the confusion, he hadn't remembered his rifle. If he ran into Jack Cornwall, he would need to be armed. Let the man so much as touch Chipper, and Seth would blow his head off.

No. Rosie had said that wasn't the way. No violence.

Then how was he supposed to win his son? Cornwall would never stop pursuing Chipper. Seth would have to kill the man to stop him.

Kill Mary's brother? Murder her beloved Jack? No, he couldn't do that.

God, help me! Seth's heart cried out again and again as he wandered the creek bank calling his son's name. In response he heard nothing but the quiet murmurs of the prairie. An owl hooted. A raccoon scurried from the water's edge. Crickets stopped their chirping the moment they sensed his footfall. The moon rose in the black velvet sky, but even its bright light revealed nothing but clumps of bluestem grass and the trunks of cottonwood trees. It was no good. The boy was gone, and Seth knew he would have to ride after his son and the man who had stolen him away.

He turned back toward the soddy. By the time he reached the barn again, most of the families had packed up and driven away. Jimmy and some of the others were still searching the roads, Sheena told him as she herded her children over the bridge. The rest of the men had given up the hunt. The yard was empty of wagons. The fire had been reduced to ashes.

Rosie moved out of the shadows into the moonlight. Her bun had come down, and the hem of her blue gingham dress was muddy. He could tell she had been crying.

"Any sign of him?" she asked.

He shook his head. "I'll ride out at dawn. Cornwall will be heading for the Missouri border. After the war, the family was planning to move to the southeast part of the state. Jack's father owns a little plot of ground near Cape Girardeau. At least I'll know where to start looking."

"You'll be going after him then?"

"He's my son."

She covered her mouth to stop the sob that welled up. "I'll stay here. I'll tend the homestead until you come back."

"I may be gone for months. You go on over to Rustemeyer's place where he can look after you. He'll find a preacher somewhere. You'd be better off getting married to him early in the summer when you can do him some good in the fields."

"Marry Rolf . . . but . . ." She knotted her fingers. "But . . . but you'll want me to hoe your fields, won't you? What about your crops?"

"If need be, I'll start over again next year."

"You won't have seed money." She followed him into the barn. "If you don't bring in a harvest this fall, you won't have the money to outfit yourself for next spring. And you'll need cash to travel. Take the bridge tolls, Seth. Rolf and Jimmy won't mind."

"All right. I'll take my share. Divide the rest between the other two, but keep back some for yourself. You earned it." Seth studied the interior of his barn and shook his head. Too bad Cornwall had spoiled the party. "Where did you move my saddle?" he said as he walked toward the back of the barn. "I'll need to take both mules so I can travel faster. Did you get a look at what Cornwall was riding? Did he have a horse?"

"I didn't see him come into the barn. I just turned around and there he was." Still searching Seth's face, she stopped beside the large chest in which she stored the supplies she traded for bridge tolls. He could tell she was struggling hard to hold back her tears. "You must take some blankets, and there's a little molasses. . . . Seth, before you go, I want you to know . . . I didn't intend to dance the first dance with Rolf. I wanted to dance with you. But . . . but he pulled me into the barn—"

"Never mind about what happened." He looked into her brown eyes, wondering if this was the last time he would see her, trying to memorize those beautiful eyes and sweet lips. "You did right to organize the search and come after me."

"But I want you to understand. It's not Rolf. It's you. It's you that I . . . that I care about. I never meant to—"

"Don't talk about it, Rosie. Rustemeyer's a good man. You'll be happy with him. He'll take care of you."

"I know he would, but—"

"That's how it has to be. There can't be anything else. I need to go, Rosie. Do you have any ammunition left?" Seth looked down into the open storage chest.

There lay Chipper. Huddled into a ball. His cheek nestled against a wool blanket. Sound asleep.

"Chipper! Chipper, you little rascal!" With a groan of disbelief, Seth scooped the drowsy boy up in his arms and hugged him tightly. "Thank God! Thank God, you're here!"

"Oh, sweetheart!" Rosie threw her arms around both of them. "We were so worried about you. We couldn't find you."

"Really?" Chipper blinked sleepily and rubbed a little fist in his eye. "Were you lookin' for me again?" He yawned, then he drew back and stared solemnly at his father. "Are you mad at me? Are you gonna yell an' scold me?"

Seth nestled his cheek against his son's warm skin. "No, no," he murmured, trying to dam the emotion that welled like a fountain in his heart. "Chipper, you had me so worried, son. I walked up the creek all the way to Rustemeyer's place looking for you."

"You did?" A smile crossed the boy's mouth. "An' I was right here in the blankets all along. I guess I fooled you, huh?"

"I reckon you did."

Seth sensed that Rosie had moved away, and he missed her presence. Yet at this moment he wanted nothing more than to hold his son. Hold him on and on. He lowered the lid on the storage chest and sat down, cradling the boy against his chest. "I don't want to lose you, Chipper," he murmured. "You're my only son."

"I wasn't lost. I was just sleepy."

"I bet you were." Seth brushed a strand of hair from his son's forehead. The baby-softness of the skin startled him. He ran a finger from the boy's brow to his cheek. Soft. So soft. How was it possible this child was his own flesh and blood?

Blue eyes that matched his own gazed up at him. "You sure you ain't mad?"

"Nope. Truth is, I'm mainly feeling real happy right now. I don't ever want to lose somebody I care about as much as I care about you. See, when I was a little boy—not too much bigger than you—my papa decided to go away on a trip. And he never came back."

"Not ever?" Chipper pondered this for a moment. His long black lashes fanned his cheeks. "Like mama did. She went away, an' she ain't never coming back."

"A little bit like that, I guess." As he ran his hand over the boy's dark silky hair, Seth turned over the comparison in his mind. Finally he decided it was accurate enough. His own father had left—run off and abandoned the family. Chipper's mother had died. But the loss was the same. The emptiness was the same. The need for a parent's love was exactly the same.

"That's why I left the other kids playing prisoner's base," Chipper said. "I heard that music, an' I got to thinkin' about my mama. She just loved to dance."

"I remember. I used to dance with her a lot."

Chipper glanced up, startled. "I forgot about that. You knew her too, didn't you?"

"I sure did. I loved her."

"Me too. I looked an' looked for her in the barn, but then I remembered all over again that she wasn't comin' back. That's when I got sad an' grumpy an' tired. So I thought about Rosie's wool blankets that she traded for bridge tolls, and I climbed into the old storage chest to listen to the violin music and think about mama. I wanted to cry where nobody would see me." Again, the blue eyes searched Seth's face. "Do you ever do that?"

Seth nodded. "Yes. I do that sometimes."

At the admission, Chipper smiled and snuggled closer into his father's arms. Seth could hardly believe the sensation. The boy's little legs curled up tight, fitting perfectly into the curve of his father's lap. A pair of matching bare feet—tiny toes peeping out from the hems of his overalls—rested on Seth's denim jeans. Tentatively, the father reached out and touched one of those little toes. How small. Amazingly small. And as perfect as a pearl.

Then his wondering gaze moved upward to the child's thin arm. Lightly scattered with pale, downy hair, the arm was propped in perfect position to admit the boy's thumb into his mouth. Was it all right for children to suck their thumbs? Seth had no idea. But something told him that a little boy whose mama had died deserved whatever comfort he could find.

Poor Chipper. Again Seth stroked his fingers through his son's soft warm hair. The scent the boy carried on his skin drew the father like the aroma of baking bread. It was the smell of little boy—of sunshine, winds, dust, green grass, and puppy dog. Two months Seth had lived near this child, and he had never come close enough to smell that smell. That wonderful smell. Seth laid his cheek on his son's head and gathered him tightly in his arms.

"I'm sorry, Chipper," he began, and then he realized he couldn't go on. "I'm sorry I—"

"It's OK." The boy laid a small hand on his father's arm and caressed the coarse dark hair in the same tender way his own arm had been stroked. "You know something?" he said. "You gots a lot of hair, Papa."

Seth gulped back the lump that threatened. *Papa.* Chipper had called him Papa. Amazing.

"You'll have a lot of hair, too, when you get bigger," he managed.

"Will I look like you when I grow up?"

"You already look like me."

"Do I?" Chipper examined Seth's face. "I don't think so. You gots little black whiskers all over your chin."

"You'll have whiskers, too."

"You reckon?"

"You're my son, aren't you?"

"That's what everybody tells me." Chipper snuggled back into the fold of his father's arms. "You know something else? I don't think you're too bad of a Yankee. I bet Gram an' Gramps just didn't know you very good."

"They didn't know me very well at all. They were scared I wouldn't make a good home for your mama and you. If things had turned out differently, I would have brought both of you out here to live."

"I don't think mama would have liked it out here too much. No mirrors."

Seth laughed at the image of Mary Cornwall attempting to dress herself without a gold-framed pier mirror. "That might have been a problem."

"There's not even a town with sidewalks where she could say hello to everybody an' show off her new dresses an' bonnets."

"Well, that's true, too."

"Now, Rosie is really different from mama. Rosie don't care about mirrors an' showin' off. She fits just right out here on the prairie."

"She sure does."

"Rosie gots lots of good ideas about things. Like bridge tolls. An' barn painting. An' cooking squirrels. An' making clothes out of grain sacks. I love Rosie a lot. Do you?"

Seth looked around, saw that Rosie had left the barn, and nodded. "I reckon she's a pretty special lady."

Chipper leaned around and looked into his father's eyes. "Maybe you ought to marry Rosie and get you an' me another good mama."

"I might just do that, Chipper," Seth said softly. But as he spoke the words, he read the pain of loss in his son's eyes. Taking a wife would bring Chipper the comforts of a mother's love. It would bring Seth the joy of marriage. But it would also bring the risk of loss. For a woman, life on the prairie meant hardship, disease, and the dangers of childbirth. Could he and Chipper bear to lose another love? Was the hope worth the risk?

And what about Chipper himself? Seth had no guarantee that he could keep his son nearby. Cornwall threatened that hope for happiness. If the man stole Chipper, life would seem empty—all but unbearable.

"How come you're always thinkin' you lost me?" Chipper piped up. "How come you always go runnin' up an' down the creek like a chicken with its head cut off? You don't let me go nowhere by myself. Not even to sleep in the old storage chest. How come?"

Seth lifted his son's chin. "You know your uncle is looking for you, Chipper. He wants to take you away with him. But I don't want you to go." He gently kissed the child's forehead. "I love you, Chipper. I love you very much."

Chipper wriggled around in his father's lap until he could slip his arms around Seth's neck. "I love you, too, Papa."

When Seth lifted his focus, he saw Rosie had returned to the barn. She was standing in the doorway, a lantern in one hand and a pitcher of milk in the other. Her brown eyes were misty as she studied the father and son.

"I thought we might as well make use of some of this food that was left behind," she said softly. "Chipper, would you like a big slice of strawberry pie before bed?"

"Strawberry pie!" The child slid off his father's lap and raced across the floor. "I was sleepy before, but now I'm hungry."

Seth stood. As he watched Rosie cutting pie and pouring milk and as he studied his son's dark head and bright, happy eyes, he knew the answer in his heart. Yes. He wanted to marry Rosie. He wanted to take the risk.

But as he approached, she leaned toward him. "Seth, Jack Cornwall was inside the soddy while we were all out searching," she whispered in his ear. "He's stolen your rifle."

CHAPTER 12

ROSIE?" Sheena's high-pitched voice rose at the end of the word. "Rooo-SIE?"

Rosie watched through the soddy's open front door as her friend came scurrying over the pontoon bridge like a mama duck with her five little ducklings in tow. Bonnet ribbons flying, Sheena waved a sheet of white paper over her head. "I've had a letter from Ireland! All the way from God's country. Rosie, where are you?"

Rosie wedged the final loaf of bread into the hot oven and pushed the door shut. The little soddy felt warm enough inside to bake bread without the oven, she thought as she mopped the back of her neck with a cool, damp handkerchief. It would be a welcome break to talk with Sheena for a few minutes—even though it was less than an hour to lunchtime and Seth would be looking forward to a meal.

"I'm here, Sheena." Wiping her hands on her apron, she stepped out of the soddy. It was almost July and not a breath of breeze stirred the still summer air. Across the prairie, the tall grass stretched out like a vast, golden-threaded blanket shimmering in the heat. The limitless surface was marred only by the small green patches that made up Seth's fields. Rosie mused that even though the cultivated acres broke the God-created symmetry of the prairie, they offered the promise of food and sustenance for his people.

As she walked toward Sheena, Rosie turned over in her mind the amazing fact that she had come to love the prairie. Every spare moment she could carve out of the day, she wandered out across the majestic plains—picking wildflowers for the dinner table, watching the antelope graze, marveling at the glorious sky that rolled overhead in waves of depthless blue. The thought of ever returning to the confines of a brick orphanage, high limestone walls, and air darkened by smoke made her shudder. Yet she had made up her mind to obey God's direction, no matter where he led.

"It's just as I'd hoped," Sheena called, puffing up the last few yards to the soddy's front yard. "Better than I'd dreamed! I've had a letter from Caitrin. You know my little sister? My beauty? My sweet, precious Caitie?"

"Yes, you've told me about Caitrin," Rosie said, dragging a bench into the scant shade of the little soddy's overhanging roof. "Sit down and give me all the news."

"Better yet, I'll read it to you!" Sheena shooed the children off to find Chipper in the fields. Then she set a pair of spectacles on her nose, unfolded the letter, and spread it across her lap. "Sure it's taken me all morning to make sense of the writing, but I believe I have it. Listen to this." She began to read in a slow, halting voice. "'My dearest Sheena, All is well with the family and me. How are you? How is Jimmy? How are all the wee ones?'"

Here Sheena paused and took off her spectacles. "Caitie's never met any of them, you know. Not even Erinn, and she's already eight years old. Can you imagine? I've not clapped eyes on my dear Caitrin for more than eight years."

"I know you've missed her terribly."

"Haven't I?" Sheena shook her head and went back to the letter. "'I have made up my mind . . . not to wed Seamus Sweeney—'" Again Sheena stopped reading. "Seamus Sweeney is a fisherman's son and a rotter, if I do say so myself," she confided. Her green eyes flashed. "I never knew what Caitie saw in him. Of course, it was our papa who set the whole thing up, so he did. Papa is the fishmonger in our town, and he thought it would make a good partnership to join with the Sweeney family in business and in marriage. You know, Caitie's always been such a good girl, Rosie. She's always done everything she was told, so she has. I feared she would marry that *sherral*, even if she didn't want to. But now she hasn't after all!"

"Good for Caitrin."

"So you say, but can you imagine what my papa thinks about this? Sure, he'll be in great kinks. At any rate, I'll read again. Now where was I? Oh, yes. 'Dearest Sheena, I am . . . com-coming . . . to see you.' There you have it! She's coming to see me, Rosie! Coming here—to America. Can you credit it? I'm sure I can't. Listen to this. 'I shall see you in . . . August.' Now isn't that what it says, Rosie? August?"

Rosie leaned over Sheena's shoulder and studied the letter. For the difficulty her friend was having in reading it, Rosie had expected a poorly written document. Instead, the handwriting was neat, the words crisp, the message carefully spelled out.

"Yes, it's August," Rosie said, reading quickly through the message. "Caitrin's coming to Kansas at the start of the month, and she wonders if there might be a teaching position anywhere near you."

"Is that what she's written? Teaching. Well, I couldn't make out that word at all. *Teaching*. Why would you put an *a* in a word like that, Rosie? Sure it ought to have a double *e* by all rights. You know I never went to school but a year or two. But Caitie—well, she's been all the way through, so she has. She's very smart. Yes, indeed. Our Caitrin is a well-rounded young lady. I suppose she believes she could earn wages as a teacher in America."

Rosie considered the situation for a moment. "You have five children, Sheena. As you said, Erinn's already eight years old, and

Will is six. Chipper's five. Then there are the youngest of the Rippeto children. Mr. and Mrs. LeBlanc have all those daughters, too. Casimir Laski might even want to send his son."

"Sure, the boy is seventeen!"

"But he can't read a word. At the start of the barn dance, I handed him a list of the guests and asked him to mark off who had come. He couldn't even read his own name, Sheena. How will he make anything of himself without an education?"

"A man doesn't need to know how to read and write to plow a field. My Jimmy couldn't spell his name if he tried. But it's all the same to me. I love him anyway." She studied the letter for a moment. "Still, it would be wonderful if our Caitie could teach the children in the winter months, wouldn't it, Rosie?"

"Yes, it would. It sounds like she needs some kind of work to do now that she's not going to marry."

"Oh, she'll marry. Caitie's a fine, beautiful girl, so she is. She was only fourteen when I left Ireland, but she's twenty-two now and well into the age where she ought to find a husband. Besides that, she's a stunning lass. Red hair in grand big curls falling all over the place. And such eyes. Sure, you never saw such pretty green eyes in all your days. I have no doubt the young farmers will scramble to court Caitie the moment she gets here. She won't have any trouble finding a husband. But no . . . no, I think teaching would be a nice diversion for her. I believe I'll send a message to the Rippeto and LeBlanc families. Do you suppose Seth would let us use his barn for the school?"

Rosie shifted on the rough-hewn bench. The idea of a red-haired, green-eyed beauty charming Seth Hunter into marriage had caused her an uncomfortable pang. Even though Seth had not given many hints as to his feelings about her, Rosie had sensed that things between them had begun to change—soften—ever since the night of the barn dance.

Now Sheena wanted her beautiful red-haired sister to use Seth's barn as a schoolhouse? To see him every day? The barn was Rosie's home, her only place of solitude, her haven of rest. . . .

"Sure you won't be needing the barn by winter, will you?" Sheena asked. "You've told me you might well be wedded to Rolf Rustemeyer by that time. And if you don't marry the German, Seth means to cart you back to Kansas City—not that I'd want you to go, of course. But the barn would be free, wouldn't it?"

"Well, the cows—"

"Caitie could teach the children in the loft! There's lots of room up in the loft, so there is. Oh, Rosie, I cannot wait for you to meet my little Caitie. She's the prettiest thing! A fair flower! I shall have to plan a party to welcome her. Glory be, that reminds me of the second bit of news. There's to be a picnic on the Fourth of July. An Independence Day celebration—and it's hardly a week away. LeBlanc is hosting it, so he is. His wife is planning to hold a box-lunch auction for all the unmarried girls. You know the LeBlancs have all those pretty daughters. I'm sure the missus is hoping to hook a husband or two at the picnic. But the box-lunch auction will include you, too! And won't you be in demand with all the young farmers? Sure you will! Now if Caitie were here, there'd be a fair brawl over her, so there would. I'm half glad she isn't, aren't you?"

Rosie nodded, her mental image of the young green-eyed Caitrin transforming moment by moment into the most glorious creature who ever walked the earth.

"The money is going to a very good cause," Sheena explained. "LeBlanc wants to put up a church, so he does. If we can raise enough to buy the lumber, perhaps the men will build it in the fall."

"A church!" Rosie cried. "But where? Will it be beside the mill?"

"No, no. LeBlanc owns only the land his mill is sitting on and the water rights. It's not a proper homestead. No, he's asking someone else to donate an acre or two for the church. Sure, I'm going to press my Jimmy for it. Wouldn't that be wonderful? A church on our own homestead. Perhaps we'd even have a minister for it one day."

Rosie couldn't imagine the reticent Jimmy O'Toole wanting a church full of people on his property. But if Sheena made her case forcefully enough, it could happen. A church . . . with hymns and preaching and evening socials. The thought of it fairly transported Rosie.

"You're in a dream world," Sheena said, elbowing her friend as they sat together. "What do you think of LeBlanc's proposal? Our very own church, right out here on the prairie."

"It would be wonderful, Sheena. And with all the people passing through, the minister could touch so many lives."

"Aye, the traffic across our bridge has nearly doubled by my count."

"*More* than doubled in the last two weeks." Rosie glanced across the fields to see if Seth was coming. Then she leaned closer to her friend. "The storage chest in the barn is already full again, and I've traded for two more big trunks. Every time someone wants to trade instead of pay the toll, I have to haul everything out and set it all up. I'd love to leave the merchandise out for view—put up pretty displays and even build counters. But I don't want to worry Seth. He's so concerned about Jack Cornwall showing up again, and I don't want him to think my trading post would draw trouble."

"Your trading post, is it?"

Rosie shrugged. "Sheena, I could put a stop to it all. And I would—if I thought this might harm Seth or Chipper in any way. But I-I'm afraid I will have to go away one day, and I want to leave them with something. I know Seth doesn't really like my trading. But it's what I have to give. If I could get a post office commission, I'd have so much traffic I would have to put up a hotel."

"Great ghosts, that reminds me!" Sheena tugged a second letter from her pocket. "LeBlanc brought this along with my letter from

Caitie the last time he picked up the mail in Topeka. Look, it's for you, isn't it?"

Rosie stared at the travel-stained white envelope. "It's from the Christian Home. It's from Mrs. Jameson."

"Well, stop casting sheep's eyes at the thing and read it."

The letter was Rosie's first contact with the place where she had lived so many years. They had been years of struggle, loneliness, and an aching hunger for love. Half of her heart commanded her to pitch the letter into the stove and burn it up. Destroy that part of her life forever and look forward. Only forward.

But those years had been good ones, too. She had learned about her heavenly Father. She had gone to school and read the fairy tale book. She had made her way in a world where only the toughest survived.

Taking a deep breath, she slit open the envelope. "'Dear Miss Mills,'" she read aloud. It was Mrs. Jameson's handwriting. "'Thank you for the iron skillet. By this generous gift, I see you are making something of yourself in the world. I trust that in your efforts to improve yourself you have not strayed from the straight and narrow path—'"

"What does she mean by that?" Sheena cut in. "Does she think you earned the money for the skillet in some low manner?"

"Mrs. Jameson is very strict. She wants the best for me." Rosie read again. "'I trust that in your efforts to improve yourself you have not strayed from the straight and narrow path that was paved for you at the Christian Home for Orphans and Foundlings. I must tell you that your presence is sorely missed.'" Rosie lifted her head. "They miss me, Sheena!"

"Of course they do. You're a wonder, you are."

Rosie began to read again. "'Your presence is sorely missed. The main cook quit her position, and you are needed to fill in, along with Jenny and Pearl. I am counting on your return in the fall, as Mr. Hunter assured me. I do not like to think that we at the Home have given you all these years of care and sustenance only to have you walk away from us in a time of need.'"

"Of all the—!"

"'If you manage to earn any money while you are away,'" Rosie read on, "'I expect you to bring it when you come. We need a new washtub. Sincerely, Mrs. Jameson.'"

"Ooo, I should like to get my hands around her neck!" Sheena exclaimed, demonstrating just what she would do to the orphanage director. "She wants your money for a new washtub, does she? She expects you to race back to that dreadful place just because she gave you a bed and a little food all those years? Well, I've news for her. You deserve a life better than that, so you do. You're a good girl, a hardworking girl, a fine Christian girl. You're going to marry Rolf Rustemeyer and live in his soddy and have yourself a home and a family. And that's that." She clapped her hands over her knees. "You won't give that letter another thought, will you, Rosie? Rosie?"

Rosie stared down at the sheet of white paper. "Sheena, Mrs. Jameson is right. They do need me at the Home. I did run off and leave them in a difficult position. From the moment we drove away from Kansas City in Seth's wagon, I sensed I had been willful and selfish. I certainly didn't pray about coming out to the prairie before I took the first step, and I'm not sure I've done a bit of real good for the Lord since I've been here."

"Of course you have! You're the best cook, the most caring—"

"And I don't think I want to marry Rolf Rustemeyer after all."

"Really, now? I can't say I'm surprised, though I thought you had your mind made up on it. What about Seth then? You know I've wanted you to marry him all along."

"Sheena, I care about Seth. Truly I do."

"You love him."

"Maybe I do. But he loves his wife."

"She's dead!"

"I know that, but it doesn't make any difference to Seth. No woman can take his wife's place. I think he's afraid."

"Afraid of what?"

"Afraid to let someone into his life in that way again. He was hurt so badly by what happened. Now all he can think about is keeping Chipper safe from Jack Cornwall and trying to get his crops in. Sheena, I have to accept the truth that Seth is never going to love me. He's never going to marry me. And my heart . . . my heart doesn't want to marry Rolf Rustemeyer."

"Your heart? I thought you said the heart had nothing to do with marriage. Didn't you tell me that all a woman needed to do was find a good, hardworking, honest man?"

Rosie shrugged. "I think . . . I think I might have been wrong. There may be more to it than that. I've come to believe there's a certain feeling people sometimes have. It's like in Mrs. Jameson's fairy tale book when the story says, 'The prince took Cinderella in his arms and began to dance with her. The rest of the evening, he had eyes only for the beautiful, mysterious woman.' And in Beauty and the Beast: 'though she knew he was outwardly a beast, she saw the good in his heart, and her own heart beat the faster for it.' You know, Sheena, I always thought eyes gazing at each other and hearts beating too fast were just pretend. Make-believe stories for children. But now I'm not so sure."

"Who taught you differently, Rosie?" Sheena took her hand. "Was it Seth?"

"It wasn't Rolf, I can tell you that." She let out a deep sigh. "It's all beyond me. God knows I'd best be back at the Home, where I'm certain of what I'm supposed to be doing and I can't get myself into any greater trouble than climbing trees."

"Does God know that? How can you be so sure?"

"He's been watching what a poor job I'm doing out here. Oh Sheena, I'm such a wreck." Rosie bent over on the bench and buried her face in her hands. "I do love Seth," she whispered. "I love him so much I can hardly stand it. I love Chipper, and I want to try to be a mother to him. I want to marry Seth and feel his strong arms holding me close. I want to know what it's like to kiss . . . to kiss him. Oh, Sheena, this is just awful."

"Fräulein!" Rolf's booming voice brought Rosie upright in an instant. At the edge of the yard, the big blond German was climbing down from his mule. "Happy lunschtime to you!"

"Hello, Rolf." She blotted her cheeks with the corner of her apron. "How are you today?"

"I *komme* eaten vit you!"

"The bread!" Rosie gasped. She hadn't given a thought to the midday meal since Sheena came traipsing over the bridge. A glance out to the fields confirmed that Seth, Chipper, and all five O'Tooles were trudging toward the soddy. "The bread is probably burned to a cinder. All they'll have for lunch is ashes. Oh Sheena!"

"Go on then, Cinderella. I'll take my wee *brablins* home with me whilst you feed your two Prince Charmings." Sheena gave her friend a squeeze. "You must talk to God about this matter of your love for Seth. He'll find you a way through it."

"Thank you, Sheena," Rosie said as she left the bench and made for the soddy door.

Rolf caught her hand just as she stepped inside. "Fräulein, I vill *mein* money haf. Dollars."

"Rolf, my bread is burning. I don't have time to figure out what you're trying to say." She resorted to Seth's habit of shouting at the German. "The . . . bread . . . is . . . burning!"

"Dollars," he repeated. "Britsch money of Hunter, O'Toole, *und* Rustemeyer. You gif me? *Ja,* you gif to me *mein* money?"

"You'll have to wait, Rolf. I must get my bread." Rosie pulled away from him and hurried into the soddy to find black smoke billowing from the oven door. Her bread was ruined. Ruined! There would be nothing for lunch but a few slices of cold salt pork. Everything was a mess. Rolf wanted his money. Sheena's entrancing sister was coming to Kansas. Jack Cornwall was trying to steal Chipper. And Seth . . . oh, she had confessed out loud that she loved Seth. Now it was in the open, and she felt as confused and upset as though a hive of bees had taken up residence in her stomach.

"Rosie?"

She whirled around, the smoking lump of bread clamped in a hot pad. Seth stood in the doorway, a tall silhouette framed by golden noon sunlight. "Rosie, are you all right?"

"No! No, I'm not all right." She thunked the loaf pan on the table and marched toward him through the smoky haze. "You want me to marry Rolf. Rolf wants his money. Sheena's beautiful sister is coming. Cornwall is trying to take Chipper away. Mrs. Jameson needs a new washtub! And worst of all . . . I-I've burned my bread!"

At that, she burst past him and ran right out the front door. She ran by Sheena and Rolf and Chipper and all the gaping little O'Tooles. She ran all the way down to the creek, halfway to Rustemeyer's homestead, and straight to the biggest, tallest tree she could find.

Then she yanked off her apron, kicked off her shoes, and began to climb. Straight up. Up to the very highest branches of the cottonwood tree. And there she sat—thinking, praying, even crying a little—until the sun sank below the prairie. She didn't go down for lunch. Not even for supper. Seth had cooked meals before she came, she reasoned. He could do it again. She needed time to put her world back in order.

When everything seemed quiet at the homestead, she finally returned to the barn. She climbed the ladder into the loft to get ready for bed. And Seth walked in to check on her.

"Are you there?" he asked, holding up the lantern.

"Yes," she said.

"Did you talk to God up in the tree?"

"Yes." She could see him through the chinks in the floorboards, though she knew he couldn't see her. It hardly mattered. Just the sight of him brought everything back in a rush. And she knew that all her hours in the cottonwood tree had been for nothing.

"Did you and God get everything worked out?" Seth asked.

"No."

"Do you want to talk to me about anything?"

"No."

He fell silent for several minutes, and she used the time to study him. It was all as true as she had feared. He was handsome and wonderful and kind. Her heart beat helter-skelter every time she looked into his blue eyes. Her thoughts, dreams, hopes were filled with him. She loved Seth. Loved him in the strongest possible way she could ever imagine. And she could do nothing about it. Nothing.

"Good night, then, Miss Mills," he called up.

"Good night, Mr. Hunter."

Rosie was acting mighty strange, Seth mused as he loaded a stack of blankets into his wagon on a bright Independence Day morning. She wouldn't look at him. Would hardly talk to him. He had asked her if there was a problem. But she always got a look on her face like a big grizzly bear was after her. She sort of shrank inside herself and told him she just couldn't talk about it.

After a while, Seth had decided it must be one of two things. Either she was upset that Rolf had taken his part of the bridge money, or she had gotten worried about going back to the orphanage.

He had spotted the letter lying on the ground that day after she burned the bread and ran off to climb the tree. He had read the letter, even though it wasn't his business, so he knew that the Jameson woman wanted Rosie back. Or maybe she just wanted a new washtub.

On the other hand, Rosie's consternation could have something to do with Sheena's little sister coming out to the prairie to teach school. Maybe Rosie was worried about having to give up the loft. Seth knew she was pretty attached to her little room. She'd decorated it with flowers and bows and little things she found out on the prairie. He wasn't about to make her give up her bedroom, but every time he tried to reassure her, she told him she had something to do. He was beginning to think lassoing a dust devil would be easier than talking to Rosie Cotton Mills.

"Are they going to have races at the picnic, Papa?" Chipper asked, tugging on his father's pant leg. "Three-legged races and sack races?"

"I'm not sure, son. We'll find out when we get to the mill."

"Can we bring Stubby with us? He wants to come. Please, Papa?"

Seth glanced down at the dog. Long-legged, lanky, and growing about an inch a day, the mutt certainly belied his name. His feet were the size of saucers, and his wagging tail had become a downright hazard. Seth had the feeling Stubby might end up the approximate height and weight of a small bear.

"Sure, we'll take Stubby," he replied, lifting the boy into the wagon. "Where's Rosie?"

"In the barn. She's fixing up her box lunch."

"She already packed the lunch." Seth glanced down at the large basket with its cheerful red and white checkered cloth. Rosie must be confused. Lately, she had been doing absentminded things like that a lot. Put salt in the rhubarb pie instead of sugar. Dropped a sack of beans all over the floor. Pulled up a whole row of radish sprouts and left the weeds to grow in their place.

"Naw, *this* ain't Rosie's box lunch," Chipper said, peeking into the basket. "This lunch is for us. You an' me. Rosie gots her own."

"What for?"

"Don'tcha know? Whoever pays the most for Rosie's lunch gets to eat with her."

"Well now, what kind of a crazy idea is that? She doesn't need to make money that way. She's already got all those bridge tolls. And the barn is beginning to look like a bona fide mercantile. Why would she need to sell her picnic lunch?"

"It's for the church, Papa. The money goes to the new church. Ain't you heard about it? Sheena's been telling everybody." His blue eyes brightened suddenly. "There's Rosie! Tell Papa about the auction, Rosie. He don't know a thing about it."

Seth turned, and for the second time that summer, his breath dammed up and his heart flopped over in his chest. Pink. Rosie was pink! She came strolling out of the barn, her dress a billowing, bouncing butterfly of pink calico. Tucks and ruffles and bits of lace and ribbons dangled everywhere. A frill of white eyelet petticoat peeked out from the hem. A fringed cotton shawl draped over her shoulders. She had piled her hair up on her head and pinned white ox-eye daisies into the loops and curls. And in her arms she carried a small woven basket covered with a matching pink calico cloth.

"It's a box-lunch auction," she said, setting the basket into the wagon. "Mr. LeBlanc is hoping to raise enough money to build a church."

Tongue-tied as a gigged frog, Seth helped Rosie onto the wagon bench, then climbed up beside her. Where had she gotten the dress? Had she done her hair up by herself? And how come she smelled so good? Half stupefied, he flicked the reins and set his mules on the trail for the five-mile drive to the mill. His hands felt clammy. He wasn't even sure he could remember the way.

"I bet all the men are gonna put down money for Rosie's lunch," Chipper said. "She's the best cook around."

"Why thank you, Chipper," Rosie said. "I just hope we can bring in something to help with the new church."

"You're gonna put down money, aren't you, Papa? You're gonna try to eat lunch with Rosie, aren't you?"

"Your papa eats lunch with me every day," she reminded him.

"Breakfast and supper, too. I'm afraid he wouldn't find it very exciting."

Exciting? Seth was feeling something closer to panic as he glanced at the beautiful woman beside him. He had looked forward to this day ever since he'd heard about the picnic. Maybe he would finally have the chance to talk to Rosie a little. Possibly even collect that dance she owed him.

And now? Now he would have to be the highest bidder just to eat lunch with her. A cold sweat broke out down his back as he thought of the leather wallet he kept in his pocket. He had brought a little money in the expectation there might be lemonade for sale, or ice cream. What did he have on him—twenty-five cents? Fifty?

"You want to eat lunch with Rosie, don't you, Papa?" Chipper asked. "Look how pretty she is. All in pink. You won't let somebody else get her, will you? Somebody like Mr. Rustemeyer?"

"Chipper!" Rosie said with a laugh. "Leave your papa alone. I've packed you both a big lunch of fried chicken and hard-boiled eggs. It doesn't matter to your papa who eats with me today."

Seth clenched his jaw. It did matter. It mattered a lot. How much was Rustemeyer likely to bid? Seth stiffened. The big German had emptied his third of the savings. And now Seth understood why.

CHAPTER 13

FOR the first time in her life, Rosie felt pretty. Her hair looked just right for an Independence Day picnic. She had spent hours raveling and knotting threads on a white flour-sack shawl to make a fringe. And the dress Sheena had let her borrow could not have been more perfect. Oh, she'd had to take in the side seams a few inches, and the hem was so short that her petticoat kept peeking out, but truly she felt just like Cinderella at the ball.

In fact, it appeared many of the young homesteaders at the picnic had decided to vie for the role of Prince Charming. If Rosie chanced to sit on the swing that Mr. LeBlanc had hung from an oak branch, five men appeared in a cluster to ask for the privilege of pushing her. If Rosie walked toward the front steps of the LeBlanc house, three men were at her side to escort her up to the porch. If she commented on the sunny day, four umbrellas shot up to shade her. If she mentioned a slight thirst, six glasses of lemonade were thrust in her direction. She felt silly and flattered and, most of all, amazed. Could a pink dress do all that? Were these men desperate to find eligible single women? Or did she actually look as pretty as she felt?

"Sure, you're the belle of the ball," Sheena whispered as Rosie placed her box lunch on the long table set up for the auction. "I wager you'll earn the most money for the new church, so you will."

"I hope I can help. But as for earning the most money—haven't you noticed Yvonne LeBlanc? She's lovely. And don't forget Maria Rippeto."

"Aye, they'll win a few bids, I'm sure. All for the good of the church. But who have you cast your eye on, Rosie? Is there a man you'd especially favor to win the privilege of your company? I hear Gabriel Chavez has been speaking favorably about you. He's a good-looking man, though I understand his farm is very rocky."

Rosie studied the dark-haired immigrant from Mexico. Mr. Chavez was indeed a dashing fellow. So were several of the other young homesteaders. But all morning Rosie had been conscious of one man in particular. Seth Hunter.

Seth remained oblivious to Rosie's attentions. Concerned that Jack Cornwall might use this public gathering for another kidnapping attempt, he kept his concentration on Chipper. He had borrowed a pistol from Jimmy O'Toole. He had mentioned to a few other men to keep an eye out for trouble. And he had spent every moment of the morning with his son.

Father and son ran together in the sack race and the three-legged race. They even tried the wheelbarrow race—though Chipper collapsed so many times that Seth finally scooped up his son and dashed the rest of the way to the finish line. They were disqualified, of course, but everyone cheered as Chipper gave his papa a noisy kiss on the cheek. Only once or twice did Rosie catch Seth looking at her. And then he averted his eyes so quickly she wondered if she'd been mistaken.

"It's auction time, messieurs, mesdemoiselles!" Mr. LeBlanc called out when it was nearly noon. "Everybody gather around."

Instantly the whole crowd moved toward the long table where seven pretty baskets sat in a row. The four eligible LeBlanc daughters and Rosie stood in a line to wait their turns. Mrs. Violet Hudson made the sixth contestant. A widow with three children and a baby on the way, she was struggling to hold onto her homestead after her husband's death. The seventh basket belonged to Maria Rippeto, a black-haired beauty with flashing eyes who was reputed to be a terrible cook.

The bidding began with the LeBlanc girls, and as Rosie waited her turn, she searched the crowd for Seth. *Please. Oh, please. Where are you, Seth?* She considered praying over the matter and decided such a small thing wasn't worth God's attention. Then she remembered her Father was interested in every part of her life, and she began to lift up such fervent prayers that Sheena had to caution her to stop muttering out loud or everyone would think she had gone around the bend.

Before long, the proposed community church could boast twelve dollars and sixty-five cents in its building fund, and all the eligible LeBlanc daughters had earned themselves company for lunch. Rosie was next in line. She stepped up behind her basket and looked out over the crowd. Seth and Chipper were sitting at the back of the gathering, their matching blue eyes pinned on her. She took a deep breath. *Please, dear God. Please give him courage. Please let him make an offer for me. Just the smallest offer. That's all I need.*

"What am I bid for the pleasure of taking lunch with Miss Rosie Mills?" Mr. LeBlanc called out. "I understand she is a fine cook. And very pretty, too. Who will start with ten cents? There. Mr. Williams bids ten cents. Do I hear fifteen? All right then. Mr. Hill has fifteen cents. How about twenty? Twenty?"

"Twenty-five cents," Seth called out.

Rosie's heart leaped into her throat. A whole quarter! *Thank you, Father!*

"I hear twenty-five cents from Mr. Hunter. Do I hear thirty?"

"Thirty," Mr. Hill called.

"Forty," Seth answered back.

"Fifty," two other men said simultaneously.

"Seventy-five cents," Seth called out.

For a moment, all was silent. "Eighty cents!" Mr. Hill shouted.

"One dollar!" Mr. Chavez hollered back.

Rosie stood numbly as the price of her lunch box went up and up. One fifty. Two dollars. Two seventy-five. Seth and Chipper picked up their basket and walked away with Stubby. In the deep shade of a pine tree, they spread out the red checkered cloth and began to sort through the pieces of fried chicken Rosie had cooked early that morning. Her eyes filled with tears. Three dollars. Three twenty-five. Four dollars. Five dollars.

"Five seventy-five!" Mr. LeBlanc called out. "Mr. Hill has offered five dollars and seventy-five cents for Miss Mills's lunch box. Do I hear six dollars?"

"Ten dollars," Rolf Rustemeyer boomed, coming to his feet. "I gif ten dollars for lunsch of Fräulein Mills. Fery goot lunsch. Tank you."

The crowd sat in stunned silence as Rolf walked up to the table, hooked one beefy arm through the handle of Rosie's picnic basket and gave her a curt bow. "*Ja*, Fräulein Mills? You eaten lunsch vit me?"

Rosie cast a last look at Seth and Chipper and nodded. "Thank you, Mr. Rustemeyer. The church will be very grateful for your donation."

Her heart aching, Rosie shook out a blanket and spread the lunch under a shady tree. Rolf tucked a napkin into the collar of his blue work shirt and beamed at her. She did her best to smile in return. *Is this what you want from me, Father? Do you want me to learn to love Rolf? Is this your plan?*

"Was you maken?" Rolf asked, peering into the basket. "Chicken? Fery goot. *Ist* goot, *ja?* You eaten togedder vit me?"

"It's very nice."

After she murmured a brief prayer of thanks, Rosie filled the two plates with fried chicken, boiled eggs, and fresh strawberries. Rolf took off his boots and crossed his legs. One big toe poked through his worn sock, and Rosie felt her heart soften toward him. Poor

Rolf. He needed looking after. And who better for it than a woman who longed for a home and a husband?

"Fery goot chicken," he said around a mouthful. "I zo hoppy to eaten vit you."

"It's a pleasure." Rosie realized she didn't have much else to say to Rolf. After all, how many times could he tell her that he liked her cooking? She glanced at Seth. He and Chipper were getting up from their blanket, their attention trained on the auction table.

"Mrs. Hudson has made a fine lunch of ham sandwiches and potato salad," Mr. LeBlanc was saying. "Now who'll start the bidding? Can we start with ten cents? . . . Do I hear ten? . . . Well, how about five?"

"Ten!" Seth called out.

"I hear ten cents from Seth Hunter. Do I hear fifteen? . . . Come on boys, this is for the church."

Violet Hudson, a small woman with light brown hair and big olive eyes, stared bravely out at the crowd. The swell of her stomach lifted the front hem of her dress so that her worn-out boots and darned stockings showed. Seth and Chipper paused at the back of the gathering. "Fifteen cents," Seth said.

"You can't bid against yourself, Mr. Hunter," LeBlanc said. "All right, we've got fifteen. Do I hear twenty?"

"Twenty," Seth said.

"Twenty cents. Do I hear twenty-five?"

"I bid fifty cents," Seth said.

Everyone laughed, even Violet Hudson, whose pale cheeks had flushed to a bright scarlet. LeBlanc declared the bid a winner, and Seth marched forward to take his prize. Rosie watched as the delighted woman picked up her basket and handed it to Chipper. The little boy grinned.

"I vill *ein Haus* builden," Rolf said, tapping Rosie on the arm. "Vit britsch money."

"A house? You're going to build a house?" Her heart sank as

Violet, her three children, Chipper, and Seth gathered in a circle to eat lunch. "You already have a house, Rolf. Don't you?"

"*Ja, ja, ja*. But I vill *ein* voot *Haus* builden."

"Voot?" Rosie shook her head. "What do you mean? What's a voot house?"

"Voot. From trees."

"Wood!"

"*Ja, ja, ja.*" He laughed. "You liken voot *Haus*, fräulein?"

"Yes, I suppose so. I don't mind our soddy, though." She looked over her shoulder. Seth and Violet were chuckling about something. Violet rubbed Stubby's ears. "We've been very happy."

"*Ja?* You vill be hoppy togedder vit me?"

"You and me?" Rosie focused on Rolf again. "I'm having a lovely time now. Thank you for buying my lunch."

"You vill lif in *meinem* voot *Haus?* Cooken, vaschen clothes, maken *Garten* grow?"

"Live in your house?" At the sudden change of tone in Rolf's questioning, Rosie felt nervousness prickle up her spine. She fanned herself. "Well . . . I-I don't know exactly what you mean."

"*Ja? Ist* goot?"

"I don't know, Rolf. I mean, when would your wood house be built?"

"Vinter."

"There's the problem then. I have to go back to Kansas City by wintertime. I'm very sorry."

"*Nein, nein*. You *kommst* vit me. You helpen me."

Rosie felt so hot she was sure the daisies in her hair would start dropping petals any moment. Was this a marriage proposal? Did Rolf actually want her to become his wife and move into his house? *No, dear Lord. Please not this. Not now.*

"You want me to work for you?" she asked. "For room and board? Like I work for Seth?"

"*Ja, ja.*" He nodded. Then, seeming to realize the significance of her question, he shook his head. "*Nein!* Not vorken only. You marry vit Rolf Rustemeyer. Haf baby. *Ja?*"

"Wife."

"*Ja.*" He smiled, his warm gray eyes filled with hope. "*Ist* goot? Voot *Haus*. Vife. Childrens. *Ja? Ist* fery goot."

"I don't know, Rolf. I thought I knew. A month ago I would have said yes just like that." The words gushed out of her—all her pent-up emotions. "I should probably say yes right this very moment. But so many things have happened. I suddenly feel so strange inside. I'm sure you can't understand, because I don't think you've felt this feeling before, Rolf. If you had, you wouldn't be asking me to marry you. It's clear you don't feel it. You're talking about cooking and washing, and all the things I thought marriage was about. But it's more than that. At least I think it ought to be more than that. There ought to be some sort of passion between a husband and wife. Do you know what I mean? Rolf?"

"*Ja, ja, ja.*" He nodded absently. "Danz? *Ist* danz now? You danzen togedder vit me, *ja?*"

He grabbed Rosie's hand and pulled her to her feet. A space had been cleared in the mill yard, and many of the young couples were hurrying to form squares. The makeshift band struck up a tune. People began to clap. Rolf whirled Rosie onto the floor.

She danced. In fact, she danced all afternoon with hardly a moment to sip at her glass of lemonade. She danced with Rolf and Mr. Hill and Mr. Chavez and all the young men who had bid on her box lunch. Then she danced with all of them again. Every time she danced with Rolf, he talked about his voot *Haus*. But she managed to avoid giving him an answer to his marriage proposal.

In fact, she realized that the more she talked, the less Rolf understood. This provided a perfect solution to her dilemma because every time Rosie became nervous, she talked too much. Their attempts at conversation shut down, and the focus returned to dancing.

Rosie knew she needed to pray. Desperately. But she couldn't very well run off and climb a tree. And she couldn't concentrate on anything with all these young farmers bidding for her attention. Finally she resorted to quick whispered pleas—accompanied by furtive glances at Seth. He had taken a seat at the edge of the dance floor. Violet sat beside him, and they talked. They laughed. They pointed at things and laughed some more.

Rosie had never considered that playing the part of Cinderella at the ball could be a miserable experience. As the sun set, Mr. LeBlanc lit lanterns around the dance floor. By that time, Rosie's feet felt like lead weights. Her shoulders wanted to sag. A length of eyelet lace trailed from her petticoat where Rolf had accidentally stepped on it.

Worst of all, she couldn't find Seth. He and Violet had disappeared long ago. How could she blame them for enjoying each other's company? They had so much in common. Both had lost spouses. Both had small children. Both were trying to manage farms on the prairie. They made a perfect match.

As Gabriel Chavez bowed to Rosie after a particularly spirited dance, she spotted Rolf eagerly elbowing his way toward her. *No.* She couldn't take it anymore. Not another dance. She swung around and stepped out of the circle of light.

A warm hand cupped her elbow. "Miss Mills? Would you care to dance with me?"

"No, please. Thank you, but I'm . . . I'm—"

"Are you too tired, Rosie?"

She looked up into Seth's blue eyes. Her heart spun around, and the pain in her blistered toes evaporated. "Tired? Me? Of course not. Never."

"Are you sure?"

"I'm fit as a fiddle."

"Well, come on then. I reckon it's my turn with the fairest flower of the prairie."

Rosie gave a silly, dizzy giggle as he escorted her onto the floor. Just then, the band struck up a waltz. A collective gasp came up from the crowd. Waltzing was considered by many a sinful and wicked thing. Some of the elderly glowered at the change in the music to three-quarter time. Some stomped off in disgust as the tempo slowed down, the squares dissolved, and couples began to move in time to the dance. Rosie herself had heard that waltzing was the devil's tool. But she and some of the girls at the orphanage had practiced the steps and turns in the attic, and none of them had felt the least bit sinful afterward.

"I reckon it's OK to waltz at a church benefit," Seth said, taking Rosie into his arms. "Don't you?"

"It's for a very good cause." Wild horses could not have dragged her away.

Rosie felt exactly like she was floating. Seth's blue eyes gazed down at her. His dark hair gleamed. One hand slipped around her back and the other clasped her fingers. Her feet positively had wings.

"I don't think God has a specific command against waltzing," Seth said. "Although if we looked hard enough we might find it someplace in Deuteronomy."

She laughed. "If it's a sin in the Bible, Mrs. Jameson could probably find it for us."

"Mrs. Jameson is in Kansas City. You're here."

"Yes, I am."

"I'm glad of that." He leaned close to her ear. "You're beautiful, Rosie Mills."

She thought her knees were going to buckle. "It's . . . it's Sheena's dress."

"It suits you."

"My petticoat shows."

Oh, that wasn't polite. She shook her head, embarrassed. She was talking about her underthings! In front of him!

"The dress is a little short, is what I meant to say," she mumbled, and she could hear her own voice begin to speed up in her nervousness. "I really don't mind. About the petticoat, I mean. I'm not ungrateful. In fact, I'm very grateful. I had the blue gingham, but then Sheena said she had brought this pink one all the way from Ireland. She couldn't fit into it anymore after all the children, so the dress was wasting away in her trunk. She suspects her sister Caitrin might be able to wear it when she arrives. Caitrin is coming from Ireland next month for a long visit, and I'm . . . I'm talking too much, aren't I?"

He was smiling at her, the corner of his mouth tipped up just a little and his gaze lazily studying her face. "I like the sound of your voice."

She couldn't think of anything to say after that, so she just drifted along in the soft, sweet music and enjoyed the sensation of Seth Hunter standing so close and holding her in his arms. He smelled very good. Like lemons. She felt the greatest urge to lay her cheek on his shoulder. God had given Seth such strong shoulders—shoulders that could hold up the world. Her daisies began to drop out of her hair one by one, but she didn't care. Seth whirled her around and around until her feet lifted off the ground, her dress billowed, and her heart soared.

When the music stopped, she was so surprised she let out a little gasp. Like coming out of a dream. But it wasn't a dream, and the reality of persistent Rolf Rustemeyer was bearing down on her again. "His wood house," she said, taking a step toward Seth. "He'll want to talk about his wood house."

"Rustemeyer's building a house?"

"He took all his money out of the savings, you know."

"I know."

"Please. Can we go home now?"

Seth tucked Rosie's arm under his. "We're . . . going," he shouted at Rustemeyer. "Chipper . . . is . . . tired."

Rosie could feel Rolf staring at her as she and Seth left the dance floor and walked toward the old pine tree. Good manners dictated that she thank Rolf for his company and for the bid that won her lunch box. She should give him some response to his proposal of marriage.

But she squeezed her eyes shut against her conscience and let Seth guide her away from the gathering. *Forgive me, Lord. If you want me to marry Rolf, I'll try. But not now. Not yet. Please, not yet.*

Chipper was curled up asleep on the blanket, his head on Violet's lap and Stubby at his side. Seth knelt beside the young widow and picked up his son. "Thank you, Mrs. Hudson," he said in a low voice. "I enjoyed the afternoon."

Her eyes deepened. "You're so kind, Mr. Hunter."

"Good night, then."

"Good night." As he turned away, her fragile voice stopped him. "Mr. Hunter, you'd be . . . you'd be welcome to stop by our place anytime. If you're passing thataway. Or if you'd just like to come . . . to come calling on me. Me and the children, I mean. You could bring Chipper to play."

"Thank you, Mrs. Hudson. I'm much obliged."

As Rosie and Seth walked toward the wagon, she reflected on the plight of the lonely widow with her three children and a baby on the way. Guilt began to eat at her again. Maybe it wasn't right to ache so deeply in the hope of winning Seth's love for herself. Violet Hudson needed him more than she did. And Rolf was a good man—an honorable man—who wanted Rosie for his wife.

Back in Kansas City this would all have seemed so simple to her. The widower marries the widow who needs a father for her children. The German bachelor marries the homeless woman who has always wanted a house and a family. How much more logical could the arrangement be?

But then Seth slipped his hands around her waist and lifted her up onto the wagon seat, and Rosie laid a hand on his broad shoulder—and Seth, only Seth, was right for her! He tucked a blanket under his sleeping son's head, loaded the dog, and walked around the wagon to join her.

As the mules pulled them onto the road home, Seth reached over and draped Rosie's fringed shawl over her shoulders. "Cold?" he said.

"Mm."

It was the hottest night of the year. But he left his arm around her, and she snuggled against him. Never in her entire life had she known a feeling so wonderful. So secure. So absolutely perfect.

"Did you enjoy the picnic?" Seth asked.

"Mm." Rosie felt like she was drifting on a soft white cloud. She didn't care about the picnic. She didn't care about anything.

"That fried chicken you made sure was good."

"Mm."

"I guess Rustemeyer liked it."

"He likes everything I cook," she murmured.

Seth fell silent for a moment. "I reckon Rustemeyer took his money so he could outbid everybody."

Rosie's cloud began to fade just a little. "He wants to build a wood house. That's why he took his money."

"A wood house. What's he want to do that for? Doesn't he think a soddy is good enough for him?"

"He's just thinking of the future, Seth."

"The future? What else does he have in mind for the future?"

An alarm bell went off in Rosie's head, and her fluffy cloud vanished completely. "A wood house," she said. "He's been thinking about a wood house."

"I think he took the money in order to win you at the auction. And I think he wants to build a wood house so he can put you into it."

"Rolf didn't win me at the auction. He won my box lunch."

"And the right to your company."

"Are you angry because he outbid you?"

"Angry? I'm not angry." He removed his arm from her shoulder and flicked the reins. "If that hound dog wants to spend his hard-earned money on a box lunch, that's fine with me. I just don't see the point of spending ten dollars on a few pieces of cold fried chicken."

"The money goes to the new church. And what's wrong with my fried chicken?"

"Nothing. There's nothing wrong with the chicken you made. It was good chicken. Better than Violet Hudson's ham sandwiches, that's for sure. But ten dollars? Ten hard-earned dollars."

"Those were bridge-toll dollars. The hard work Rolf put into the bridge was paid off a long time before those ten dollars came along. If he wants to put ten dollars into the new church, why shouldn't he?"

"If you hadn't kept on with those bridge tolls of yours, he wouldn't have ten dollars to pay for a box lunch."

"You don't like it that I take the bridge tolls, do you? You never have liked that. But I've been doing it for you. You and Chipper. I want to give you what I can. I want to leave you something."

"We have all we need." He let out a hot breath. "We have you."

Rosie grabbed the edges of the plank wagon bench. *Please, Father, help him to open his heart. Let him see how much I care.*

"Rolf Rustemeyer's ten dollars mean nothing to me," she said carefully. "Though I'm glad they'll help build the new church. And as for his wood house—"

"I'll build a wood house one of these days." Elbows on his knees, Seth stared out into the darkness ahead. "I have big dreams for my place. I want fences and cattle. I want a better plow and a new seed planter. I plan to chink the barn, and put a floor in the well house, and buy a horse. And I'll build a frame house, too—double storied with real glass windows and a big front porch. I'd like a new wagon. Maybe I'll even get myself a carriage with a black-cloth top and a pair of big, shiny—"

"Seth." Rosie laid her hand on his arm. "Wood houses don't matter. Not to me."

He turned and studied her for a long time. She could feel his eyes searching her face in the moonlight. He dropped the reins and lifted a hand to her hair. Slowly, very slowly, he sifted his fingers through the loose strands. He picked a daisy out of a curl and rolled the stem between his thumb and finger. Then he leaned forward and touched his lips to hers. The kiss was gentle, firm, and over in a breath.

"Rosie," he said. "I meant what I said. Chipper and I . . . we're glad you came. Both of us. Me, especially."

"Especially you?"

"Especially me." Then he bent over and his hands cupped the back of her head. When his lips met hers in a long, satisfying kiss, her breath hung in the back of her throat. She slipped her fingers up his arms to the solid round muscle of his shoulders. He pulled her closer, and his mouth found hers again.

"Rosie," he whispered.

She started to answer, but something popped against the side of her head—a tiny lead pellet. And then another hit her in the cheek. On the neck. In the ear. She drew back in pain.

"Shotgun!" Rosie cried. "It's Jack Cornwall!"

Waving her hands over her head, she fought the hundreds of tiny missiles that suddenly came at her from every angle. Was Chipper all right? She could hear him wailing in the back of the wagon. Stubby began to howl. Oh, Lord! They would all be killed. "Seth, he's shooting at us!"

Seth kept one arm around Rosie as he struggled to capture the reins of the bolting mules. "It's not Cornwall," he shouted. "Take cover, Rosie. We've got grasshoppers!"

CHAPTER 14

IT TOOK all the strength Seth could muster to keep the frightened mules on the track. Chipper screamed in terror as Rosie hauled the boy into the front of the wagon and wrapped him in a blanket. Stubby raced around in circles, yapping and howling. All around them, invisible except for the teeming shadow they cast over the moon, the grasshoppers flew. They settled on Seth's hatband. Climbed up the legs of his jeans. Nestled in Rosie's hair. Rode the leather driving lines like a long string of hideous ornaments on a monster's necklace.

While Chipper whimpered and Rosie cringed against the bench, all Seth could think about were his crops. Would the grasshoppers eat his corn? He had heard the stories, of course. Terrible tales of devastation from the few homesteaders who had been in Kansas long enough to remember the insect plagues. If he lost his crops, he'd be all but ruined.

"Giddap!" he shouted, flicking the reins and sending the hoppers off in every direction. "Come on, Nellie. Don't quit on me now, Pete."

But the mules wouldn't take another step. All around their long ears the grasshoppers flew, their wings buzzing, crackling like the rush of a prairie fire.

"We'll have to walk home," Seth said to the bundle of blanket that was Rosie and Chipper. "You go on ahead, and I'll catch up. Can you manage the boy?"

The bundle nodded. As swarms of grasshoppers flew into his face and hit him on the head, hands, and chest, Seth climbed down from the wagon. Crunching his way over the insects that had landed on the trail, he grabbed the mules' bridles and spoke whatever soothing words he could think of.

Stubby snapped at the insects as Rosie helped Chipper out of the wagon. They walked past Seth, a moving shroud. He put one arm around them and peeked under the drape covering Rosie's face. "You know the way to the soddy?" he said.

"I can find it."

"Here, take the gun." He pressed the pistol Jimmy O'Toole had given him into her hand. "If you see Cornwall, don't stop to think. Protect yourself and the boy."

He knew Rosie would rather do anything than carry a gun. But she took the weapon in silence. "Seth," she whispered, "what will we do?"

He said the only thing that came to mind. "Pray."

Then he kissed her cheek and lowered the blanket to cover her face. She moved away into the swarm, and he returned to his team. Frightened and confused, the mules were straining to escape the harness. Old Nellie had made up her mind to stay put, and she was doing her best to sit down between the leather trace lines. Pete wanted nothing more than to run. He pulled against the neck yoke, thrashing his head around in torment as the hoppers assaulted him.

Seth muttered a prayer for Rosie and Chipper and then concentrated on the mules. He had invested most of his army savings in the mule team and wagon. If they ran off, hurt themselves, or overturned the wagon, he'd be in deep trouble. Crushing grasshoppers with every step, he worked to calm the terrified animals. Pete's mouth grew bloody from straining against the bridle bit, and Seth's heart sank. Even if the grasshoppers didn't eat up his crops, Pete wouldn't be much use until he healed. Nellie kept trying to sit.

As the moon climbed through the night, the swarm in the sky gradually began to taper off. But Seth realized he couldn't afford to relax. The grasshoppers hadn't flown away. Instead, they had settled. Everything Seth touched—the driving lines, the wagon, the road—was covered in tiny, restless insects.

"God!" he groaned as his team finally began to pull the wagon forward. "Why, God? Why this? Why now?"

Seth walked along, his boots crackling like a trek across an icy field. *Pray*, he had told Rosie. Pray? What for? What good had God ever done him?

Seth thought about the Deuteronomy verse and how deeply it had hurt Rosie. She had made peace with it somehow. She felt an absolute assurance that God was her Father—and that knowledge made her whole life worthwhile. Maybe God was Seth's father, too. But truth to tell, God didn't seem that different from the earthly father he'd known.

Just when Seth had needed him most, his father had run off and left the family—abandoned them. Left them to their own devices. Sure, the family had survived. Barely. Seth had begged God to send his papa home. The man never returned.

Then a second crisis in his life had led Seth to cry out to God. When Mary's father had run him off the farm, Seth had been sure his life was over. What had God done to answer a desperate prayer for reconciliation? He had tossed Seth into the Union army to fight one battle after another, march thousands of miles—so far away from Mary that he hadn't known she was expecting a baby. Hadn't known when she died. Hadn't even known she was sick.

On his own, Seth had fought his way back from the edge of despair. He had signed up for a homestead, bought a team, built a soddy and a barn. Then he had traveled back to Missouri and had taken what was rightfully his. His only son. Along the way, Rosie had dropped into his life. Rosie—an unexpected, unearned gift from God if ever there was one.

And now—now he could lose her, lose his land, lose his son. Lose everything.

"God!" he shouted again into the black sky. At the cry, old Nellie stopped in her tracks. Seth pulled on the collar. She balked, shaking her head from side to side. Frustration boiled up inside him. He slapped the mule on her rump. She sat down.

Heat pouring through his veins, Seth dropped to his knees. "God, take these confounded grasshoppers away!" he said through clenched teeth. "Keep them off my crops. Keep them out of Rosie's garden."

He angrily backhanded a tear off his cheek. "I want Rosie, you hear me, God?" he said. "I want Chipper, too. He's my son. I have a right to him! If you let Cornwall have him, I'll kill . . . that . . . that . . ."

He couldn't go on. He brushed a handful of grasshoppers off his thigh and set his hand in their place. Rosie wouldn't like it that he was shouting at God. He doubted she would call that praying. But it was the best he could do.

If he was honest with himself, Seth had to admit he hated God. Hated him just the way he hated his own father. Maybe God had created the world, but he'd sure bungled up the rest of the job. He was never around when a man needed him. It was a lot easier for God to let people struggle against impossible odds than to step in and protect them. Take these vexatious grasshoppers for a perfect example.

"God!" Seth shouted upward again. "If you let these bugs eat my crops, I'll never talk to you again. You hear me? I'll know you're no better than my good-for-nothing papa. I'll know you don't care what becomes of me. You hear?"

Seth grabbed a grasshopper that was wandering down the back

of his collar and hurled it to the ground. Then he got up and brushed the squashed grasshoppers off the knees of his jeans. Old Nellie had decided to stand up again. Seth took her and Pete by the harness and led them toward the bridge. Ahead, the sun was just beginning to rise.

"They're eating up your scarf, Rosie," Chipper said. He stood beside her outside the door of the soddy and held up the tattered scrap of cotton. Six grasshoppers clung to it, their tiny mouths working furiously at the thinly woven fabric.

"They're eating everything."

"What are we gonna do, Rosie?"

"Pray. That's what your papa said we should do. I've been praying ever since the first grasshopper hit me in the head last night. I'm not going to stop now."

"I reckon you might as well stop. God ain't listening."

"A good father always listens to his children. And God always answers our prayers."

"I don't think God's gonna answer this prayer, Rosie. It's too late. The hoppers are eating up most of Papa's corn—an' your potatoes, an' the beans, an' everything we gots."

Rosie knelt down amid the grasshoppers clustered around the soddy. "The thing you must always remember is this, Chipper: God *always* answers our prayers. Sometimes he says, 'Yes, my child, I will do that for you because it fits in with my plan for the way I want the world to go.' And sometimes he says, 'You'll have to wait awhile. I'm not ready to do that yet.' And sometimes . . . sometimes, Chipper, our Father says, 'No, that is not what I'm going to do, my beloved. I have a better plan for you, so please try to trust me through this difficult time.'"

Chipper studied the fields beyond Rosie's shoulder. His blue eyes were troubled, and the corners of his little mouth turned down. "Which way you think God's going to answer us this time, Rosie?" he asked. " 'Cause it sure looks to me like them grasshoppers have ate up everything Papa planted."

She turned and looked out over the stretch of land Seth had so carefully plowed and planted. Bare stalks covered with living, moving insects pointed upward like knobby fingers accusing God of betrayal. The willow tree by the creek was stripped bare. Nothing remained in the garden beside the kitchen but a few pale yellow stems. The grasshoppers had even eaten the pith out of the pumpkin vines.

The pests had attacked the soddy, too. Rosie's broom lay on the ground, chewed from handle to bristles. Holes riddled her storage baskets. Her cleaning rags were nothing but tatters. If not for the stream, she, Seth, and Chipper would have nothing to drink. Even the top of the well was filled with grasshoppers.

The animals had suffered beyond belief. The cows refused to eat, and Rosie was concerned that their milk might dwindle to nothing. The mules stood forlornly in the barn, their brown eyes speaking of their misery. Stubby squeezed himself under the bed and wouldn't come out.

"Chipper, we are going to have to wait on the Lord," she said softly. "Though I'll admit I can't imagine what he can do about this."

"He better think of something quick. 'Cause here comes Papa."

Rosie stood as Seth strode through the grasshoppers toward the soddy. His eyes red-rimmed, he grabbed Rosie's hand and set a knobby, half-chewed potato into her palm. "They got into the root cellar," he said. "That's all I could find."

"I'll make dinner," she said. She put on the best smile she could come up with, but Seth shouldered past her into the soddy.

Rosie and Chipper hauled water from the creek and built a fire using their cache of stored buffalo chips. She decided to make a big pot of potato soup—something that might warm their stomachs and clear their heads. But the moment she lifted the lid on the stew pot, fifteen grasshoppers jumped into the steaming water.

Finally, she pushed the potato in among the buffalo chips and left it to bake. At least the grasshoppers wouldn't be able to get through the coals to eat it.

The grasshoppers stayed for nine days. They ate the cornstalks. They ate the wagon ropes. They ate the wooden milk bucket. They ate every leaf, bush, blade of grass, and weed in Seth's one hundred sixty acres of homestead. They even ate up the old dress Rosie had worn from the orphanage to Kansas.

And then one morning a wind blew in from the west. All the grasshoppers took wing. Within an hour they had gone—a great black cloud of buzzing, swarming pests that nearly blotted out the sun.

Startled at the sudden silence, Rosie stepped out of the soddy to see what had happened. Stubby slinked out from under the bed and stood beside her. Chipper and Seth were walking up from the stream carrying a bucket of water between them. Rosie crossed her arms over her stomach and stared at the two of them, fighting tears. For nine days, they had lived from one moment to the next—fighting for survival with little time even to think.

Now . . . now what?

"Didja see that, Rosie?" Chipper asked. "The grasshoppers went away! They flew right straight over me an' Papa. It was like black smoke—only real loud. I got scared, thinkin' the hoppers couldn't find anything left to eat and was gonna come after us next. But Papa said to hold on tight to his hand. So I did. Sure enough, they left us alone."

Chipper and his father set the water pail down in the yard beside Rosie. She picked a few grasshoppers out of the water and tossed them onto the ground. Then she looked up at Seth. Neither of them had slept much since the invasion. Instead, they had sat together on the bench just outside the soddy. Saying nothing, they had joined hands and waited. Waited through the long, swarming nights until the hot, swarming days began again.

"Now whatcha gonna do, Papa?" Chipper asked. "What's next?"

Seth looked down at his son. Then he lifted his head and met Rosie's eyes. "I'm ruined," he said.

"No." She shook her head. "Please, Seth, don't say that."

"Pack up."

"Seth, why? What are you saying?"

"I'll take you back to Kansas City."

"Kansas City! But I don't want to go."

"It doesn't matter what you want. It doesn't matter what I want. I don't have anything to offer. When you came out here, I promised you room and board in exchange for looking after Chipper and keeping house. Your bed's half eaten up. And God knows I don't have anything but what I can shoot to feed you. You'd best go."

Rosie sank onto the stool beside the front door. In the distance she could see the O'Toole family filing over the bridge. Rolf Rustemeyer was coming from the other direction. No doubt they would all want to compare and assess the damage now that the hoppers had finally gone.

"Lord, what does this mean?" she murmured, bending over and squeezing her eyes shut as Seth and Chipper went out to meet their neighbors. "Were the grasshoppers your sign of wrath against us, Father? Are you punishing me for coming out to the prairie without asking your permission? Is it my willfulness in not letting you choose my husband for me—for loving Seth so much? Was it something Seth did? Or Rolf? Or Jimmy? Why Lord? Why did you allow the grasshoppers? And why are you sending me away now?"

"Great ghosts, has she lost her mind?" Sheena asked Seth. "Did the pestilence send her over the brink?"

Rosie looked up. "I'm praying, Sheena."

"She does it all the time," Chipper piped in. "Out loud, too. She says God answers all our prayers. Sometimes yes, sometimes wait awhile, and sometimes no. But he always makes everything turn out good for the people who love him."

Sheena, Seth, and Jimmy all stared down at Rosie as though she had indeed lost her mind. She picked a grasshopper out of her pocket and gave a little shrug. "I do believe it," she said. "The Bible says it."

"What good can God make of our troubles now?" Jimmy asked. "Sure, the lot of us are finished. Finished clean. It's as bad as the potato famine in Ireland, so it is. Only this time I've my wee *brablins* and hardly a thing to feed any of them."

"No foot *für* eaten?" Rolf Rustemeyer asked.

"No food," Sheena said. "We've eaten the last of our salt pork. Do you have any food, Mr. Rustemeyer?"

"*Nein.*" The German shook his head. "No foot."

"We gots oysters," Chipper said. "Rosie gots 'em in the barn in her big tradin' box."

Rosie glanced at Seth, and the look in his eyes made her heart begin to hammer. "Yes, we *do* have oysters. Now why didn't I think of that before?"

"What else is in there?" Seth asked.

"Coffee. And canned brandied peaches."

"I've got pickles at our place," Sheena added. "Shortening, too. They didn't get at that."

"I have a jug of maple syrup," Rosie went on. "And mackerels—big fat ones in cans. And a keg of lard."

"I haf tea," Rolf said.

"What with oysters and mackerel and canned brandied peaches, we will be a fancy lot, won't we?" Sheena said. A grin tugged at the corners of her mouth. "At least we've something to get by on."

"Until what?" Seth asked. "We won't be able to make it through a Kansas winter on a few oysters and some lard, Sheena. The crops are ruined. There won't be a harvest. That means no winter stores.

No produce to sell in Topeka. No grain to haul to LeBlanc's mill. And no money to buy seed."

"We have a little money," Rosie said. "The bridge tolls. Rolf took his already, but there's forty-three dollars and seventy-five cents each for the Hunters and the O'Tooles."

Jimmy O'Toole's face went from white to pink to bright red in the space of three seconds. Seth's mouth dropped open. Sheena fanned herself with both hands.

"Forty-three dollars, did you say?" she puffed.

"I'm pretty sure of it. I counted it out for Mr. Rustemeyer right before the picnic."

"By all the goats in Kerry, my sweet lass, you've saved us!" Jimmy O'Toole cried. He grabbed Rosie's hands and pulled her up from the bench. "You and that wobbly pontoon bridge have saved us!"

"Forty-three dollars *each?*" Seth asked.

"And seventy-five cents." Rosie hugged herself tight, hoping against hope that the light in Seth's eyes meant what she thought. She had done the right thing. She had helped him.

"Rosie!" He threw his arms around her and swung her up into the air. "You crazy girl! Taking bridge tolls left and right. Trading for oysters and mackerel. Going on with it even when you knew I didn't like it. You did it! You saved us!"

He planted a big kiss right on her cheek. Rolf laughed and gave her a kiss on the other cheek. Then Jimmy O'Toole kissed her hand. Chipper kissed her elbow. Stubby started barking. Pretty soon the whole group was dancing around the yard, stepping on squashed grasshoppers and singing and shouting at the top of their lungs.

"We'll go to Topeka," Seth said. "Rolf and I. There isn't time to go all the way to Kansas City. We'll bring back whatever we can lay our hands on to plant. If we're lucky, we can all put out winter squash, bush beans, cabbages, and even tomatoes."

"Will you buy carrots?" Sheena asked. "We can still plant those. It's only mid-July."

"Carrots. Collards, too. They can take cold as low as fifteen degrees. We can put out mustard greens. It's too late for onions and potatoes, but we might get turnips."

"I'll stay here with the women and *brablins*," Jimmy said. "Every day I'll plow under the ruined crops and get the fields ready. I'll plow two or three acres for me one day. Three for Seth the day after that. And then three for Rustemeyer."

"Chipper, you'll be coming with me." Seth took his son's hand. "We'll leave right away. The sooner we get going, the sooner we can come back and start planting again. Rustemeyer, go get your things. Rosie, it's time to clean out the savings."

The gathering dispersed with far more enthusiasm than when they had assembled. But Rosie couldn't prevent the wave of despair that swept over her as she watched Seth and Chipper head into the soddy. Yes, her bridge tolls had saved them. Yes, she had done her part to help.

But what would it all mean? Just moments ago, Seth had been ready to send her straight back to Kansas City. Were his feelings for her so shallow? Did his affection depend on healthy crops and lots of money? Did he still see her as merely someone to look after Chipper and keep the house?

Brushing aside fragments of dead grasshoppers, Rosie dug her fingers into the corner of the barn floor where she kept the bridge tolls hidden. In moments she had unearthed the heavy crock in which she stored the precious cache. Silver dollars gleamed in the bar of sunlight that filtered between the barn siding.

"Father," she whispered as she touched the cold metal. "I may have saved Seth's homestead with these dollars. But I haven't made him love me. We haven't become a family. We're still just three misfits. Four, if you count Stubby. I don't have a home to call my own. Chipper doesn't have a mother to care for him. Seth doesn't have a wife to share his love. Nothing seems settled between us. I promised Chipper you would turn all our troubles into good. But, Father, oh Father—"

"Still praying, Rosie?" Seth was standing at the far end of the barn, a chewed-up leather bridle in his hands. "I thought you might have given up on that by this time."

She stood beside the heavy crock. "No, Seth. I still believe."

"Believe what?" He walked toward her. "I asked God to get rid of those grasshoppers—"

"And he did."

"Nine days too late."

"Our Father never promised to do his work by our timetable."

"*Your* Father sure has a funny way of showing his love. You'd think if he cared the least bit about you, he wouldn't have let those grasshoppers head in this direction."

"Our Father never promised a life free of trouble."

"Then what's the use of praying?"

Rosie bent down and picked up a silver dollar. "Praying is talking to God. Praying is how you let him know you love him. It's how you know you can trust him."

"Trust him for what?"

"Trust him to be with you—through grasshoppers and whatever else life on this earth brings us."

"You really think God is out here on the prairie with you? How can you go on believing that?"

"Because praying is also listening. And when I stop to listen, I can hear God's voice speaking to my heart. I feel his comforting presence. He's my rock. My redeemer. He has saved me from a fate much worse than grasshoppers, Seth. It's the least I can do to trust him with my earthly troubles."

She tossed the coin to him. "I wanted to help you," she went on. "I thought this would do it. But now I understand it takes much more than forty-three dollars and seventy-five cents to save a man. It takes faith. It takes hope."

"It takes love," he said. He was silent a moment, regarding her with intense blue eyes. When he spoke again, his voice was low. "Do you love me, Rosie Mills?"

She looked away quickly, wishing for a bonnet to hide beneath. Her cheeks flushed at his bold question. But he wanted an answer. She would give it to him.

"Yes, I do," she said, squaring her shoulders and meeting his gaze. "I love you, Seth."

"How?"

"What do you mean?"

"How do you love me? The way you said you'd find love when we talked back at Holloway's Station? Look at me. I'm a good, honest, hardworking man—just like Rolf Rustemeyer. Just like Gabriel Chavez, David Hill, Matthew Smithers, and most of the rest of the homesteaders. You danced with me. You danced with them. You let me kiss you. You let Rustemeyer kiss you. Is that how you love me, Rosie? The same as all the rest of them?"

She gulped down a bubble of air. *What do I say? How do I tell him?* "I love you as my Father loves you," she managed.

His eyes hardened. "Your Father doesn't love me a lick."

He slung the bridle over one shoulder and turned to leave the barn. Rosie caught his sleeve. "Do you want to take me with you as far as Topeka?" she asked. "Do you want me to go back to Kansas City, Seth?"

He swung around and grabbed her shoulders. "I want what no one can give me—a guarantee they won't leave . . . or die."

"Oh, Seth, I—"

He was breathing hard. "Go back to Kansas City, Rosie. Or stay here. The choice is yours."

"Seth," she said softly, "true love involves trust. It's all about faith—trusting the one you love and trusting God to protect your union. The shield of faith in our Father helps us endure."

"Do you still think that's all there is to it? Endurance? Just signing the pledge on the marriage license and then working together day in and day out?"

Rosie shook her head. "No," she whispered. "I think it's more."

"Are you willing to give your heart to a man?"

"Do you have the courage—the faith—to make a pledge?"

He dropped his hands from her shoulders and looked away, struggling against emotion she could barely comprehend. "I'm trying," he said.

She blinked back the tears that threatened. "Then I'll stay."

CHAPTER 15

THE TRIP to Topeka should have taken a day and a half. But Rustemeyer had insisted on hitching his horse alongside Seth's mule to pull the wagon—and the two creatures could not have been more unsuited. Pete was a plodder. Seth had always been able to rely on the mule, whether it was to pull a plow across three acres of tough sod in a day or to haul a loaded wagon over the uneven prairie trails. Rustemeyer's feisty mare, on the other hand, thought she had the world by the tail. She pranced, she flirted, she complained about the heat, she shied and balked and generally made poor ol' Pete miserable.

Seth couldn't help but compare the mismatched team to his marriage to Mary Cornwall. She had enchanted him, but he couldn't deny that in time her lightness would have worn thin. As much as he had adored her, Seth understood now that Mary would have made a poor partner in the life he had always dreamed of for himself.

Rosie Mills, on the other hand, was perfect. She actually enjoyed the prairie. Not only had she accustomed herself to the daily chores, she had taken on the extra labor of managing the bridge. Though the stream of strangers crossing his land bothered Seth—especially where Chipper and Jack Cornwall were concerned—he knew Rosie's ingenuity had saved his farm.

Leaving her there with nothing but Stubby to protect her had been hard. Now all Seth could think about was loading his wagon with supplies and heading back to the homestead. Though he wasn't quite sure he was ready to marry Rosie, he couldn't imagine life without her.

Three days after they'd left the homestead, Seth, Rolf, and Chipper finally arrived in Topeka. During the following seven days, they traveled from mercantile to feed store to farm, and they bought whatever seed and healthy plant stock they could lay their hands on. It was a tough assignment. Every grasshopper-eaten farmer in Kansas who had put a little money back seemed to have the same idea. The town teemed with men, prices rose, tempers flared. But finally Seth and Rolf managed to fill their wagon and set off on the return trip.

"Are we really goin' home now?" Chipper asked as they crossed Soldier Creek one evening and headed toward the Red Vermillion River. "Or are we goin' out to another farm to buy plants? I wanna go home, Papa."

Seth smiled. *Home, Papa.* He had never thought two words could sound so beautiful. *Home . . . Papa.* Even if the crops completely failed this year, Seth knew he had accomplished something far more significant. To Chipper, the Kansas soddy was home. And Seth was Papa.

"We're on our way home," he said, ruffling his son's thick dark hair. "If we can get Pete and Gertrude to cooperate, we'll be there late tomorrow night. How does that sound?"

"Sounds good. I can't wait to see Rosie. How 'bout you, Papa? Have you missed Rosie?"

Seth didn't have to ponder that one. "I sure have. I've missed Rosie a lot."

"Fräulein Mills *ist* goot cook, *ja?*" Rolf said.

Seth shook his head. *Food* again. It seemed like they'd spent half their time in Topeka searching out boarding houses and hotels where the German could buy himself a hearty meal.

"Rosie's more than a good cook, Rustemeyer," Seth told him. "She's a good woman."

"*Ja,* vasch clothes. Grow potatoes *und* carrots in *Garten*. Sew pretty dress. Pink, *ja?* Maken britsch money. Goot fräulein."

"Rosie's a good fräulein, all right. But there's more to her than cooking and gardening and sewing."

"She's pretty," Chipper said. "She gots all that hair!"

"Dances good, too," Seth added. "And she's smart."

"Schmart? *Was ist* schmart?" Rolf asked. "*Schmatz?* A big kiss?" He demonstrated the German word by making loud smacking noises with his lips. This sent Chipper into fits of laughter.

"No, no!" the boy said. "Not kissin'. Rosie's *smart!*"

"*Schmerz?* Fery sad?" Rolf gave a big frown and pretended to cry.

"Not *Schmerz!*" Chipper giggled. "Smart. Smart!"

As Seth watched the sun sinking into the sea of rippling bluestem grass, he wondered how to explain Rosie's complicated intelligence. For one thing, she had good old horse sense. The woman could take a pile of grain sacks and decorate a whole house. She could make a meal out of a single potato. She could turn wood ashes into lye for soap or pigment for paint. And she wasn't afraid to try where others might have failed.

But there was more to Rosie. The woman thought about things. Deep thoughts. She was interesting to talk to. She'd read some books, and she liked to discuss ideas she had. Seth had never met a woman like that, and Rosie's intelligence was something he treasured.

"She thinks," he said, tapping his head to illustrate his point to Rolf. "She's smart."

Rolf frowned. "Schmart? I can not . . . not unterstanden." Then he shrugged. "Rosie *ist* goot fräulein. Vill be *meine* vife."

"Your *wife?*" Seth and Chipper said at the same time.

"Vife, *ja*. In vintertime Rosie vill *komm* to *mein Haus und* marry vit me. *Ist* goot, *ja?*" He gave them a broad smile. "I build voot

Haus, und Rosie vill babies haf. Rosie *und* Rolf: *die* family Rustemeyer."

Seth stared out at the long flat trail ahead. Had Rosie actually agreed to marry the German in the winter? Had she accepted a proposal of marriage from Rolf and never bothered to tell Seth?

Maybe she hadn't thought it important to tell him. After all, more than once that summer Seth had made it clear he was going to take her back to the orphanage in Kansas City in the fall. Sure he had kissed her once, but the grasshopper infestation had kept him from courting her properly. Maybe that kiss hadn't meant to Rosie what it had meant to Seth. Maybe the whole time she was kissing Seth, she had already agreed to marry Rolf Rustemeyer.

"Rosie's gonna marry *you?*" Chipper asked the brawny German. "Are you sure about that?"

"*Ja, ja, ja.* She marry vit me. I build *Haus für* Rosie. Haf childrens togedder. Big family. *Ja?*"

Chipper looked up at his father. Seth could feel the blue eyes boring into him. "I thought *you* liked Rosie, Papa."

"I do like her."

"I thought you loved her."

Seth clenched his jaw. "I do love her."

And she loves me, he wanted to add. But what had Rosie told him in those hurried moments before he left her to go to Topeka? *I love you as my Father loves you.*

What kind of love was that? Surely not the marrying kind. Maybe she was saving that kind of love for Rolf Rustemeyer.

"Why don't you marry Rosie, Papa?" Chipper asked, tugging on his sleeve. "We need a mama."

"Rosie's not *my* mama, Chipper—"

"She's not mine either, but it don't matter. We need her. We like her. We want her."

"Stop your team, Seth Hunter!" The unexpected voice behind the wagon startled Seth. He swung around. Jack Cornwall had ridden his horse to within ten yards of the wagon, and his shotgun was leveled straight at Seth's head.

"I said stop your team, Hunter," Cornwall repeated. "Stop or I'll blow you straight to kingdom come."

"Don't do that, Uncle Jack!" Chipper shouted, standing as Seth pulled on the reins. "Don't shoot him!"

"Get down, Chipper," Seth barked. White heat poured through his veins. He grabbed his son's arm and pushed the boy to the floor of the wagon. "Put down your weapon, Cornwall. You can see we're unarmed. You're scaring my son."

"*Your* son? Chipper no more belongs to you than my sister did. Turn him over to me, and maybe I'll think about letting you live."

"Not a chance." Seth stood slowly, his heart hammering. He knew Cornwall had been lurking. Now the predator had cornered his prey. In moments, Seth could be lying in a pool of blood. Unless . . . *dear God, help me* . . . unless he could calm the man, reason with him, persuade him to let them go.

"Give up this craziness, Jack," Seth said, squaring his shoulders. "You know I don't want any trouble with you. I'm a peaceable man, and I'm taking good care of the boy. Why don't you go on back to Missouri? Your daddy and mama need you a whole lot more than Chipper does."

"A lot you know! They raised that boy from the time he was born. I won't leave this trail tonight without him. Now turn him over."

"I won't do it."

"I'll kill you."

"Don't kill him!" Chipper cried, jumping to his feet again. Tears ran down his cheeks. "Uncle Jack, don't shoot. Please don't shoot!"

"Get down, Chipper. Rustemeyer, hold him!" Seth glanced at the German. In Rolf's lap lay a gleaming coat pistol. Seth's focus flicked to Rolf's gray eyes. Understanding passed between them.

"I want you to keep Chipper covered," Seth said, leaning over and pressing the boy under the seat. As he did, he palmed the pistol. "Stay down now, Chipper, you hear me?"

"Don't make me kill you, Hunter!" Cornwall shouted. "Though I reckon your Yankee hide wouldn't be too sorely missed."

"You're not going to kill me, Cornwall. You're going to turn your horse around and head back east. You're going to tell your daddy you tried your best to get Chipper, but I wouldn't turn him loose. And then you're going to make a life for yourself in Missouri where you belong."

"I don't belong in Missouri," Cornwall said, cocking the shotgun. "My home was lost, Hunter. The likes of you stole my land. The likes of you burned our family house and ruined our crop fields and robbed us blind."

"Is that what this is all about? Are you still fighting the war, Jack? Well, I got news for you. It's over. You killing me and taking Chipper to Missouri isn't going to change that one bit. The war is over. Now it's time to get on with life."

"I'm aiming to get on with life. My life includes that little boy you kidnapped. He's my sister's son, in case you forgot. Mary's son. He's all we've got of her. And we mean to have him."

"You won't get him," Seth said. He cocked the pistol he had kept hidden behind his thigh. "Now turn around and head east. Chipper stays with me."

"You good-for-nothing Yankee!" Cornwall lifted the shotgun to his shoulder. "I'll take him if it's the last thing I do!"

"Don't do it, Jack!" Seth raised the pistol.

The shotgun roared in a flash of fire and black smoke. Seth squeezed the pistol trigger as he flung himself over the seat into the wagon bed. A cry rang out. The animals bolted. Chipper screamed. Rustemeyer jerked at the reins and struggled to keep the wildly racing team on the road.

Among the seed barrels, Seth elbowed himself to his knees.

He'd been hit. He could feel the pain in his left thigh and calf. But he was alive. Chipper was alive. Rolf was alive.

In the dim light, Seth could see Jack Cornwall's horse cantering behind the wagon in crazy circles as its rider fought to stay in the saddle. A bright red stain blossomed on Cornwall's right shoulder.

"Go home, Jack!" Seth shouted at his assailant. "Don't make me kill you! Get on home where you belong."

As the wagon swayed down the trail into the twilight, Seth clambered back over the seat. "You OK, Chipper?" he asked, hauling the little boy up into his lap. "You all right, little feller?"

"I thought he was gonna kill you, Papa," Chipper sobbed.

Seth's heart warmed. "I won't let him do that. I've got to stick around to take care of you, remember?"

"But I don't want you to kill Uncle Jack either, Papa. Please don't hurt him. Promise?"

Seth let out a breath. His leg was beginning to throb, and he had noted a red stain on Rolf's sleeve. The German had taken some buckshot, too. They would need to find a farmhouse and get some warm water and bandages. He rested his cheek on Chipper's head. "I'll do my best not to hurt him, son," he said gently. "I reckon you care about your Uncle Jack. And your Gram and Gramps, too. Maybe there'll come a day when all of us can make our peace. But until then, I aim to keep you with me. See . . . I love you, Chipper. I love you."

"I love you, too, Papa." The soft lips touched Seth's cheek.

"*Mein* arm *ist* bad," Rustemeyer said. "Bloot *kommt*. You haf blood *kommt*, too, Hunter."

"We'll head for the stagecoach station on the Red Vermillion. They'll doctor us." Seth studied the German. The big hound dog. His rival. "Hey, Rustemeyer," he said. "You saved my life by pulling out that coat pistol. Thank you."

"Tank *you*." Rustemeyer smiled. "*Ist* goot haf *einen Freund, ja?*"

"*Ja,*" Seth said. "It's good to have a friend."

While Seth was away, Rosie poured herself into her work. When she wasn't milking the cows, gathering eggs, cooking, washing, or mending, she plowed. Seth had taken Pete to Topeka, but old Nellie seemed to understand the gravity of the situation.

The mule patiently bore Rosie's attempts at putting on the harness and hitching the plow. She even accepted Rosie's first counterclockwise rows—and she didn't grumble too much when Jimmy pointed out that all the ground would have to be plowed again in a clockwise direction. In fact, old Nellie seemed to appreciate Rosie's gentle touch. She only sat down once or twice a day. And when she ate up the last scrap of Rosie's scarf, she acted as if she had done her new mistress a favor.

So Jimmy loaned Rosie a straw hat and taught her how to turn under the grasshopper-eaten corn stubble. Every afternoon, when the rest of the chores had been done, she and Stubby trudged out into the field. With each row Rosie plowed, she said a prayer. She felt as though she were knitting her prayers into the very soil of Seth's homestead.

Bring him peace, Father.

Open his heart, Father.

Strengthen his faith, Father.

As the fields were transformed from desiccated ruin into fertile black soil again, Rosie felt her own heart grow ripe. It wasn't just hope that strengthened her. It was love.

She missed Seth. Missed him desperately. Even though he was gone, she realized he had become a part of her every waking hour. She could hear his voice in the rush of Bluestem Creek. In the shimmering haze of the summer heat, she could almost see him working—his shirt cast aside and his muscles straining as he hammered the planks that would link his homestead to the world or guided the plow that would ensure his future. She could smell his essence in the strong, fresh breeze that drifted over the prairie grasses. And every time she thought of his sweet kisses, the ache inside her heart grew stronger.

When Stubby began barking at two men driving a wagon into the yard one afternoon, Rosie's heart leapt. Abandoning the plow and old Nellie, she picked up her skirts and hop-skipped over the loamy rows, the dog scampering behind her. But as she ran toward the wagon, she realized the two men weren't Seth and Rolf at all.

A gentleman with a thick brown beard and no mustache lifted a hand in greeting. "Miss Rose Mills?" he called.

Rosie slowed to a walk, a lump the size of a sourdough biscuit forming in her throat. It wasn't Seth. Almost two weeks had gone by, and July was drawing to a close. Where was Seth? How could she keep on going when the hunger in her heart was so great?

"Mills—is that your name, ma'am?" the man asked.

Rosie approached the wagon. "I'm Rose Mills. What can I do for you, sir?"

"We hear you got a mercantile out here. Is that right?"

She studied the two men from a safe distance. Though they looked peaceable enough, she began to wish she had brought Jimmy O'Toole's pistol with her. What if they were friends of Jack Cornwall?

"I take bridge tolls," she said. "Sometimes travelers want to trade goods with me instead of paying cash. It might seem like a mercantile to some. But it's not."

The man climbed down from his wagon, took off his hat, and extended a hand. "My name's Bridger, and I'm from Topeka."

"Topeka!" Rosie's heart contracted in fear. "What's happened to Seth?"

"I don't know nothin' about anybody but you, ma'am. Word is, you got a mercantile out here on the Bluestem. Folks tell me you trade fair, and you do honest business."

"Are you from the government? Have I done something wrong?"

"Matter of fact, I *am* from the government. I'm with the United States Post Office, and I got a proposal to make you. Since late spring, about ten, fifteen folks come into my building in Topeka—seems like three or four of 'em a week here lately—and they been askin' me to give you a post office commission. And now that half my people under contract went bust after the grasshoppers came through, I'm aiming to do just that. How's it sound to you?"

"A post office? Here? But I don't know if . . . Seth might not . . . what about Mr. Holloway's station?"

"Gone belly up. Your place put him out of business, and the grasshoppers finished him."

"Oh, my." Rosie couldn't help but pity the man, even though he had been unpleasant to her. "Mr. LeBlanc might want a post office."

"Already asked him. Says he's got enough to keep him busy runnin' the mill."

"But I don't really have a mercantile."

"I don't much care if all you got is a cowshed. If you'll let me send the mail out here so folks around can come and get their letters, I'll give you a commission."

Rosie lifted her chin. A United States post office. That sounded mighty respectable. What could Seth find wrong with it? In fact, it would be an honor.

"Yes, sir," she said, feeling almost as though she should salute the bearded gentleman. "I shall be much obliged to serve my country in that fashion."

The man's mouth twitched a little. "Very good. Now, I'll need a little information from you." He pulled a piece of paper from his back pocket and took a pencil from behind his ear. "What's your full name?"

"Rosenbloom Cotton Mills."

He scowled. "Like the place over in Illinois where they make stockings and such?"

"Yes," she said, trying not to let shame overcome the pride of the moment. "But everyone calls me Rosie."

"Age?"

"Let's see. I reckon I must be twenty by now." She hoped he wouldn't ask what day she was born.

"Birthplace?"

"Kansas City."

"You got any warrants out against you? Ever been in trouble with the law?"

"No, sir."

"All right, then. Miss Rosenbloom Cotton Mills, you're now hereby an official commissioner of the United States Postal Service." He handed her a sheet of paper. "You got a name you want to call this place?"

"A name? What for?"

"So's folks can put an address on their letters."

Rosie pondered. Seth had not liked it when she'd called the barn Hunter's Station. But she wouldn't feel right about naming the post office after herself.

"Well, you think about it," the man said. "Meantime, I want to hand over the first mail delivery to you." He hauled a sack out of the back of his wagon and set it in her arms. "There you go. This covers the territory in a good part of this county."

"But how will people know to come here for their mail?"

"We'll put out the message from headquarters in Topeka, and you can let folks know as they pass across your bridge. Word'll spread quicker'n you think. Now, ma'am, this post office is gonna increase your traffic by a goodly bit, so I reckon you ought to be prepared. You might want to keep an eye on them fine-lookin' chickens of yours. Folks has been knowed to take just about anything that's not nailed down. And if I was you, ma'am, I'd set me up a real mercantile double-quick. This commission is your key to some good business."

He tipped his hat and climbed back onto his wagon. Rosie hugged the bag of mail. She could only hope Seth would understand. The mail could bring customers and their money—money that could help during hard times on the prairie. Mail also meant contact, a chance to touch the lives of hundreds of other people. Maybe she could even share her faith—the hope of a future of joy through Jesus Christ. Hope for a bountiful future. Hope for Seth. Hope in God.

"Wait!" she called. She waved at the men on the retreating wagon. "Wait, please! I have the name. I want to call it Hope."

"Hope?" The post office man considered for a moment, then he gave an approving nod. "All righty. I'll be back in a week—bringin' the mail for a town called Hope."

CHAPTER 16

A *TOWN!*" Sheena hooted as she plunked a crock of fresh honey on the makeshift counter in Rosie's barn. "Here it is barely two weeks Seth has been gone, and already you've taken a post office commission, set up a mercantile, and founded a town! He'll be fit to be tied, so he will."

"I'm afraid you're right." Rosie set a basket of eggs beside the honey and propped up a hand-lettered sign: *Eggs: 50 cents a dozen*. "But Seth will have to accept the facts. He can't deny prairie farming is uncertain business. Without the bridge toll money, Seth, Rolf, and Jimmy might have gone under just the way Mr. Holloway did. If God gives us the opportunity to secure the future by granting us a post office, why should we throw the gift back in his face?"

"But a *town?*"

"This is not a town, Sheena. It's one soddy and a barn. The gentleman needed an address, so I invented a name."

"Aye, and the first time Seth sees a letter addressed to Hope, Kansas, arriving at his barn on the postal coach—"

"Halloo!" The high female voice cut off Sheena's warning of doom. "Is anybody home?"

"It's a traveler," Rosie whispered to Sheena. "So, are you with me in this, or not? Together we can run this mercantile and divide the profits. It's hope, Sheena. Hope."

"I'm with you. Although when Jimmy gets wind of it, there'll be the devil to pay."

"Come on then. Let's greet the first customer to the Hope Mercantile." Rosie smoothed down her apron. She wished she had a bonnet. For all the trading she'd done, she had not been able to part any woman from her headgear. It seemed every female traveler had been forewarned about the prairie sun and its propensity for baking skin to a leathery brown.

Patting her bun, Rosie stepped out of the barn, Sheena at her side. A woman in a bright green dress threw her arms open wide and ran toward them.

"Glory be to God, Sheena!" the woman cried. "The *brablins* said I'd find you here! Don't you know me? I'm Caitrin!"

"Caitrin?" Sheena's eyes went wide. "Caitie? 'Tis really you?"

"Aye, Sheena! I'm here. I've come at last!"

Laughing, the two women flung their arms around each other. Each kissed the other on both cheeks, and they began to weep. "*Cead mila fáilte!*" Sheena cried. "A hundred thousand welcomes, Cait! Oh, Rosie, she's here. My sister is here!"

"Sheena, Sheena, let me look at you!" the woman said, turning Sheena around and around. "You're so lovely!"

"Me? Aye, 'tis you Caitie! You're all grown up, so you are, and as pretty as a shamrock in your green dress. Look at your hair! What have you done with it? Oh my, aren't you the stylish young thing in all your ringlets and silvered combs? Have you ever seen such *shingerleens* as these, Rosie?"

Rosie shook her head, but Sheena paid no attention to her friend's response. She was completely enraptured at the arrival of her sister. And no wonder. Rosie herself could hardly believe such a beautiful creature existed—let alone that she had deigned to set her delicate feet on the prairie.

Caitrin's curling hair glowed like a red-hot fire. Her emerald green eyes sparkled with life. Her cheeks flushed with the most delicate shade of damask rose, and her lips shone in a perfect porcelain pink.

Anyone could see that Sheena and Caitrin were sisters by the turn of their noses and the tilt of their eyes. But where Sheena was short in stature and had been pleasingly rounded by years of childbearing, Caitrin stood tall and elegant, as fine-figured as a queen.

And her dress! Rosie gaped at the wondrous creation in emerald green lawn. The full-hooped skirt had been trimmed in ribbon and braid. Fabric-covered buttons ran up the fitted bodice in a neat row. A loose coat with a small ribbon at the neck had been crafted of matching green fabric. And perched on that glorious mass of long red curls sat the most elegant pillbox hat.

Abashed at her own faded blue cotton dress, Rosie backhanded a smudge of dirt from her forehead and shoved her work-worn hands behind her apron. Lucky to have a petticoat, she had never even considered the luxury of hoops. As for buttons, Rosie had managed to put together a collection of odd-sized fastenings—not one of which matched the other.

As she sized up Sheena's sister, Rosie sensed something unpleasant—and all too familiar—rising inside her heart. It was envy. She had learned the voice of envy well in her years at the Home. Now it was whispering again, and she could hardly deny the truth of its message. She felt like a skinny, bedraggled little prairie dog next to this astonishing creature.

"Isn't she lovely?" Sheena cried, turning Caitrin in Rosie's direction. "Isn't my sister the most elegant lass in all the world?"

"I believe she is," Rosie agreed.

"Nonsense, Sheena. You're as full of blarney as you always were!" Caitrin laughed, and it was the merriest sound Rosie had ever heard. "In all your chatter you've failed to introduce me to your friend, so you have. I'm Caitrin Murphy and pleased to make your acquaintance."

The young woman extended one of her gloved hands. Rosie

shook it in wonderment at the woman's friendliness. Could it be possible that Caitrin was not only beautiful but kind? This was worse than Rosie could have imagined.

"And you are—?" Caitrin asked when Rosie remained tongue-tied.

"She's Rosie, so she is," Sheena explained. "Rosie Mills. She's my dearest friend in all the world. Not only that, but she's a bold young thing with a good *killeen* of God's common sense between her ears. I'll have you know she's built a town, so she has—and all by herself."

"A town?" Caitrin glanced around at the flat prairie. "But where is it?"

"Sure, you're standing directly on the main street of Hope, Kansas."

The young woman looked down at her feet. "I don't see a street, Sheena. I only see . . . dirt."

"It's a post office," Rosie said. "We have a post office here. And that makes it a town. Sort of."

"And where do you live in town?"

Rosie's envy couldn't quite suppress the warm feeling that filled her at Caitrin's valiant attempt to accept the absurd situation. "I live in there. In the barn."

"That's not a barn," Sheena said. "It's the town mercantile."

"Sheena?" Caitrin reached out and took her sister's hand. "Are you feeling well?"

At this comment Sheena burst out laughing and gave her sister another bear hug. "I'm well enough to be sure, Caitie. Has Jimmy clapped eyes on you yet?"

"Not yet. The children told me he was away in the fields."

"I'm not surprised. He's been working day and night. I never have a spare moment with the man. Sure, he's taken on the farming for two other fellows while they've gone off to fetch supplies—Rolf Rustemeyer and Rosie's Seth."

"You're married?" Caitrin asked, turning back to Rosie. Her green eyes were wide with interest. "Have you any children?"

"No, I'm—"

A shriek from Sheena cut off her explanation. "Glory be to God—it's them! It's my Jimmy, so it is! And look who he's leading. Seth and Rolf!" She picked up her skirts and started running in the direction of the approaching wagon, Stubby running behind her as fast as his lanky legs would take him. "They've come home! Jimmy! Jimmy, look who's here! It's our Caitrin. Our beautiful Caitie! She's come all the way from Ireland. Everyone's here together at last. What a day, what a glorious, wonderful day!"

Rosie grabbed her apron and quickly dabbed the perspiration from her neck and cheeks. Seth was home! She could see him sitting tall and straight on the wagon, his black hair gleaming in the sunshine. The very sight of him told her that her heart had not lied. He was everything she had been dreaming of. Beside Seth sat Rolf Rustemeyer. And little Chipper between them.

"The men have been to Topeka," she explained to Caitrin. "They've come back with seed and plant stock. We had a grasshopper invasion, you see, and we thought we were all ruined, but then—"

"You must run to your husband and son, Mrs. Mills. They'll be anxious to see you. Don't mind me in the least."

"Oh, Seth is not . . . he's not my husband."

"No? But I thought Sheena said—"

"I'm only Mr. Hunter's employee." Rosie bit her lower lip as she studied the fair creature who was even now assessing Seth as the wagon pulled up to the barn. Every fiber of Rosie's heart warned her to build a barrier of protection around Seth and Chipper. They were hers. They belonged to her by right.

"Seth and I . . ." she began. But she knew what she wanted to say wouldn't be true. Seth had never given her the hint of a promised future with him. Though her heart claimed him, he was free. And for all Rosie knew, God might have brought Caitrin Murphy to the prairie to become Seth's wife. It would be wrong to step out against that plan. She must submit to his will, not her own.

"Seth and I don't . . . he hasn't courted me. I work for him, that's all."

"But he's looking at you as though you were a honey rose and him starving for sweetness." Caitrin elbowed Rosie. "Go to him, now. Sure, I know a moonstruck man when I see one."

"Miss Murphy, you don't understand—"

"I'm Caitie to you. Here, let me pin up your hair." The young Irishwoman reached up and poked on Rosie's bun for a few moments. Then she whipped a small silver comb from her own cinnamon curls and slipped it into Rosie's brown hair. "There now. It won't matter a whit that you haven't a bonnet. You look as fine as any lady in Dublin."

She gave Rosie a prod. Stunned at the young woman's act of kindness and equally dazed at the sight of Seth Hunter, Rosie found it was all she could do to move her feet in the direction of the wagon. Seth walked slowly toward her, a slight hitch in his gait.

"Afternoon, Miss Mills," he said. A grin tilted one corner of his mouth. "I hope Rustemeyer and I don't owe you a toll for crossing the bridge back there."

"No, of course not . . . no." She felt so silly inside. Like a jar of jelly left out in the sun. "Are you limping?"

"We had a little run-in with Jack Cornwall a couple of days ago. Low-down snake peppered us."

"Jack Cornwall!" Rosie glanced at Chipper. "Was anyone badly hurt?"

"Well, I winged Cornwall with Rustemeyer's pistol. I don't think it killed him. But maybe he'll think twice before coming after us again. And Rolf took a couple of pellets in his shoulder."

Rosie let out a breath. There was more to this story, and she intended to hear it—later. "I see you found seed," she said.

"Everything we went after. And then some."

"Hallo, Fräulein Mills," Rolf said, stepping up beside Seth. "How you are?"

"I'm fine, Mr. Rustemeyer." A sudden thought occurred to Rosie. A bright hope. A brilliant plan. "Sheena's sister has come from Ireland. Caitrin Murphy."

The German's gray eyes shifted their focus to the vision in emerald green. So did Seth's blue eyes. Both men instantly swept off their hats as Caitrin glided forward on her little kid boots.

"Pleased to meet you, I'm sure," she said tilting her pretty head of red curls at the two men. But her attention turned quickly away. "Jimmy O'Toole! How well you look! Sure you've put on weight since I saw you last—and all of it muscle."

Jimmy—as skinny as a fence rail—flushed bright red when his sister-in-law swirled over and gave him a warm embrace. "Caitrin Murphy, welcome to Kansas," he said. "We're happy to have you with us, so we are."

"Hi, Rosie!" It was Chipper. Rosie looked down to find Seth's son gazing at her. "How you been, Rosie?"

"I've been fine," she said, kneeling to wrap her arms around him. "But I've missed you, sweetie."

"We missed you, too. Look!" He opened his mouth and pointed to the gap where a lower front tooth had been. "Notice anything different about me?"

"You lost another tooth!"

"Yep. It was hangin' by a thread, and I couldn't eat nothin'. Papa pulled it out. I didn't even cry."

"Good for you. You're a brave boy." Rosie allowed herself a glance at the adults. Everyone had clustered around Caitrin Murphy—even Rolf and Seth. "What do you think of Sheena's sister?"

"Purty. She gots the same green eyes as Sheena an' all her kids, huh?"

"Yes, she does."

"You been plowin', Rosie? You gots dirt on your face."

"I do?" Rosie grabbed her apron and swiped the hem across her cheek. "Did I get it?"

"Naw. It's sorta all over."

"All over." Rosie shut her eyes. It was useless to feel envious of Caitrin Murphy. There was not a way on God's green earth that Rosie could compete with the Irish beauty. What little affection she had earned from Seth she was bound to lose now. After all, he had made it clear that true love sprang from passion. And what man in his right mind wouldn't feel passionate about Caitrin Murphy?

"Sure, I'm looking forward to meeting everyone in town," the young woman said in her singsong Irish accent. Rosie's heart nearly stopped.

"Town?" Seth looked around. "Nearest town is a fair distance from here."

"Nonsense! Sheena tells me I'm standing on the main street of a fine Kansas town." Caitrin gave Rosie a warm smile. "A town with a mercantile *and* a post office. And it has all been built by one very clever young lady by the name of Miss Rose Mills."

Everyone turned to stare at Rosie. She wished she could sink right into the hard prairie sod. She shrank into herself, her eyes pleading with Sheena for a rescue. But Sheena was suddenly preoccupied with her children.

"A mercantile?" Jimmy said.

"A post office?" Seth said.

"A *town?*" Rolf said.

"Right here!" Caitrin lifted her arms and turned around and around. "Surely Rosie, Sheena, and I are not the only ones who see it. It's Hope, of course. A town called Hope!"

Rosie had never known that things could go so very well—and so very badly—all at the same time. On the good side of things, August and September brought the planting and healthy growth of a whole new range of crops. Chipper and Stubby at his side, Seth worked the fields from sunrise to sunset, stopping only to wolf down the meal Rosie had packed for him in an oak splint basket.

Rosie had more to do than she could possibly accomplish. The post office and mercantile brought a stream of visitors day and night across the pontoon bridge. The stash of bright silver dollars rose to the top of the buried crock again—and Rosie was obliged to bury a second crock. And then a third.

Jimmy had flat-out forbidden Sheena to have anything to do with the enterprise. She was a mother, he reminded her, with five children who needed corralling. But every morning Caitrin Murphy strolled across the bridge bearing goods to sell to the travelers—baskets of hot bread Sheena had baked and bowls of fresh eggs the children had gathered.

Invariably, the young Irishwoman stayed most of the day at the barn. Not once did she mention a desire to set up a school or begin soliciting students. She loved the work of selling, bartering, and trading, and in the process, her greatest talent blossomed. Caitrin Murphy, as it turned out, was a genius in the art of transformation.

"We need windows," she announced one afternoon in early October. "Do you know what I mean, Rosie? Grand big windows right in the front of the mercantile. With glass panes to show off all our merchandise."

"Don't forget this building is really a barn, Caitie," Rosie said. She was folding bolts of fabric to stack on the row of shelves Caitrin had nailed up and down the barn walls. "I don't think Seth would like the idea of glass windows in the same place he'll be housing his livestock this winter."

"Livestock. Oh, the very thought of it! Sure we can't have the nasty beasts in here. They'll ruin all our work."

"It's a *barn*, Caitrin."

"Not anymore it isn't. Look at this place! We've put the chickens to roost in the new coop. The cows are out in the pasture. The mules work in the fields every day. We've carpets on the floor and even these glass-topped counters. It's not a barn anymore. Truly it's not."

"You're right," Rosie acknowledged. "You've changed it."

She still could hardly believe the way Caitrin Murphy had managed it. In the two months since arriving from Ireland, Cait had talked Rolf Rustemeyer into building a large wire chicken coop. She had talked Jimmy O'Toole into hauling three enormous counters across the trail from Holloway's station—after she had persuaded Rosie to buy them from the family who had taken over the Holloway homestead. She had talked Carlotta Pippeto into lettering a big wooden sign that read *Hope Mercantile and Post Office*, and she had talked Sheena into painting the sign in bold black strokes.

In fact, Rosie sensed the whole enterprise had gotten completely out of hand. And that was the bad part of the way things were going. Ever since Seth had returned from Topeka, he had retreated farther and farther from Rosie. He worked all day in the fields. In the evenings, he went out to the barn to cut shingles, sharpen tools, or build furniture.

When he did chance to cast a glance Rosie's way, his blue eyes were inscrutable. What was he thinking? What did he want? Why wouldn't he say it in words?

She could only assume he resented the mercantile and post office. She knew he didn't like people traipsing across his land any more than Jimmy did. And she had the feeling he was still concerned about Jack Cornwall. No rumors of the man's whereabouts had filtered out to the homestead, but Rosie couldn't imagine that any person so determined would give up.

Rosie sighed. "Mr. Hunter will be the one to decide about putting plate-glass windows in his barn," she told Caitrin.

"Mr. Hunter this. Mr. Hunter that!" Caitrin set her hands on her hips. "Why do you care so much what that man thinks?"

"I work for him."

"You love him!"

Rosie drew in a deep breath. "Caitrin, the harvest is starting to come in now. In a week or two, I'll probably be on my way back to Kansas City to work at the Christian Home for Orphans and Foundlings. My feelings for Mr. Hunter don't matter in the least. Winter is coming, and I won't be needed anymore."

"Not needed! That man needs you more than he needs his own life's blood."

"You sound just like Sheena."

"Of course I do. And I'll tell you the truth. If I were you and I had found a man as good as Seth Hunter, I'd marry him double-quick, so I would. But you go about your work, and he goes about his, and the two of you are just like a pair of courting chickens—dancing this way and that and never getting down to the business of it."

"Caitrin!"

"The business of *marriage* I mean. That's what this is all about, isn't it? Anyone with two eyes in her head can see that the two of you belong together. You should marry him, Rosie, and the sooner the better."

"I notice you didn't marry the man intended for you in Ireland, Caitie."

"That oaf? Not likely. Besides, I love a man I'll never marry." A wounded glaze came over Caitrin's green eyes. "Sean O'Casey is his name, and he's the finest man that ever lived. I love him. I'll love him always. My heart belongs to no other, nor shall it ever."

Rosie smoothed her hands across the flat folds of fabric. Caitrin's words mirrored her own feelings for Seth exactly. "Why didn't you marry Sean O'Casey?"

"Because he's already married, that's why. Don't look so shocked. Nothing wicked ever passed between us. Sean's father is a rich man. Four months ago, Mr. O'Casey forced his choice of a bride on his son.

It wasn't me. My own father had picked out my bridegroom, you see. But how could I live the rest of my life in that little village? Watching Sean and Fiona together day after day? Loving Sean as I do—and him loving me? No, I told my father I wouldn't do it. I would go to America to live with Sheena instead. And here I am. Bound to live alone the rest of my life and happy with my choice."

"Oh, Caitrin." Rosie didn't know when she'd ever heard such a woeful tale. It made her think of poor Rapunzel locked up in the tower by the wicked witch.

"But *you*," Caitrin said, "you have nothing to keep you from the man you love."

How little the Irishwoman understood, Rosie thought. "In many ways my problem is just like yours," she said. "You see . . . I believe that in his heart, Seth is still married to his late wife. Even though their marriage was difficult from the beginning, he must have adored her. When she died, I think something must have died inside Seth. He's afraid to let himself truly love again. He holds back. He throws himself into his work—night and day—anything to keep away from me and the feelings. . . ."

"That settles it," Caitrin announced. "The two of you belong together—never mind the man's long lost wife, God rest her soul. What we need is a grand occasion." She pondered a moment, then she snapped her fingers in delight. "I have it! We'll hold a harvest feast, so we will. We'll have it right here in the mercantile, and we'll invite all the farmers from miles around."

"Caitrin, if you want to have a party, why not hold it in Jimmy's barn? I'm afraid I've already pushed Seth too far with all these changes."

"But this is the perfect place for a feast. Two weeks should give us enough time."

"Enough time for what?"

"Enough time to get ready. Enough time to convince Seth Hunter he can't go on living without you."

"Oh, Caitrin, you don't know what you're saying! You don't know what you're doing. You're trying to change everything, but you can't! It isn't right. You can't just go around changing everything that doesn't fit with your dreams. You can't change barns into mercantiles. You can't turn a bit of prairie sod into a town. And you can't make Seth Hunter want to marry me. Besides, in two weeks, I'll be gone."

"Nonsense, Rosie. You'll be right here." Caitrin pressed a slender finger into the button at Rosie's collar. "I'm going to see that you wear the prettiest dress on the Kansas prairie. I'm going to arrange for music, dancing, and the perfect evening for a proposal of marriage. We'll have lanterns strung around the mercantile, hot cider, fried doughnuts, bobbing for apples, pies—lots of pies—and sticky buns with raisins on top, and . . ."

For a few moments, Rosie drifted in the scene that this genius of transformation painted with her words. It would be lovely indeed. The fragrance of cider and cinnamon drifting in the air, the aroma of freshly baked pies and cobblers, the scent of candles, the laughter of children. The feel of Seth's arms as they slipped around her and drew her onto the dance floor. So perfect.

Yes. She would wear one of Caitie's beautiful Irish gowns. Something in a pale silvery blue or deep russet . . . or plum, velvet plum. Caitie would pin up Rosie's hair and set jewels in the curls. Maybe she could even dust a little of Caitie's cologne across her skin. Seth would be entranced. He would fall under her spell. And then—

"Mail, Miss Mills!" Mr. Bridger from the Topeka post office marched into the mercantile and flopped a heavy sack of letters across the counter. "Got a letter for you this time. Seems like there might even be two."

Rosie sank out of her daydream like a hot cake in a drafty window. *Silly*. How silly to live in fairy tales. Seth hardly looked at her these days. Their conversations were short, matter-of-fact, and all about the business of daily life. If she had been right and working amicably side by side was all it took to make a marriage, it would be an empty lot in life. Now she understood how much more was needed to make a marriage truly fulfilling. Gentle touch. Quiet conversation. Longing looks. Passion.

No, Seth was not a man in love. And a harvest celebration was unlikely to change that. *Lord, help me to let him go. Please help me to do your will. . . .*

"Let's see now," Bridger said. "This letter here is for Rippeto. It come all the way from Italy. You ever seen such crazy writin' as this?"

Rosie studied the letter. She must concentrate on the here and now. And she must prepare herself for whatever God would lay in her future. "I can't read a word of it," she said. "Only the address."

"Hope," Bridger said. "Hope, Kansas."

Rosie rolled her eyes at the name and began to help him sort through the mail. "Here are two for Mr. LeBlanc," she said. "They look like business letters. Probably payment for milling. This one's for the young widow Hudson. Violet loves to hear from her sister in Ohio. This ought to cheer her up as the time for the baby draws near. And here's one for Jimmy, and two for Rolf Rustemeyer. Look at that writing. It's German, you know."

"Good thing that feller's been learnin' how to talk," Bridger said. "It ain't halfway hard to understand him now."

"Mr. Rustemeyer is a good man," Caitrin put in. She was sliding the letters into the cabinet of wooden mail slots she had talked Mr. Bridger into hauling all the way from Topeka for the mercantile. "He's a very hard worker."

Rosie chuckled. "I used to think that was enough in a man."

"Ain't a hardworkin' man good enough for you women?" Bridger asked. "Surely you don't figure to get good looks, a charmin' personality, manners, education, and all that out of a prairie farmer, do you? 'Cause if you do, you're gonna be in for a long wait. Here's your letter, Miss Mills. Looks like it come all the way from Kansas City."

Rosie held her breath as she took the letter. She recognized the handwriting at once. "Mrs. Jameson," she whispered. She tore open the envelope, and a scrap of paper that had been tucked inside fluttered to the floor. Scanning the letter, she absorbed the information.

"What is it?" Caitrin asked.

Rosie lifted her head. "I've been offered a position at the Christian Home for Orphans and Foundlings—where I grew up. The director writes that she has purchased a one-way coach ticket to Kansas City at great expense. I'm to be the head cook and earn three dollars a week plus room and board."

"Three dollars a week?" Caitrin exclaimed, sweeping the stagecoach ticket from the floor. "Why, that's highway robbery, so it is! You can make twice that in an hour with your bridge tolls. And the mercantile—"

"You don't understand, Caitie," Rosie said, taking the ticket. "They need me at the Home. They need what I have to give. Money is not, and never has been, the reason I work. I want to do God's will. I want to go where I can be most useful. And the children need me, Caitie, truly they do."

"*We* need you!" Caitie said. "We all do. Don't we, Mr. Bridger?"

"Hate to lose you, Miss Mills," Bridger said. "You sure have brightened up the prairie since you came along. Well, take a gander at this letter. Maybe it'll change your mind. Looks like it went all the way from here to Topeka and back again. That figures. It's from that German feller. Rustemeyer."

"From Rolf?" Rosie took the note and scanned it silently. English and German words were jumbled together, but the meaning was perfectly clear.

"Well, what does he write?" Caitie asked. Her green eyes flashed. "He doesn't want you to cook something for him, does he? The man eats like a horse, so he does."

Rosie looked again at the letter—so well-meaning and earnest, just like Rolf. These words would demand an answer. Confusion overwhelmed her, and in the end she could only chuckle and shake her head. "As a matter of fact, he does want me to cook for him—and wash his clothes, tend his garden, and have his babies. It's a formal proposal of marriage, Caitie."

"To that great *glunter?* Well, well, well. So you *are* needed out here after all."

"And in Kansas City, too. As a cook in both places." Dismay mingled with humor at the situation into which she had stumbled. "That skill seems to have emerged as my greatest offering to the world."

"What are you going to do, Rosie? Will you go and look after the fatherless children? Or will you marry that big hungry galoot? Or will you let me organize the harvest feast for you and Seth Hunter?"

Rosie slipped the letters into the pocket of her apron. "You can plan the feast, Caitrin," she said. "What I'm going to do is pray. In two weeks, I'm sure I'll have my answer."

CHAPTER 17

AFTER his return from Topeka, Seth had made up his mind to focus on his farming. His fields demanded his constant attention. And farming was a good way for him to spend time with Chipper. In the two months since their trip, the little boy had become his shadow. They plowed together, planted together, even hoed side by side down the crop rows. With three good rains and plenty of sunshine, it was beginning to look like Rosie had chosen a good name for the place. "Hope" was thriving.

But in his heart, Seth felt the coming of winter. Dormancy. The end of growing things. The long silences. The cold.

Would Rosie go away? Would she marry Rolf Rustemeyer? As Seth knelt to check his turnip crop, he turned the situation over in his mind. Rolf had insisted that Rosie was going to become his wife. Though Seth had doubted the German at first, he now felt sure it must be true. One day he had spotted a scrap of paper lying below the hook where Rosie hung her apron. As he picked it up, his eyes fell across the message. A marriage proposal from Rustemeyer. Had Rosie answered? Why not? She had nothing to turn to but a life in the orphanage where she'd grown up. She deserved more than that.

Seth longed to give Rosie a new life. A better life. Did he dare? He ran his fingers over the bright green leaves of his turnips. What kind of a future could he offer Rosie? Not much better than what she would have at the orphanage. Hard work. Children to mind. Clothes to wash. Meals to cook. Only real difference was that she'd have a house to call her own.

He looked up at the little soddy he had built. Not much to speak of there. A house made of dirt. No glass in the windows. Not even a real wood floor to sweep. When winter came, the place would be snug and warm enough. But there would be no idle pleasures—no trips to church or visits to a row of bright shops. Nothing but sitting by the woodstove and quilting or darning socks.

"Whatcha think of them turnips, Papa?" Chipper asked. "You been studyin' long an' hard over 'em."

Seth looked up at his son and realized the boy had been examining the crop as diligently as his father had been lost in thought. "I reckon we'll be pulling these turnips in a couple of weeks, Chipper. What do you think?"

"I think so, too. I bet Rosie'll put 'em into a big stew for us." He sobered for a moment. "A long time ago, Rosie told me she'd be goin' away in the fall. Is that true, Papa?"

"I don't know, son. There's not much to hold her here."

"There's me!"

"Yep, there's you. Rosie loves you an awful lot. But she's got to think about the rest of her life. She might not want to call a prairie soddy home, you know."

"I reckon she wants a family. And out here she gots me. She gots you, too, Papa."

Seth scratched the back of his neck. "I doubt I'm much of a catch, Chipper. I don't have a barrel of money to offer, or a big fancy house, or a carriage and team. Truth is, I'm about as poor as the dirt this turnip's growing in. So if Rosie had her druthers, I kind of doubt I'd be her first choice."

He stood and slapped his hands on his thighs to brush off the dust. As he and Chipper started toward the soddy, Seth glanced in the direction of the barn. Silhouetted by the setting sun, Rosie stood on tiptoe taking laundry off the line. Her slender hand reached for the pegs, plucking them one by one and dropping them into her apron. Across the field, Seth could hear her humming a hymn—something she did all day, every day. He tried to remember how it had been around his place before Rosie. Mighty silent, he recollected.

Lord, he breathed, lifting a prayer as he had seen Rosie do so many times when she thought he wasn't looking. *Lord, I've been awful angry with you. The grasshoppers and Cornwall and all. But I reckon Rosie was right when she said love took faith. Faith in you. Lord . . . I love that woman. I think . . . No, I know I love her enough to take the risk that I might lose her one day the way I lost Mary. But, Lord, dare I ask Rosie to take on this hardscrabble life? Show me. Somehow teach my heart the truth. Would Rosie want to mother a child who's not her own son? Could she love a man who is secondhand goods? And the house? Lord, could she ever come to feel that a dark, dusty, cramped soddy was a home? Her home?*

Seth sighed deeply and lifted his head. As he studied the little house he had built, he spotted something he had never noticed. Outlined by the pink sky of sunset, a large cluster of bright purple flowers nodded in the evening breeze—flowers growing on the soddy roof.

"What's that up there, Chipper?" he asked. "Up on the roof. Looks like some kind of weeds or something."

"It's purple coneflowers," Chipper said. "Don'tcha remember? You gave Rosie a seed head on our trip out to the prairie. She put it in her treasure bag that she wears around her neck. Back in the spring, she planted the seeds on the soddy roof."

"On the roof?" Seth gazed in amazement at the simple, natural beauty of the dancing purple wildflowers. "Why did she plant them on the roof?"

"So the soddy wouldn't be a house anymore." His voice took on a note of disgust. "Don'tcha know *anything* about Rosie, Papa?"

"Maybe not."

"She says you got to have flowers," Chipper said. "Rosie says flowers make a house into a home. That's why she planted them, Papa. 'Cause now we don't just live in a house anymore. We live in a home."

"Exquisite!" Caitrin Murphy crossed her arms and stepped back to admire her latest transformation. "Miss Rose Mills, you are a true beauty!"

"That you are, Rosie!" Little Erinn O'Toole fingered the ruffles on the deep claret-colored gown her Aunt Caitie had loaned away for the evening. "You look like a fairy princess."

"Snow White," four-year-old Colleen announced. "Rosie looks like Snow White."

"Where are the gloves?" Sheena asked. "Cait, you must let Rosie wear your gloves. The white kid ones with all the buttons. Where are they?"

Rosie stood in front of the stove in Sheena's house and stared down at the rippling, purple-red silk gown. Her waist, cinched tightly with a borrowed corset, curved inward and then out into the billow of a great hooped petticoat. She took a step forward. The skirt bobbed and swung. Beautiful! Oh, it was beautiful!

"Now the garnets," Caitie said, snapping her fingers. "Erinn, pass me the garnet necklace."

Rosie gasped as the chilled metal slipped around her throat. A narrow cascade of deep red garnets dripped down her bare skin to the delicate point of her bodice neckline. She had barely accepted the reality of wearing her first necklace ever, when Caitrin began screwing a pair of dangling earrings onto Rosie's lobes. Earrings! What would Mrs. Jameson say to such luxury? Such extravagance!

"Now my shawl," Caitie said. "The black one. Not that. The one with the fringe, Erinn dear."

Caitrin draped the soft wool shawl around Rosie's shoulders and gave a gentle squeeze. "There you are. Perfect. If only we had a looking glass, you would see you're a very queen tonight. Sure, your hair will be enough to send poor Mr. Hunter straight over the brink."

"You look like Snow White," Colleen said again.

"I think she looks like Cinderella," Erinn said.

"How do you feel?" Caitrin turned Rosie around and around on the packed dirt floor of the O'Toole soddy. "Do you feel like a queen?"

Rosie nodded—but not too hard. She was afraid her hair might fall down. Caitie had done it all up in loops and braids and curls. Then she had piled it so high and stuck it with so many combs and jewels and *shingerleens* that Rosie feared the slightest breeze would send the creation crashing like a great Christmas tree, scattering ornaments left and right. She wove her gloved fingers together. "I feel very . . . very wonderful."

"And you look it!" Caitrin clapped her hands together. "Now for the grandest surprise of all. A gift to you, Rosie. Can you guess who sent it? Seth! It's from Seth himself, so it is. He said, 'Give this to Rosie when she's getting ready for the dance. I think she'll like it.'"

"Seth said that?"

"Every word of it." Caitrin set a small flat box on the bed and gave Rosie a quick kiss. "We won't stay to see you open it. Sure, the rest of us must hurry over to the mercantile and join the guests. Rosie, you're to make your entrance at seven o'clock exactly. Not a second sooner. Erinn, the moment she walks through the door, you're to gasp loudly, so you are. Do you remember how we practiced?"

Erinn let out a loud gasp. "How's that?"

"Perfect. And Colleen, what are you to say?"

"I'm to say, 'Look at Rosie! She's magni . . . si . . fi . . shent. Magnishifent.'"

"*Magnificent*. Oh, just say she's lovely." Caitrin smoothed out the flounces on her own gown of deep blue. "Come along then, everyone. Rosie, we'll leave you here. Be sure to study the time. Don't be a moment late. Seven o'clock!"

Rosie stood, half afraid to move, as the O'Toole women traipsed out of the house toward the bridge. She gingerly took a single step toward the fireplace. The clock on the mantel read six-thirty. Half an hour to wait. She eyed the package on the bed. But she couldn't sit down to open it. If she did, how would she manage to keep from flipping the hoop straight up to the ceiling?

Rosie bent over carefully and picked up the flat box tied with a pink ribbon. For two weeks, she had watched the world turn upside down around her. Caitrin and Sheena—and even Seth himself—had slowly altered the character of the barn. While the two women were busy filling the front with lanterns and tables and paper decorations sent in the mail from Topeka, Seth was piling the back with radishes, lettuce, collards, cauliflower, carrots, and cabbages. His biggest cash crop would be the beets he was just beginning to harvest, and Rosie knew he had great hopes for them.

Three times Seth had stopped Rosie and asked if he could have a moment of her time. There was something he would like to say to her. But twice Caitrin had cut in—calling Rosie to help with customers or to rescue her from some little emergency. Once, just as Seth had been about to speak, Rolf Rustemeyer had dropped by. The moment had vanished—and Rosie had too. She was terrified that Rolf would ask for an answer to his letter. She wasn't ready to give it. She hadn't prayed hard enough yet. She didn't have an answer. She didn't know what to do.

With shaky fingers, she tugged apart the pink bow. Gingerly, half afraid to see what was inside, she lifted the box lid. Fabric lay flattened on a sheet of newsprint. She pulled it out into the light and let out a gasp of delight. It was a bright yellow calico bonnet!

Crisp and brand-new with long ribbons and a firm round peak, the bonnet had a gathered crown that would easily hold all her hair.

A bonnet! *Oh, Seth—what do you mean by giving me this? Is it a thank-you for my hard work? A farewell present? An apology for the loss of the old bonnet?* Or could it be . . . did he understand how much a new bonnet would mean to her? And did he want to please her with a gift that would draw her heart to his?

She needed to pray! *Dear Father, what do you want from me?* Rosie turned toward the door, and her dress spun like a carousel. How could she even concentrate enough to pray in this getup? This wasn't her. This wasn't Rosenbloom Cotton Mills. She should be cooking a big hot stew for Chipper and Seth. She should be tending a bowl of rising bread. She should be piecing her quilt. She should be seeing to the six-forty-five stagecoach from Manhattan. The stagecoach . . .

Father! Am I supposed to get on that stagecoach? Am I supposed to go back to Kansas City and help Mrs. Jameson?

Oh, she didn't know the answer. Why couldn't God hurry up and tell her what to do? She'd given him two weeks!

Maybe she was supposed to marry Rolf Rustemeyer. She could tell him her answer tonight at the harvest feast. *Yes, Rolf. I will marry you. We will be the Family Rustemeyer.* Washing clothes and growing potatoes and bearing him babies.

No! That wasn't right.

Rosie wrung her hands. What did Seth's gift mean? What had he been trying to tell her in those vain attempts to have a private word? Did he want to discuss her trip back to Kansas City? That must be it. What else could he have on his mind? The harvest was coming in. Winter was in the air. It was time to go back to the orphanage—and a new bonnet would send her off in style.

Oh, why was she wearing this silly outfit? She didn't belong in silk and garnets. She belonged in calico and gingham.

Father, what shall I do?

Knowing only what she *couldn't* do, Rosie stripped off the white kid gloves and threw them onto the bed. Then she began to pull the combs and ribbons from her hair. With every stage of her transformation from Cinderella-dressed-for-the-ball to Cinderella-of-the-ashes, Rosie felt better and better.

She unbuttoned the scores of tiny buttons down the back of Caitrin's dress, stepped out of it, and laid it across the bed. Then she took off the hooped petticoat. Then the corset. In seconds, she had slipped on her faded blue gingham dress and run her fingers up the mismatched buttons. She twirled her long hair through her hands and wound it into a familiar, comfortable bun. Slipping the new bonnet over her head, she tied the long ribbons into a bow under her chin.

Yes, the voice in her soul said. *Yes, Rosie. This is who you are, my child.*

In the distance, she could hear the six-forty-five stagecoach approaching, hoofbeats and wheels clattering down the trail. In moments it would pass the O'Toole house and cross the pontoon bridge. Then the driver would stop at Seth's barn to pay the toll.

If Rosie got on the coach, she would leave behind everything she had come to love—Seth, Chipper, the little soddy. But how could she ask more of Seth than he had to give? And how could she turn away from the orphans and foundlings who needed her?

The stagecoach. Yes, she should be on the stagecoach. She grabbed a piece of charcoal from the edge of the fireplace. *Dear Sheena*, she scratched out on the wood table. *I have gone back to Kansas City to help the orphans. It is the right thing to do. I love you all. Rosie.*

Yes, she loved them all. She did. But in the time she had spent on the prairie she had done little more than create havoc. Seth had never wanted a post office or a mercantile—or even her. She had forced her way into his life. It was time to go.

She shrugged her old white shawl over her shoulders and

stepped out into the darkness. Half blinded by unexpected tears, she reached into her pocket and pulled out the stagecoach ticket. As she started for the bridge, the coach passed her.

She waved and began to run behind it. The coach would stop at Seth's barn for only a moment. Rosie would speak to Mr. Dixon, the driver. She would get on with the other passengers. *Father, help me to leave! Help me to have the strength to leave this place!*

Rosie ran across the pontoon bridge. Up ahead she could see the barn strung with lanterns. Guests milled around the open front doors and gathered at the tables inside. The little band was tuning up. Children played hide-and-seek around the wagon wheels.

The stagecoach pulled to a stop. In the dim light, Rosie could see the driver talking with Caitrin. She took his toll money and chatted for a moment. Then he sauntered back toward the stagecoach. *Time to go, time to go*. Rosie brushed a hand across her wet cheek, lifted her skirt, and hurried up to him.

"Mr. Dixon," she said, thrusting out the ticket. "I want to book passage with you to Kansas City."

"Well, howdy there, Rosie. Kansas City, huh?" He looked her up and down. "You ain't stayin' for the festivities tonight?"

"No. I need . . . I need to go."

The driver raised an eyebrow. "If I was you, I'd stick around. Smells like some mighty good cooking's been done for this shindig."

"No, sir. I won't stay."

"Suit yourself then." He took the ticket. "Climb in round to the other side. I'll give the horses a quick check, and we'll be on our way."

Nodding, Rosie glanced inside the barn. She could see Seth talking with Violet Hudson. The widow was showing him her newborn baby. The look on the man's face was soft. Caring.

Let him go! Father, help me to let Seth go. Others need him more.

Rosie spotted Chipper in the doorway gnawing on a candied

apple. Will O'Toole had slung his arm around his friend, and the two boys were laughing at some shared joke.

Let him go! Let the child go. Others can care for him as well as I.

Where was Rolf? She really should say something to Rolf. There wasn't time. As he had written to her, so she would write to him from Kansas City—a kind letter, full of respect and admiration for him, yet firm in her refusal of his offer. She put her foot on the coach step and her hand on the door. As she leaned into the stagecoach, someone touched her elbow.

"Rolf?" She swung around.

"Miss Mills." Jack Cornwall took off his hat. "I'd really hate to accost you as I did once before, but I do need my nephew. So, if you'll just come with me now."

Seth's stolen rifle was slung across the man's back. He cradled his own shotgun in his arms, one hand resting loosely near the trigger. Her tears transforming instantly to icy fear, Rosie stepped back onto solid ground. Cornwall linked his arm through her elbow.

"Fine night for a party," he said. "You weren't thinking of leaving, were you?"

Unable to speak, Rosie walked beside him toward the barn. She could see Chipper and Will still munching on their apples, completely oblivious to the threat. In the half darkness, it would be easy to lure the boy away from the barn. Cornwall would use her to do it. She guessed he would take them both—using her as insurance—in his flight across the state. So she would return to Missouri after all . . . if Cornwall let her live that long.

"Call the boy," he said, prodding her forward a little. "Go on. Call him."

Rosie swallowed. "Chipper!"

"Hi, Rosie! Erinn said you were all gussied up. But 'cept for that bonnet, you look the same as ever to me." Chipper walked across the lighted open doorway of the barn and into the semidarkness. "Who's that with you?"

"It's your Uncle Jack," Cornwall said. "Hey, Chipper. How've you been?"

Chipper stopped and stared. "Hi, Uncle Jack. Did you come here for the harvest feast?"

"I just came to get you." His voice was soft, beckoning. "You want to go home to Gram and Gramps? They sure have missed you this summer."

Chipper took two more steps toward Cornwall. "I miss them, too. How are they?"

"I haven't seen them in a while. You know what happened? That ol' Yankee you've been staying with shot me. Right in the shoulder."

"Papa shot you?"

"You don't call that fellow papa, do you? Aw, he's just been tricking you. He's an ol' Yankee, don't you remember? He shot me, and I haven't been able to get home yet. But I'm ready to go now. Come on, and let's head out together, Chipper. You and me. I bet Gram will bake us one of her apple pies when we get home. You remember Gram's apple pies, don't you?"

"I love Gram's apple pies," Chipper said. "Can Rosie and Papa come with us?"

"We'll take Rosie part of the way at least. How about that?"

"OK. If Rosie's goin', I'll go, too. Lemme tell Papa good-bye first, Uncle Jack. He don't much like me to go off without tellin' him."

"Wait! Don't go. If you tell him you're leaving, he might try to stop you. Come on. Let's ride out. Just the three of us."

"Chipper—" Rosie began.

"Come on, Chipper," Cornwall cut in, squeezing her arm hard to silence her. "Let's go, buddy. I'll let you ride on my black horse. You'd like that, wouldn't you?"

Chipper stood for a moment. He studied Rosie. Then he eyed his uncle. Finally, he shook his head.

"Naw, Uncle Jack," he said with a shrug. "I reckon I'll just stay here with Papa. You can tell Gram and Gramps to come over for a visit. Know what? Papa says maybe we can all make peace one of these days. I sure would like that, 'cause me and Papa an' Rosie would really be happy if you lived near us. Wouldn't we, Rosie?"

Rosie did her best to nod. "Chipper, why don't you step back—"

"Come over here, Chip," Cornwall said. "Give your Uncle Jack a hug before I head off."

"Chipper, no!" Rosie said.

Cornwall jerked her with him as he lunged at the little boy. Chipper tumbled to the ground beneath his uncle. Behind him, Will O'Toole let out a howl. As Rosie fell, the shotgun barrel jabbed into her stomach. Shouts filled the air.

"Chipper!"

"Let go, Uncle Jack!"

"Stop, or I'll shoot!"

"Rosie, Rosie!"

"Seth, where are you!"

"Help them!"

Rosie struggled to move the gun barrel that was wedged beneath her ribs. She could hear Chipper shrieking in terror. *Father,* she prayed. *Father, help us!*

"Get off my boy, Cornwall!" Seth's big hand clamped onto the man's jacket. Cornwall sprang at his adversary. The shotgun jerked and went off. Rosie screamed as pellets peppered the dirt beside her.

"Chipper!" she shouted. "Chipper, where are you?"

"Rosie!"

In half a breath, the boy was in her arms. She scooped him up and struggled to her feet. Without a glance behind her, she ran with the child through the darkness, dodging around the stagecoach toward the bridge. *Get away. She must get Chipper away. Take him to safety.*

"Rosie! Rosie!" the boy cried.

"I've got you, Chipper. You'll be all right."

"Stop runnin', Rosie! We gots to go back. I don't want Papa to kill Uncle Jack!"

Rosie set the sobbing boy on the ground at the edge of the bridge. "Chipper, you can't save them both," she whispered, kneeling in front of him. "You have to let them see it through. Let God settle this thing."

"No, Rosie! Sometimes we gots to do what's right, even if we ain't had time to pray it over. Now come on with me!"

Taking her hand, the little boy pulled her down the trail, back toward the half-circle of light in front of the barn. She could see the two men there, slugging each other, fists flying left and right. Blood spattered into the air—a shower of droplets—and the gathered crowd drew back. Seth fell to the ground. Cornwall leapt at him, but Seth rolled over and came at his assailant from the side. They tumbled across the trampled earth.

Rosie and Chipper pushed through the crowd toward the two men. Chipper was sobbing, crying out, begging them to stop. Seth came to his feet again. Cornwall lunged. This time Seth was ready with a swift blow to the man's right jaw. Cornwall crumpled and sprawled backward.

"Uncle Jack?" Chipper rushed forward and fell to his knees beside the fallen man. "Are you all right, Uncle Jack? Papa, is he going to die?"

Seth limped over and looked down. He prodded his rival with the toe of his boot. "I reckon he's still with us, Chipper, though that shoulder doesn't look too good. Must be the place where I winged him a couple of months back."

Chipper ran a hand over his uncle's forehead. "You OK, Uncle Jack?" he asked. The man's eyes fluttered open. Chipper bent and kissed him on the cheek. "Uncle Jack, you didn't have to hit Papa just 'cause I said I wanted to stay here. Papa's been good to me. I love him, Uncle Jack. I love my Papa."

Rosie looked over at Seth. Though he was still breathing hard and a trickle of blood ran from the corner of his lip, he knelt beside Chipper. One big hand slipped protectively around the boy's shoulders.

"Jack," Seth said. "Can you hear me?"

The man's eyes slid open again. "I hear you."

"This boy is my son. I know you care about him. I know you loved . . . loved his mama. But I did, too." Seth wiped the blood from his mouth with the side of a finger. "Chipper's the child of my marriage to Mary. He's half of me. Maybe you don't like to hear that, but it's God's truth. I mean to keep Chipper with me, give him a home, raise him up right. He's my boy, and I love him. Three times now, you've tried to take him. I won't let you do that. Not ever."

Jack Cornwall struggled up to his elbows. The pain in his face told of an agony that went beyond his bruised jaw and wounded shoulder. "All right," he said, his words slurred. "I surrender. You win, Hunter. But it's not because of Mary. And it's sure not because of you. The only reason I'm giving my word I'll back off is because Chipper's made his choice." He turned to the boy. "You want to stay out here on the prairie with him, Chipper? You don't want to come live with Gram and Gramps?"

Chipper's lower lip trembled. He looked at his father; then he searched the crowd for Rosie. When he caught her eye, he let out a deep breath. "I want to stay here," he said. "I love my papa, Uncle Jack."

"All right, Chipper." Cornwall edged up onto his knees and then stood. Rosie was sure the man would collapse. Blood had soaked his shirt around his shoulder. He clamped a hand over the wound. "I'm going back to Missouri now."

"Uncle Jack, why don't you stay with us for a while?" Chipper said. "You look awful bad hurt."

"That's OK, little feller. I'd best be getting home to help your grandpa bring in the harvest."

The man staggered away from the barn and made his way through the gathered guests. As he vanished into the darkness, the crowd began to murmur and swarmed around Seth. "You done it, Hunter!"

"You whopped him good!"

"You sure gave him what-fer!"

"You got your boy back for good now, Hunter!"

Rosie slowly let out her breath. She could see Chipper clinging to his father's hand, his blue eyes shining up in adoration. It was going to be all right now. Cornwall wouldn't come back. He had given his word.

"Ready to head out, Rosie?" Mr. Dixon touched her elbow. "I held up the coach to see how this thing came out. But I'd best be pulling out. The next station's a good piece off."

"Yes," she whispered. "It's all right now. I can go."

CHAPTER 18

ROSIE squeezed between two men in the backward-facing seat inside the stagecoach. She tugged her shawl tightly around her shoulders and tucked her hands in her lap. As the coach began to move, she shut her eyes tight and swallowed the lump in her throat.

Yes, it was time to go. She had done everything God could possibly have wanted her to do. She had looked after Chipper during the difficult months of summer. She had helped Seth learn to be a good father to the child. She had kept his household running—food on the table, clothes washed and mended, floor swept clean. She had assisted in saving the homestead after the grasshopper plague. The toll money was safely stored away in the buried crocks, and Seth, Rolf, and Jimmy could use it as they saw fit. Her goal of leaving Seth and Chipper with something of value had been met. It was time to go.

"Quite a little to-do there," the gentleman next to her commented. He was clad in a fine gray coat and matching trousers. "Did you know the man who prevailed, madam?"

"Not very well." Rosie struggled to hold in her tears. Truly, she hadn't known Seth well. The pieces of his soul he had revealed to her, she had grown to love. But he kept back his heart. Always his heart. "I worked for him, that's all."

That was all. She had worked for Seth. Worked hard. Done her part. That was enough. It had to be.

The stagecoach clattered down the trail, and Rosie bid a silent good-bye. Good-bye to Sheena and Jimmy. Good-bye to all the children. And good-bye to Caitrin Murphy. Envy had not won a victory. Rosie truly liked Caitrin. They had become friends.

"Where are you off to, then?" the man asked. "Topeka?"

"Kansas City. I have a job there."

"A job? May I inquire as to your new position?"

"The Christian Home for Orphans and Foundlings. I'll be the cook."

"I should imagine they could find someone in Kansas City to do their cooking, couldn't they?"

"I am someone," Rosie said. "I'll do it. They need me."

"I'm sure you know best, but—"

His words were cut off by the sound of rifle fire. Rosie clapped her hands over her ears as the stagecoach began to sway. "It's Cornwall!" she cried out. "He's after us!"

"Cornwall? The man in the brawl?"

"That's him. He's come after us!" Rosie could hear men shouting outside as the horses whinnied and the coach began to slow. "Don't stop!" she hollered out the window. "Don't stop for him, Mr. Dixon!"

The stagecoach had barely halted when the door flew open. "Rosie?" Seth stuck his head inside. "Rosie, what are you doing in here?"

"Seth!"

"Where do you think you're going?"

"To Kansas City."

"Is this the man?" The dandy beside Rosie pulled a small pistol from his coat pocket. "Merely say the word, madam, and I shall put a ball through his heart."

"No!" Rosie cried out. "No, it's Seth. Seth Hunter."

"Get off the stagecoach, Rosie," Seth commanded.

"I can't." She shook her head. "I have to go to Kansas City. I can't marry Rolf because I don't love him, and it's autumn, and Mrs. Jameson needs me to cook."

"I need you to cook."

"She needs me more."

"*I* need you more. I need you, Rosie. I need you to sit with me by the stove in the middle of winter and read stories to Chipper. I need you to walk through the fields by my side. I need to talk with you . . . dance with you . . . wrap my arms around you. And I'll take care of you, Rosie. I gave you that bonnet as a promise that I'll always provide for you, always meet your needs. I want . . . I want you to be my wife. Will you do that?"

Rosie gulped as Chipper's head popped through the stagecoach door beside his father. "Hi, Rosie! Where ya goin'? We need you at home."

She looked up at Seth. His blue eyes were shining. "Chipper's right," he said. "We need you at home, Rosie."

"Well, my dear young lady." The man beside her slipped his pistol back into his coat. "I recommend that you give this gentleman the courtesy of an answer."

Rosie tried to breathe. All her life nervousness had made her talk a blue streak. But now . . . now she couldn't say anything.

"Mary," she managed. "You still love Mary."

"Mary's not with us anymore," he said in a low voice. "I know that, Rosie, and I've let her go."

"I need a new mama," Chipper said. "I pick you!"

"But how?" she whispered. "How can we be a family? I didn't give Chipper life. I don't know anything about . . . about being a wife . . . a mother. I never had a family, and I don't know how—"

"We're *already* a family," Chipper said. "It don't take flesh and blood to do it, Rosie. It just takes love."

"That's right," Seth said. "There's something you need to hear,

Rosie. I love you. I love you in a way I never understood before. It's deeper . . . stronger . . . crazier than I ever thought possible. Be my wife, Rosie. Let me love you for the rest of my life. No matter what the years bring us, let me love you. Will you do that?"

Rosie closed her eyes. *Father? What shall I say? Can you give me an answer? Is this what I'm supposed to do?*

"Come on, Rosie," Chipper said. "Sometimes you just gots to do the right thing."

"Yes," she said quickly. "Yes, I'll marry you, Seth Hunter."

His face broke into a grin, and the others in the stagecoach began to applaud. Seth reached in and slipped his arms around her. "Come here, my beautiful prairie rose," he murmured.

"I love you, Seth," she whispered as she drifted into his embrace, allowing him to carry her out into the brisk autumn air. As the stagecoach started up again behind them, his lips met hers in a tender kiss that sealed their vow. Joy flooded her heart, and she wrapped her arms tightly around his neck, savoring the promise of a lifetime with this man.

Seth turned his shoulders toward home and the bridge that linked his new family with a future he had placed in the hands of his heavenly Father. Then he lifted his heart toward a vision of Hope.

AFTERWORD

Prairie Rose mirrors the story of early settlers on the Kansas prairie. Seth's small soddy, barn, and pontoon bridge are similar to structures found on homesteads where struggling farmers battled to grow their crops. Six grasshopper plagues were recorded from 1854 to 1877, eight floods occurred from 1826 to 1892, six deadly blizzards hit between 1855 and 1886, fourteen prairie fires burned between 1890 and 1916, and countless tornadoes cut across homesteads, destroying homes and taking lives. Still the farmers toiled on, holding firm to faith in God and family.

Other settlers made a living running mills, mercantiles, and stagecoach stations. Bridge and ferry tolls earned a steady income, while post offices and churches provided a welcome means of communication for lonely farmers. Immigrants brought their traditions, their foods, and their languages with them from Europe. They also brought their enmities.

Prairie Fire tells the story of Caitrin Murphy and Jack Cornwall, whose blossoming love fans the flames of a fire that threatens everyone in a town called Hope. Look for it in the spring of 1998!

To learn more about life on the Kansas prairie, please read:

Dale, Edward Everett. *Frontier Ways: Sketches of Life in the Old West*. Austin: University of Texas Press, 1989.

Dary, David. *More True Tales of Old-Time Kansas*. Lawrence: University Press of Kansas, 1987.

Hertzler, Arthur E., M.D. *The Horse and Buggy Doctor*. Lincoln: The University of Nebraska Press, 1938.

Ise, John. *Sod and Stubble*. Lincoln: University of Nebraska Press, 1936.

Massey, Ellen Gray. *Bittersweet Country*. Norman: University of Oklahoma Press, 1986.

Schlissel, Lillian, Byrd Gibbens, and Elizabeth Hampsten. *Far From Home: Families of the Westward Journey*. New York: Schocken Books, 1989.

Stratton, Joanna L. *Pioneer Women: Voices from the Kansas Frontier*. New York: Simon and Schuster, 1981.

BOOKS BY CATHERINE PALMER

A Town Called Hope series

Prairie Rose
Prairie Fire
Prairie Storm
Prairie Christmas (anthology)

Treasures of the Heart series

A Kiss of Adventure (original title: *The Treasure of Timbuktu*)
A Whisper of Danger (original title: *The Treasure of Zanzibar*)
A Touch of Betrayal

Finders Keepers series

Finders Keepers
Hide and Seek (coming in early 2001)

Anthologies

Prairie Christmas
A Victorian Christmas Cottage
A Victorian Christmas Quilt
A Victorian Christmas Tea
With This Ring